# THOSE WHO FEEL NOTHING

*A Selection of Recent Titles by Peter Guttridge*

# THOSE WHO FEEL NOTHING

The Fifth Brighton Mystery

# Peter Guttridge

This first world edition published 2014
in Great Britain and in the USA by
SEVERN HOUSE PUBLISHERS LTD of
19 Cedar Road, Sutton, Surrey, England, SM2 5DA.

British Library Cataloguing in Publication Data

Guttridge, Peter
  Those who feel nothing.
  1. Murder–Investigation–England–Brighton–Fiction.
  2. Cambodia–Antiquities–Fiction. 3. Detective and
  mystery stories.
  I. Title
  823.9'2-dc23

ISBN-13: 978-0-7278-8360-5 (cased)

*All Severn House titles are printed on acid-free paper.*

Severn House Publishers support the Forest Stewardship Council™ [FSC™],
the leading international forest certification organisation. All our titles that
are printed on FSC certified paper carry the FSC logo.

MIX
Paper from
responsible sources
FSC
www.fsc.org   FSC® C013056

Typeset by Palimpsest Book Production Ltd.,
Falkirk, Stirlingshire, Scotland.
Printed and bound in Great Britain by
TJ International, Padstow, Cornwall

*For my friend and mentor Stephen Fleming.*
*Another good man gone.*

*'The world belongs to those who feel nothing.'*

Fernando Pessoa

# PROLOGUE

You're waiting for your tailoring to arrive, sitting in the now quiet shop. Bales of silk, cotton, linen and mohair line the walls around you. It is humid. A sluggish fan above your head scarcely stirs the thick air. The sweat pops from your pores.

Under the glass top of the low table in front of you, business cards from all over the world are laid out. You have been encouraged to leave one yourself but you do not have one. You look at the ones that are there.

Alix De St Albin from some French recruitment consultancy has left his or hers. Lorenzo Monticello is in Italian water filtration. A couple of American dentists have 'selfies' with toothy white smiles on their cards testifying to their orthodontic skills. Academics from newer universities in the UK are there in abundance.

All have come to this shop in this little town on the coast of Vietnam to take advantage of its rapid, cut-price tailoring. The town of Hoi An is known for it. Cheap knock-offs of expensive western clothes and designs done in a day.

You ordered a suit last night. There were various things wrong with it this morning. Too tight on the chest. Too long in the sleeves. Pockets too shallow.

Your eye catches a card from Brighton. Brighton, Australia. Trudy Smart, Human Resources Executive.

Here's another Brighton card you almost miss. Brighton, England. You look at it intently. An address in the Lanes. You look around. Nobody is paying you any attention. You reach down and slide the card from underneath the glass of the table. You turn it over. Another office in Siem Reap, Cambodia.

Your suit arrives for your final fitting. You don't even look at it. You thrust a wad of US dollars in the hands of the startled manager of the shop and take the suit. You stumble out into the noisy street. It's hectic, bustling. The town is celebrating the full moon tonight so all electric lights are turned off. Paper lanterns illuminate the streets. Candles in hundreds of tiny paper boats have been set adrift on the river. It is a beautiful sight but you're not in the mood for beauty.

You barge your way through the crowds, rattle across the rickety boards of the medieval Japanese bridge, ignoring the soft lights floating below you to the sea.

You're in a daze all the way back to the old wooden merchant's house that is your hotel.

In a daze when you drop the suit on a chair and grab the gin from your suitcase, and when you straighten out the business card crumpled in your hand and stare at it by the wavering light of the candles that have been lit about your room.

You look at the Brighton number on the card and check your mobile for a signal. You try for an international line on the telephone by your bed. Nothing available right now. You're drenched in sweat so grab towels from the bathroom. You lie down on one and mop your face with the other, balancing the glass of gin on your chest. The man on reception phones back. He has a line and can put you through. You repeat the number to him and after clicks and tunnel sounds the number rings, surprisingly loud in your ear. You wonder what you will say if the telephone is answered.

There is another click and a voice on an answerphone message. Deeper than you remember. Older, of course. Tired, too – but then the voice has been travelling a long time. It has been travelling for thirty-five years.

# ONE

C onstable George Stanford liked the night shift. Aside from the money for unsocial hours he enjoyed the dark, especially here on the other side of the South Downs. He enjoyed the sight of a fox or a badger in the flare of the headlights. Occasionally he saw a wild-eyed deer, although he'd nearly wrecked the patrol car once avoiding one that had unexpectedly leaped out in front of him.

But three in the morning by the railway line in Hassocks on copper cable thieving watch was nobody's idea of a good time. Certainly not grumpy Constable Dennis Richardson with whom he'd been lumbered for the past six months. Stanford hated time-servers.

Richardson was grumbling about something or other – Stanford had tuned out ages ago – when they both saw a medium-height man with what looked like a heavy bag climbing over a fence on to the railway embankment.

'Where the hell did he come from?' Stanford said, nudging Richardson.

'It's where he's going we need to worry about,' Richardson said, opening his door.

Stanford followed.

Although both policemen were careful, the man turned, either at the sudden flash of light or at the sound of the car doors closing in the still night.

'Excuse me, sir,' Stanford called, his voice oddly amplified by the darkness.

The man didn't hesitate a moment. He dropped off the fence, abandoned his bag and set off at a run.

'Bugger,' Richardson said.

'You get the bag, I'll go after him,' Stanford said.

God, he hated chasing people when he was weighed down with all the stuff the modern copper was lumbered with. Clanking and clattering along, he heard Richardson get back in the car and start to follow. The man ducked away from the embankment and ran into a side street.

Stanford was a fit bloke. He ran on the treadmill in the gym three times a week. But all this bloody clobber hanging off him sapped him within a hundred yards.

By the time he got on to the side street the man had disappeared. He stopped and listened for the sound of the man's running feet. He could hear him – but where? He knew Hassocks well. A man could easily lose himself in the network of streets.

'Bugger it,' Stanford said.

Richardson pulled up alongside him. Stanford climbed back in the car.

'Judging by the clobber in his bag he's a copper thief all right,' Richardson said as he turned into the side street.

They crisscrossed the streets for ten minutes, windows down, listening for footfalls. They didn't see or hear a soul.

'Let's leave it,' Richardson said. 'We've done our duty – prevented a crime. And we can probably get some prints off the gear.'

He pulled on to the main road through Hassocks and headed towards Ditchling. As they came into the snake bend at Keymer, Stanford pointed at a car parked half on the pavement in front of the gates of Keymer church. The boot was open.

'He's after the copper in the church now,' Stanford said.

Richardson pulled up about ten yards down the road, also half on the pavement, and both policemen started back towards the car. Stanford glanced to his right, into the churchyard. He nudged Richardson. They stopped to watch as a light moved across the front of the church and disappeared around the side.

The wall was low and both men climbed over. Stanford grimaced as he splattered a slug with his hand. He wiped his palm on his trousers as Richardson pointed him to the left of the church. Richardson set off the other way to follow the torchlight.

Stanford moved cautiously between old gravestones. He had his torch in his hand but didn't want to use it yet. He didn't need to. It had been a cloudy night but suddenly a shaft of moonlight illuminated the ground in front of him.

Stanford looked at a mound of earth. He stepped closer and looked down into an open grave. He shone his torch into it. It took him a moment to make sense of the rotten planks pushed aside and the pale skull embedded in mud. Then someone pushed him hard in the middle of his back and he fell, forward and down.

Bob Watts was back. The disgraced poster boy for modern policing examined his face in his bathroom mirror as he pulled off his running gear. Not too bad, Bobby boy. The ex-chief constable of Southern Police had assumed his career in policing was dead in its tracks after the debacle of what the press dubbed the Milldean Massacre, in which armed police had shot and killed apparently innocent people. But now, thanks to stupid politicians who didn't understand policing but liked headlines, he was a law enforcer again.

Admittedly, his route was via an apathetic public, uninterested in what the politicians had foisted on them. But that didn't matter. He had won his election fair and square.

He might think the politicians were misguided but their decision gave him a new opportunity to make a difference. He hadn't thought the new, elected post of Police and Crime Commissioner (PCC) was a good fit for the way policing was done in Britain but if the Southern Force was going to have a PCC, he was going to be it. He genuinely believed he was the best man for the job. And even if he wasn't he wanted it.

He had scheduled a private meeting for late morning with Chief Constable Karen Hewitt, his deputy back in the day, but he expected to encounter her before then at the champagne breakfast for the launch of the annual Royal Escape boat race from Brighton to Fécamp. That could be awkward.

Karen had taken over when he'd been fired as chief constable. He could guess how she'd feel about him being her boss again. He was eager to get started; she would be less eager.

After his shower he stepped on to the balcony of his newly purchased Brighton apartment and breathed in the salt air. He looked at the dozens of yachts and motor boats and sailing ships bobbing on the tide a couple of hundred yards out. They would set off at seven a.m. for the annual race that notionally commemorated the famous escape to France of the future Charles II after his defeat at the Battle of Worcester. Watts knew the story well because he had heard it so many times.

Charles hid in an oak tree for one night – this act bestowing on the future a myriad of pubs called the Royal Oak – then made his desperate way to Brighton where a local fisherman, Nicholas Tettersell, had been hired to take him from Shoreham to France. When Tettersell realized who he was carrying he demanded more money.

Watts could imagine that might have pissed the future king off, but on his return to England Charles had rewarded Tettersell and the skipper had died a relatively wealthy man.

Tettersell was buried in the graveyard of St Nicholas's Church up on the Dyke Road, his memorial the oldest in the oldest church in Brighton. His grave had been despoiled a couple of years ago, one of a number during a strange black magic thing going on in the town.

Watts looked down at the seafront lights and the lamps strung along the stubby finger of the Palace Pier.

This was his city. He was back.

Breakfast for Detective Inspector Sarah Gilchrist was unusually healthy. Muesli, mixed berries, yogurt and honey washed down with a big pot of green tea. She ate it on the balcony of her flat, looking down into the pretty communal garden below.

She stretched out her long legs and wiggled her bare toes. There was redness around them. She'd done a brisk run earlier in new trainers that had chafed a bit.

It was the first day of the rest of her life. She didn't necessarily believe in such markers but a number of things had happened at once to make it seem that her life was moving into a new phase.

From today she was officially confirmed as a detective inspector, after acting the role for six months. Her friend, Kate Simpson, who had been sleeping on the sofa bed in recent months, had moved out yesterday. Although Gilchrist had been happy to help Kate, and had enjoyed her company, getting her flat back felt great.

She cleared away her breakfast things, showered and dressed in a new trouser suit she'd forced herself to shop for at the weekend. She'd gritted her teeth a few months before to buy another trouser suit that she'd thought would last her a couple of years.

However, in her job she expected the unexpected, and she had not been disappointed. That suit had been binned about a week after its purchase when a bag of faeces had been dropped on her. She gave a little laugh as she muttered to herself: 'As so often happens in life.'

She much preferred her regular uniform of jeans, T-shirt and leather jacket, but the region's first PCC was coming into the office today so she felt she should make an effort.

Daft, really, given Bob Watts, the new PCC, had seen her naked more than once during their brief and unsatisfactory affair. In recent months they'd reached a friendly, companionable state of being – albeit one with a soupçon of sexual tension. She wasn't sure how their friendship would play out now, given his new status.

She'd acknowledged him an hour or so earlier as their paths crossed running in opposite directions in tracksuit (hers) and shorts (his). She knew he'd got a swanky seafront flat with the money from the sale of his father's Thames-side house in London, but she hadn't seen it yet.

She heard the sharp beep of a car horn below her balcony and waved down at her colleague, Detective Sergeant Bellamy Heap, before locking the French windows. They were off to interview a club owner on Marina Drive.

She gave herself the final once-over in the hall mirror and let herself out of the flat. Just as she was closing the door she went back in and grabbed two chocolate bars from a drawer in the hall table. Being virtuous about healthy food was all well and good but no point being silly about it.

'Here's to Nicholas Tettersell, who made this possible.' The ruddy-faced man in the navy blazer and slacks raised his champagne flute to the assembled company.

'Nicholas Tettersell,' the company said in ragged unison as they drank his health.

Watts took only the smallest sip of his champagne. Drinking at six-thirty a.m. on an empty stomach was not something that appealed. He glanced round. That creep Bernard Rafferty, Director of the Royal Pavilion, looked like he was having trouble staying awake as he stood beside Karen Hewitt on the opposite side of the room. Well, she could be hard going.

Hewitt sensed Watts was looking and tilted her glass at him, a knowing smile on her face.

They were in a high-ceilinged, long-windowed room of a newly refurbished seafront hotel. A lavish breakfast buffet was laid out along one wall. There were about sixty people clustered near and on the room-length balcony looking out at the fleet of boats ready to sail.

Watts was with the new leader of the council, an affable but ruthless politician. 'Good to have you back in policing, Bob,' he said. 'Much missed.' He gestured discreetly towards Karen Hewitt. 'Not that the chief constable isn't doing a grand job . . .'

Watts gave a non-committal smile. He didn't expect the leader to be sexist, so he assumed there must be some other reason for the veiled comment. He looked out at the sun glittering on the water. 'That's a remarkable range of boats and yachts,' he said.

'Gaff-rigged, solo and motorised,' the ruddy-faced man said, coming up beside them. 'We've got them all.' As he shook hands with the leader he handed Watts a pair of binoculars. 'But look at that one just coming past the end of the West Pier. It's steam-powered.'

Watts took the glasses. It took him a moment to focus them so his eyes swept across the strange beauty of the burned and buckled skeleton of the once great edifice; fire-bombed, it was rumoured, by jealous competitors. Then the binoculars caught sight of a slow moving boat with sails and steam puffing from an old-fashioned funnel.

'It's beautiful,' Watts said. 'But can it get across the Channel?'

The ruddy-face man laughed. 'It was easily capable of crossing the Atlantic in the 1920s. And did so. An old rum-runner from Prohibition days. It would stock up in Glasgow and hand over its cargo a few miles off New York, just outside American waters. Years later it did God knows what in the China Seas. It was berthed in Hong Kong until independence.'

'It's beautiful,' Watts said again, handing back the binoculars. 'Is it a regular entrant?'

'First time, I think,' the ruddy-faced man said.

Watts turned to him and held out his hand. 'I'm Bob Watts, by the way.'

'The new police commissioner,' the ruddy-faced man said, shaking his hand. 'Yes, I know. Ned Farage.'

'Where is that beautiful boat berthed these days?'

The man shrugged. 'All I know is that it berthed last night in the Marina – a lot of visitors berth there the night before the Race. Owned by a man called Charles Windsor.' He saw Watts' expression. 'No, not that one.'

Watts smiled and Farage looked through the binoculars again. 'That may be the owner sitting aft.'

He passed the binoculars back to Watts. Watts focused them on a broad-shouldered elderly man sitting straight-backed in a director's chair. He had a shock of white hair and a strong jaw. His face was also ruddy. He was dressed in some oriental-style, high-collared black jacket, his matching trousers flapping in the wind against thin legs.

Sitting beside him, speaking intently into his ear, was a handsome man around Watts' age. Watts assumed he was the skipper. He was wearing shorts and a T-shirt, and his hair was crew cut. He looked fit and capable.

'I assume you mean the older man?' Watts said. 'Do you know him?'

'Not in the least. There's an antique shop with his name on it in the Lanes but I don't think he's ever there.'

Someone touched Watts' arm. He turned.

'Hello, Commissioner,' Karen Hewitt said.

The smartly dressed Asian woman was sitting on the low wall in front of the dodgems on Marina Drive, carrier bags at her feet. She scrutinized the face of every man who passed.

'What's that woman waiting for?' Gilchrist said to Bellamy Heap as they drove slowly by. 'There's no bus stop there.'

'She's waiting for her son to come back, ma'am,' Bellamy Heap said, working his way through the chicanes intended to discourage boy racers on this long, straight stretch down to Black Rock. 'She sits there every day, morning or afternoon. Been doing it for months.'

'Her son is missing?'

'Nine months ago, ma'am, as I understand it.'

'We've investigated?'

'I believe so, ma'am.'

'And she thinks he's coming back here.'

'She spoke to a fortune teller.'

Gilchrist twisted her head to examine the woman more closely. The woman looked to be in agony.

'The fortune teller doesn't seem to have been a great help,' she said, facing forward again.

'I know,' Heap said. 'Apparently he told her that her son said he was coming back to her. That she had to wait in the places familiar to him and he'd return. However, he wouldn't necessarily look the same.'

Gilchrist clenched her jaw. 'That's appalling. Has no one tried to tell her otherwise?'

Heap nodded. 'A number of times.'

Gilchrist watched the woman dwindle in the rear-view mirror. 'So sad,' she said, almost to herself.

'She does a kind of circuit, ma'am. Couple of pubs, couple of roads.'

Gilchrist looked out of the window. Heap went wide to pass a woman on a bicycle pulling a trolley with her baby in it.

'God, I hate stupid women like that,' Gilchrist said sourly.

'Ma'am,' Heap said, his voice neutral.

'She's more interested in her health and the environment than she is in her own child. When she's involved in a crash and, heaven forbid, that little love of her life dies, she's going to blame the car that crashed into her. Which may be right, except she's equally to blame because she has taken her child out on the road in a contraption that means she can't keep an eye on what may be happening to her baby.'

Heap glanced at her and Gilchrist became conscious her voice had sounded strident.

'Still, at least the mother is physically fit,' she said, trailing off.

They drove on in silence for a moment.

'How surreal is that?' Heap said abruptly.

He was gesturing to a community police car going by the other way. Painted all over it were advertisements for the latest novel by a bestselling crime writer who lived locally. He had donated the car to the police.

'If I were a villain and I got put into the back of that I might take against that bloke's writing,' Gilchrist said.

'Do you think most criminals can actually read?'

'I hope you're not stereotyping, Detective Sergeant.'

'Just observing that Milldean exists, ma'am.'

Gilchrist remained poker-faced. 'Point taken.'

Heap was chewing his lip.

Gilchrist sighed. 'What's on your mind, Bellamy?'

'Not for me to say.'

'If you don't say what's on your mind, nobody else will.'

'OK – it's Bob Watts, our new police commissioner.'

Gilchrist stiffened a little. She knew Heap was aware that she and Watts had a scandalous history. 'What's troubling you?'

'The elections for police and crime commissioners in England and Wales had an average turnout of fifteen per cent.'

'It was low,' Gilchrist agreed.

'It was abysmal.'

'What point are you making, Bellamy?'

'His appointment is not exactly a ringing endorsement of him.'

'No different to most other elected appointments then,' Gilchrist said. She saw that Heap had caught the sharpness in her tone.

'Ma'am, you know that these commissioner appointments just open the door to cronyism and nepotism.'

'Bob Watts isn't like that. You're saying he's a crony or that he's going to use nepotism or that he's not up to the job?'

'I'm saying that there is no proper job and that there are precedents. The guy who beat John Prescott appointed as his deputy the man who ran his campaign. There was no advertisement and no selection process. Both men were Tory members of the local county council. Somewhere in the Midlands an old Labour party friend of the new PCC is a deputy on sixty-five grand. Job not advertised. And she's keeping all her old jobs so will get over ninety grand a year.'

Gilchrist looked straight ahead. 'Bob Watts isn't like that.'

Next day you fly out of Hoi An heading for Nha Trang. Your itinerary then takes you to Saigon – you can't bring yourself to call it Ho Chi Minh City – then upriver to Chau Doc and Can Tho on the Mekong Delta. You had allowed yourself seven days for these places. From there you go upriver into Cambodia.

Your itinerary is both a pilgrimage and a commemoration. It charts a journey into your past. That voice on the answerphone chimed into that past but it also changed the coordinates. Now

you want to get into Cambodia as quickly as you can. Now it isn't
a pilgrimage, it's a pursuit. Not commemoration but revenge.

You have not phoned Siem Reap. You left no message on the
Brighton number. You regret phoning it at all. You do not want
him to have any warning that you are coming for him.


'You might want to hear this, ma'am,' Heap said to Gilchrist the
minute she walked through the office door. After their Madeira
Drive interview she'd gone to a community meeting – one of an
increasing number that had become part of her schedule in the
interests of community relations.

Gilchrist put her bag down on her chair and glanced at her
watch. Bob Watts would be rallying the troops shortly. She looked
at her diminutive, red-faced colleague then at the young, fit-looking
constable standing beside Heap's desk.

'Stanford here disturbed a copper cable thief last night in
Keymer,' Heap continued.

Theft of copper cable from railway signalling systems was an
ongoing and serious problem as it totally disrupted the train service
until the missing cable could be replaced. Boring as hell, though.

'Well done, Stanford. Anyone we know?'

Stanford looked at his feet. 'He got away, ma'am.'

'That happens,' Gilchrist said. She glanced at Heap. 'But why
am I being told this?'

'We got his bag of tools, ma'am,' Stanford said. 'And we got
his car registration. Well, most of it. Or should I say Constable
Richardson did. He saw the person hurrying out of the graveyard
when he came round from the back of the church and gave
chase.'

Gilchrist frowned. 'Graveyard? Why wasn't this copper thief
on the railway line?'

'He was but he got away, then we found him in the
churchyard.'

Gilchrist looked at Heap with an explain-this-to-me expression
on her face.

'There have been a number of instances of coffins being dug
up for the brass on the handles and hasps and bolts,' Heap said.

'These are desperate times,' Gilchrist said wearily. She looked
at Stanford. 'You haven't told me what your colleague was doing

round the back of the church, but never mind. Where were you
– just out of interest?'

Stanford glanced at Heap who, Gilchrist noticed, had adopted
a straight face. Stanford worked the muscles in his jaw. 'I was
face down in the grave, ma'am.'

Gilchrist nodded, also straight-faced. 'Continue.'

'The man got in his car and drove off with his boot still wide
open.'

Gilchrist frowned. 'So how did Richardson see the number
plate?'

'Our man did a U-turn. I think he must have realized that if he
went straight on to Ditchling he had very few options. We would
either have caught up with him on the long stretch of lane between
Keymer and Ditchling or on one of the three roads he would need
to take from there. Going back towards Hassocks gave him more
options.' Stanford shrugged. 'Constable Richardson almost caught
him on the turn but perhaps it was as well that he didn't as he
would probably have been run down. Anyway, he got all but two
digits of the car's registration numbers. And the make of car, of
course.'

'Good for him. Were you still communing with the dead at this
point?'

Stanford worked his jaw again. 'I was getting into our car,
ma'am.'

'And you gave chase but lost him.'

'He had a number of immediate options. Around the bend there's
a left turn down a lane that offers an immediate right then multiple
choices, or you can go on down the lane to have a further three
choices. A little further round the bend there's a right turn which
then offers multiple choices, or you can ignore the right turn and
go straight on back into Hassocks where, again, there are multiple
choices.'

Gilchrist's eyes were glazing over. 'But none that really go
anywhere, surely?' she said from her vague knowledge of the
sleepy town.

'Which is why we chose that option ourselves, ma'am.'

Gilchrist nodded. 'But he didn't. I understand. Good work,
nevertheless, the pair of you. And you've got a hit on the registration already?'

'We've got a long list of possibilities, ma'am,' Stanford said, indicating the sheaves of paper in Heap's hand.

Gilchrist looked at Heap, still wondering why he had brought this to her attention.

'Just a thought, ma'am. But in the ten minutes or so after he was spotted on the railway track he had time to dig a grave?'

Gilchrist looked back at the constable. 'A different man, then, Stanford?'

The constable looked from her to Heap. 'Quite possibly, ma'am.'

'I was wondering if it somehow was linked to all that black magic stuff of a few months ago,' Heap said.

'We're pretty confident we got everyone involved in that,' Gilchrist said. 'Aren't we?'

'We are, ma'am,' Heap said. 'But it remains a good possibility that this grave being disturbed is not about metal theft.'

Gilchrist nodded slowly. 'Look through those names, Detective Sergeant. See if any of them stand out.' She gestured to Stanford. 'You could have something interesting here.'

He didn't look interested at all.

When you land in Nha Trang you take the next flight to Saigon where you rent a car at the airport and drive six hours to Can Tho. It's hot and humid as hell out there but you move from one air-conditioned environment to another, so by the time you check into a riverfront hotel at midnight your throat is dry, your nose is blocked and your head is thumping.

You should do some yoga to right yourself but you collapse into bed. The air con is fierce and noisy. You can't figure out how to turn it off so take the extra blanket from the cupboard and put a pillow over your head.

After an early breakfast you make your way to the hotel's short jetty. There are already five tourists on board the boat tied there: a German couple and an English couple with their sulky teenage boy. You nod at the adults as they greet you. The boy keeps his head down over his tablet. You sit at the back of the boat, your duffel bag beside you.

Algae like giant cabbages and strange, foliage-like growths dip and bob on the surface of the water in the wake of the boat as you head up the Mekong Delta for Phnom Penh. You have seen similar pollution on the Nile but the Mekong is, if anything, worse: pesticides, mercury and other pollutants are at such toxic levels here that the famed freshwater dolphins of the river are almost extinct.

You watch the slow water flow, occasionally glancing at the dopily smiling German couple leaning into each other. The sullen English boy is still focusing on his tablet, his parents gazing blankly out of the windows.

Within an hour you reach the customs post on the shore at the Vietnam/Cambodia border. There is time for coffee in a small café overlooking the brown waters whilst the military fiddle with your passports. You step out into a small garden. Something in the trees is chirruping. The humidity feels like a wet sponge bathing your body.

There is a barracks across a dirt yard. It looks big enough to house six, maybe eight men. The last time you passed through, there had been twelve men at this post, mostly sleeping in hammocks strung between the trees. You and your colleagues had narrowly voted not to kill them all.

Bob Watts blethered on to the assembled coppers for a while, Chief Constable Karen Hewitt standing stiffly beside him with a fixed grin on her face. He knew from conversations with Sarah Gilchrist months ago that Hewitt's fixed grin was as much to do with cosmetic surgery as it was with her gritted teeth at the fact his role challenged her autonomy. He could still vaguely smell the alcohol on her from the champagne breakfast.

He saw Gilchrist half-sitting on a desk near the back of the room. That likeable, fresh-faced policeman, Bellamy Heap, was standing beside her although he was scarcely taller than her seated. Gilchrist had told Watts the duo had been dubbed Little and Large by their ever predictable colleagues at the nick.

His meeting with Karen Hewitt had gone . . . OK. Once he'd insisted he was not going to fire her – something the PCC had the power to do – she'd relaxed. A little. He'd assured her that he wanted to work with her, not against her. She had, quite rightly, pointed out that she'd been doing fine without any assistance in the couple of years since she'd taken over from him. However, she would be happy to work with him again.

'I have a few ideas,' he said.

'I'll be glad to hear them,' she said. 'As long as they're not operationally based, which is outside your remit – as you will know.'

Watts smiled pleasantly. 'I'm aware of that, Chief Constable.'

'I have a lot of technology types knocking on my door offering us the latest policing kit,' Hewitt said. 'Maybe that's an area you could be of real use – identifying the next generation of policing aids.'

'Happy to,' he said. He'd always quite liked the boy's toys aspect of police work. 'But what are your main operational issues at the moment?'

'The usual. Drugs, of course. You know there's talk of opening a "shooting gallery" down here for our drug addicts to shoot up legally in controlled conditions?'

'Makes sense.'

She shot him a sharp look. 'Does it? All of Britain's drug addicts heading our way for a year-round holiday?'

Watts thought it wise to move on. 'What else?'

'Teen gangs; dangerous dogs.' She grimaced – or tried to. 'Oh, and copper cable theft is still a pain in the bum. There was travel chaos for commuters last week because some clever dick nicked fifty metres of signalling cabling around Littlehampton. Trains cancelled and delayed and diverted. I'm sending out regular night patrols to try to catch them.'

'The railways have got their own police,' Watts said.

'I know that,' Hewitt said sharply. She looked down and moderated her tone. 'The rail chiefs are demanding a crackdown on copper thieves both to prevent them and to catch them. As are the commuting public. It's not our primary responsibility but we need to be seen to be responding, obviously. But then that means taking police from somewhere else.'

She sighed.

'Peacehaven has turned out to be the seagull shooting capital of the south coast. I don't know if it's to do with what happened here a few months ago, when all the fish fell from the sky, but they are attacking humans and then people shoot them and then the birds attack some more because they're defending their chicks. BB guns are the weapons of choice. We've had sixty cases reported.'

Watts laughed. 'And that's a police matter?' he said.

'Of course,' Hewitt said, almost indignant. 'People found guilty of shooting a bird can get a six-month prison sentence and a twenty-thousand-pound fine. And you think with a Green MP for the town we can afford to ignore that?'

Watts put his hands up in a placatory gesture. 'You're right, of course.'

'Experts say the birds have become "abnormally aggressive" in Peacehaven. It's like that film *The Birds* down there. People and pets have been attacked. One woman told the *Argus* she wears a hard hat when she hangs out her washing.'

Hewitt joined in with Watts' laughter this time. Then she raised her hand.

'But, in consequence, there are more crimes against gulls in Peacehaven than the rest of the towns along the south coast put together.'

'Jesus,' Watts said, still grinning.

'I know, but we do have to deal with it.'

'Noted,' he said, composing himself.

Hewitt also put on a serious expression. 'Bob, we're still going down the path you set us on. Not reactive policing but problem solving and partnerships with our different communities to forestall criminality. However, times have changed. You were able to switch the money from people into technology so we could work smarter. But these days the government is squeezing us so hard we have no money to invest in more technology. So we shed even more people without getting the technology to fill the vacuum that creates. We're stretched very tight.'

'And I'm guessing you've still got the same problem with the public and the politicians,' Watts said. 'You put all your efforts into reducing domestic burglaries and your critics moan that means some other kind of crime is being ignored.'

'Exactly.' She gave Watts a sardonic look. 'Sure you want to get drawn back into all that?'

He smiled but said nothing.

Hewitt spread her hands. 'As you say, the public isn't always happy with the choices we make dealing with the competing demands on our resources. And as you'll remember, a dissatisfied public is an unhelpful public.'

'Tell me about it,' Watts said, recalling all the public meetings he'd had to manage during his stint in her seat. He knew the importance of keeping the public onside.

Hewitt looked at her tablet. 'If you're free the Force Command Team would like to meet you on Friday. Some familiar faces; some new ones.'

Watts looked at the calendar on his own tablet. 'Sure. Let me know the time.'

Hewitt leaned forward and touched his hand on the table. 'In relation to those kind of PR exercises there's one thing you could do,' she said. 'One thing I beg you to do, actually . . .'

'I'm on tenterhooks,' he said, glancing down as she squeezed his hand.

'Be the public face of Southern Police. You're brilliant at that. I'm rubbish – plus, I hate it. If you would take over that role, among all the other things I hope we'll be doing together, I'd be really grateful.'

Bob Watts smiled as he withdrew his hand. Sure he could do that. Forgetting, in the flattering moment, that the last time he'd shot off his big mouth as the public face of Southern Police he'd swiftly lost his job.

Karen Hewitt gave her cosmetically restricted smile right back. Only when he left the meeting did he recall that she, on the other hand, was a woman who forgot nothing.

# TWO

Heap was standing by Gilchrist's desk with what looked like the same sheaf of papers as before. Stanford was behind Heap, towering over him, holding down a yawn. She saw the expression on Heap's face.

'There's someone who stands out?' Gilchrist said.

'A certain Bernard Rafferty, ma'am,' Heap said.

'Bugger,' Gilchrist mouthed.

'Quite,' Heap said.

The constable looked from one to the other of them but didn't speak.

'You don't know who that is?' Gilchrist said to him.

'Why would I, ma'am?'

'Because he's the director of the Royal Pavilion.'

'Yes, ma'am?'

'You've heard of that, I suppose?'

'Nice pub,' said the constable.

Stanford was not her type at all.

'Watch your cheek, Constable.'

'Sorry, ma'am. It's just that the Royal Pavilion itself is not a place you'd ever be likely to find me.'

'You surprise me. He's also a regular broadcaster on current affairs shows on radio and television.'

'That's not going to help me identify him either, ma'am.'

Heap interrupted again. 'In addition, he's an expert on the churchyards of Sussex.'

'I didn't think that included digging up the bodies,' Gilchrist said. She chewed the inside of her cheek for a moment. 'Was this a recent burial, Constable?'

Stanford shook his head. 'Definitely not – some one hundred and fifty years old.'

'Do we know he was the one who actually opened the grave?' Gilchrist said. 'Maybe the church was moving the body for some reason.'

'So why was he there?' Heap said. 'Was he cottaging?'

Stanford showed his teeth. 'In Keymer at four in the morning, sir? Unlikely. Lovely people there but those that aren't already in the grave have one foot in it.'

'I don't know if it's good or bad he wasn't cottaging,' Gilchrist said. 'It wouldn't be much of a scandal in this city. I saw one chief executive chair a public meeting in spandex bicycle shorts through which his Prince Albert was more than evident. However, we could still do without one of our most prominent citizens getting that kind of media attention. The council's tourist department is already hard pushed to keep the Gomorrah-by-sea tag off the city.'

'I think what he was doing is going to create enough of a scandal without his sexual practices coming into it,' Heap said. 'If it was him.'

Gilchrist nodded. 'That last remark noted. We mustn't jump to conclusions. As our new police commissioner pointed out, there's a big difference between being proactive and being predictive.'

Gilchrist looked back at Heap. 'Perhaps we should have a discreet word with him,' she said, then looked at Stanford. 'Right, Constable, you've done a good job. We'll take it from here.'

He stifled another yawn. Gilchrist got a waft of stale coffee breath.

'Suits me, ma'am. My shift ended two hours ago.'

'And you and your partner keep this to yourself. If it is him, I don't want it splashing all over the papers.'

Stanford's expression didn't change. 'Absolutely, ma'am.'

Gilchrist and Heap watched him go.

'You know, ma'am . . .'

'That I might just have put an idea into his head? Absolutely.'

'No, ma'am. That Gomorrah *was* by the sea.'

She sniffed. 'I always thought Sodom-by-sea was a bit too near the truth but had more of a ring to it.'

'Would that ring be a Prince Albert, ma'am?' Heap said.

Heap could keep a straight face like nobody else Gilchrist knew. She barked a laugh, embarrassed by how loud and abrupt it was.

'You got a girlfriend, Bellamy?' she said after a moment.

He looked startled, his face flushing.

'Scratch that question,' Gilchrist said, also flushing. 'None of my bloody business.'

'No, ma'am,' he said, giving the papers a little wave and heading back to his desk.

Gilchrist watched him go. He moved very gracefully for a short man. But he wasn't short-arsed or anything – he was actually perfectly proportioned. Just in miniature. However, she wasn't really thinking about that, she was thinking about his 'No'. Did he mean that it wasn't any of her business, or did he mean he didn't have a girlfriend?

She'd been thinking lately that it was about time she got back on the dating scene. Well, not quite that. She'd never actually been on the dating scene. But she wondered about meeting someone. Not Bellamy, nice as he was. Then she laughed. Given her job, what were the chances?

You drop your duffel at your small hotel in Phnom Penh and head straight out to the Tuol Sleng Genocide Museum. It opened in 1980, kept exactly as it was found by the invading Vietnamese a year earlier. Even though its existence revealed the horrors Pol Pot and his Khmer Rouge had inflicted upon his own people, the international community spent the next ten years denouncing Vietnam's invasion and insisting on recognising only the genocidal Khmer Rouge as Kampuchea's legal government.

Originally this place had been a well-appointed high school, with an airy set of buildings and ample open space around it. In 1976, the Khmer Rouge took it over and renamed it Security Prison-21. Guard towers were erected; the perimeter was swathed in barbed wire. Classrooms were turned into torture chambers, playgrounds into mass graves, a place of enlightenment into a place of darkness and horror.

Before you take the tour you read the plaque in the entrance hall. Some 20,000 prisoners were killed here during its time as a prison and interrogation centre. When there was no more space in the grounds to bury the bodies prisoners were transported to the Killing Fields.

You take your time walking round. There are four main buildings. Building A has mostly large individual cells where the bodies of the final victims were found. The cells contain only rusting bed frames. On the walls black-and-white photographs show the rooms as the Vietnamese found them. Each photograph shows the mutilated body of a prisoner chained to these same frames, finished off by the Khmer Rouge not long before the prison was captured.

Building B has terrible instruments of torture and leg irons on display. On the walls are paintings by a former inmate, Vann Nath, of torture being administered. Waterboarding, hog-tying and electrocutions are all represented in a naïve style in bright colours.

Building C is lined, floor to ceiling, with black-and-white photographs of some of the thousands of prisoners who passed through the system on their way to a mass grave. In one room you watch a bank of television monitors on which those who survived and those who tortured them recount their experiences. Torturer and victim are often from the same village and still live in close proximity.

On the top floor of Building D the rooms are crudely subdivided into small cells for prisoners and on the floors below large communal cells. This is the building you know best.

In the early days most of the victims had been from the regime the Khmer Rouge had overthrown: soldiers, government officials, academics, doctors, teachers, engineers plus students, factory workers and monks.

Then, as Pol Pot worried about a coup against him, he turned on his own party, accusing thousands of party activists and senior party officials and their families of espionage.

Most prisoners were held for two or three months. Some high-ranking Khmer Rouge officials were held longer. Everybody was tortured. No exceptions.

The torture methods were crude but horribly effective. Electric shocks, sometimes administered by lashing the victim with a live electric cable. Branding with hot metal. Hanging until almost choked to death then revived, again and again. Slashing with knives or machetes. Suffocating with plastic bags or by holding the victim's head under water. Waterboarding, decades before it became infamous. Fingernails pulled out with alcohol poured on the wounds to make the pain worse.

Surprisingly, rape, so often a weapon of war and subjugation, was against party policy. Rapists risked execution if they were found out. Skinning somebody alive was fine but you couldn't have forced sex with them.

Skinning alive was reserved for the most intractable prisoners. And around one hundred prisoners were bled to death in the medical unit. Every single drop of blood was drained from them in experiments to see how long a person could survive with different degrees of blood loss. Others had internal organs removed without anaesthetic.

The irony of this terrible experimentation was that there was hardly anybody capable of carrying it out professionally: the Khmer Rouge had killed most of the doctors in the country and closed all hospitals and medical centres.

You walk the perimeter. There is barbed wire all around the high walls and fences. A sign says it used to be electrified. As you walk you look up at the windows of the four buildings, still covered with iron bars and razor wire. All this to prevent one thousand five hundred prisoners getting out.

The Khmer Rouge was not expecting anyone to try to get in.


Gilchrist and Heap arrived in Kemp Town. Bernard Rafferty's tall, narrow Georgian house was mid-terrace.

A handsome young man answered the door in a sarong. He was bare-chested. He smiled but raised an eyebrow quizzically.

'We're here to see Bernard Rafferty,' Gilchrist said.

'I believe he's still in bed.'

Gilchrist looked at her watch ostentatiously. It was, after all, lunchtime.

'Late night?' Heap said.

The young man took his time looking Heap up and down. 'I wouldn't know. I was sleeping in the guest room.'

He continued to stand in the doorway, smiling at them, eyebrow still raised.

'May we come in?' Gilchrist said.

He pursed his lips. 'Well, I don't know. Shouldn't you have a warrant and all that kind of thing?'

'We don't want to search the premises, sir,' Heap said. 'Just ask Mr Rafferty a few questions. Perhaps you could tell him we're here.'

The young man turned back into the house as a tetchy voice called out.

'What's all the bloody racket out there, Roger?'

'It seems Mr Rafferty has woken,' Gilchrist said.

The young man called Roger nodded, a slight smirk on his face. 'It seems he has.'

\*   \*   \*

A familiar figure was coming out of the Bath Arms in the Lanes. It took a moment for Bob Watts to place him.

'Winston Hart – how the hell are you?'

Hart, the former chair of the Southern Police committee, was looking dishevelled. Unshaven, red-eyed. His neat little moustache had grown into a straggly bramble over his mouth. He had been trying to get past Watts without acknowledging him.

'As if you would care.'

'I'm sorry the press did a number on you,' Watts said – and meant it. 'How's your son?'

Hart's reaction was physical. He reeled back. 'He's not my bloody son,' he said through gritted teeth. 'He's the son of the anti-Christ.'

Watts was inclined to agree with him. Hart's son had killed his best friend and chopped off his head and pretty much dismembered him in a drugged and drunken stupor in a Hove flat some while ago. Hart had been obliged to resign during the press furore about his son's heinous crime, and now the PCC post that Watts occupied had replaced the committee altogether.

At the time of Hart's resignation Watts had been vengefully gleeful because Hart was one of a gang of people he blamed for wrecking his career over the disastrous Milldean Massacre. Hart had taken undue delight in lording over Watts at the meeting in which he was forced to resign.

However, that was long ago and now he genuinely did feel sorry for Hart.

'Did your son get his deal?' Watts said.

'I don't know. I don't have anything to do with him.' Hart put a sneer on his face. 'You came up smelling of roses though, didn't you?'

'I knew I could count on your vote,' Watts said evenly.

Hart spat at his feet and the sympathy Watts had for him dwindled.

'Back on the fucking gravy train,' Hart said. 'Lucky you.'

'Luck had nothing to do with it,' Watts said, more calmly than he felt. 'And the gravy long ago congealed.'

He watched Hart stumble down the alley then turned and went into the Bath Arms. It was one of the oldest pubs in Brighton. His father had frequented it during the thirties but it had been around, in some form or other, for a couple of hundred years before then. It was hosting a wine and seafood festival so he bought a large glass of muscadet and a pint of cockles, mussels and whelks.

He had the pub to himself except for an overweight man in his thirties nursing a pint at the far end of the bar. Watts recognized him as one of the men who worked on the security desk at the Brighton museum.

Watts sat on a stool at a high table by the open window. He got busy on the seafood with a toothpick whilst working on his tablet and glancing up occasionally to watch the world walk by outside.

He was thinking about his own children, Tom and Catherine. He couldn't understand how his estrangement from them could have become so complete. He'd encouraged them to become independent when they went off to university and they'd both made a good start by going about as far away as possible from Brighton.

Tom, the elder, was probably born independent. Now he was out on an archaeological dig somewhere dangerous in the Middle East. Watts had cautioned against; Tom had ignored him.

His daughter, Catherine, was freaking him out. She'd got religion. Big time. God squad: that's what they used to call it when he was at university. Bright-eyed girls and boys, all smiling a lot. A deadness behind the eyes, as with any person in a cult. He was used to the looks he'd seen on the faces of yoga obsessives in Brighton but true religious nuts took the blissful stare to scary lengths.

Her fundamentalist Christianity depressed him as he saw it as a consequence of his failure as a parent. What vast need had he and his wife, Molly, created that required filling with such madness?

As an eminently rational man, his daughter's Creationism depressed him even more. He kept up with what she was up to via her Facebook page. When he'd looked this morning her latest posting had been a photograph of a carving in Ta Prohm, a Cambodian temple. Creationists were claiming it was a carving of a stegosaur and that meant the spiky dinosaur had still been around millions of years after atheistic evolutionists claimed they had died out.

And that meant the evolutionists were wrong about the age

of the earth because they misrepresented the fossil record. And *that* meant the Creationist belief in the age of the Earth as given in the Bible was the true account. Men and dinosaurs had coexisted.

Bonkers. Just bonkers.

Watts was primarily a logical man. Much of the Bible made no sense. How could you accept the story of Adam and Eve or the fact that if God is omnipotent he allows such evil in the world? Watts couldn't. His late mum did. His mother had been vaguely religious and that 'vaguely' had driven him nuts.

'Even so,' she would say. 'Even so – there's something there.'

'Something evil,' Watts would reply. 'God is a thorough-going uncaring sadist. He feels nothing for us.'

His mother had emotional intelligence but zero logical intelligence. She couldn't string an argument together to save her life. Bob, like his brother and his father, was fiercely logical, fiercely reductive.

When they were teenagers they used that logic to shred her opposition to their doing things she disapproved of. Usually the things they wanted to do were stupid and his mother instinctively knew that, but they beat her down with their logic.

How shameful his behaviour had been. And with his wife and children too. His estranged wife, Molly, was living out her fantasy in Canada with a guy she'd been having an affair with for two weeks a year over a decade. Good luck with that, he muttered sourly.

Of course, Molly blamed him for her daughter's descent into fundamentalism.

'If you hadn't had that sordid affair with that policewoman,' she'd said during their most recent phone call.

'I think our daughter's disenchantment began before then,' Watts said. 'Perhaps your drinking had something to do with it.'

'Fuck you,' his wife said. 'My drinking came very late in the day – and it came because of you, incidentally.'

'Maybe it was our arguing?'

'Maybe it was just that you were never, ever fucking there?'

The line went dead. Before mobiles his wife had been a great smasher-of phones back down into their cradles. It must have been frustrating for her that slamming a mobile phone down would just

break it. Now all she could do was make a click, even if it was
with feeling.

Leaning against a tall marble fireplace, Rafferty looked like
someone in a Noël Coward play, without the smoking jacket but
with a paisley cravat. His head was tilted back so he was looking
down his nose at them. Or would have been if Gilchrist hadn't
been about a foot taller than him.

She introduced herself and Heap.

'I know you, don't I?' Rafferty said to Gilchrist as he gestured
for them to sit down on a deep sofa. He grinned wolfishly. 'Ah
yes. The PCC's girl.'

Heap glanced at Gilchrist.

'Hardly,' Gilchrist said, hoping she hadn't flushed. She looked
back at Heap. He seemed to be flushing on her behalf.

'We wondered if you'd mind telling us where you were at about
three this morning?' Heap said.

Rafferty stepped away from the fireplace and plonked himself
in a wingback armchair. He crossed his legs and pointed at Heap.

'And you – you investigated the theft of a picture from my
gallery some months ago?'

'The name is Detective Sergeant Heap, sir.'

'A promotion for recovering my painting?'

Gilchrist saw Heap flush brighter. He was newly promoted.
Gilchrist had brought him on to her team as detective constable
to help investigate a sudden upsurge in black magic happenings
in and around Brighton. He had proved so helpful she had immediately recommended him for promotion to detective sergeant.

Being Bellamy Heap, Boy Genius, he had done his sergeant's
exams in three months instead of a year, and when Gilchrist's
appointment as DI had been made permanent he had taken her
slot as DS. Gilchrist had asked the chief constable to assign him
to her. So here they were.

'Three this morning, sir?' Heap said.

'I was in bed, of course. I had an early start this morning – it
was the launch of the Great Escape.'

Gilchrist frowned. 'So you've been up some time?'

'My dear, I went back to bed the minute I returned home.'

'Detective Inspector will do nicely, thank you, Mr Rafferty,'

Gilchrist said. She glanced through the open door at Roger in his sarong, looking busy in the kitchen. 'Three in the morning – can anyone confirm you were in bed?'

Rafferty followed her glance. 'Alas, no,' he said softly. '*Detective Inspector.*'

'Did anyone borrow your car last night?'

'Beautiful boy,' Rafferty called. 'Did you borrow my car last night?'

Roger put down a cloth and shook his head.

Rafferty leaned forward conspiratorially. 'He thinks he's a trucker – only likes driving lorries. Thinks it makes him butch.'

'A car matching the description of yours was observed over the other side of the Downs in the middle of the night,' Heap said.

'Matching the description of mine – you mean there is some doubt?'

'Until CCTV footage has been analysed we can't be certain,' Gilchrist said.

Rafferty pushed his chest out and stuck his nose in the air again. Gilchrist wondered if such an action was the origin of *being stuck up*. She flicked a look at Bellamy Heap. He would undoubtedly know.

'I don't understand why you have come to my house then,' Rafferty said coldly. 'Is this not a little premature?'

Gilchrist glanced at Heap again.

'Do you ever do your research at night?' Heap said.

'My research?'

'You write about Sussex graveyards, don't you?'

Rafferty clasped his hands primly on his knee. 'You mean do I hang about in churchyards by the light of the silvery moon? In my younger days one or two of Brighton's town centre churchyards were popular as midnight trysting places. Frankly, I think everyone should have sex in a graveyard at least once in their lives – don't you, DI Gilchrist?' Gilchrist tried to keep her face expressionless. 'But where are those blue remembered hills?'

'That's a "no", then,' Heap said.

Rafferty swung towards him. 'Ah – the brains of the outfit. Do I hang about in churchyards? Not any more, and certainly *not* in Keymer.' Rafferty stood, hands clasped in front of him, nose in the air yet again. 'So, officers, if I may go about my business you may go about yours.'

Gilchrist gave Heap the slightest of nods. They both remained seated.

'Why did you mention Keymer, Mr Rafferty?' Heap said quietly.

Rafferty put a manicured finger to his lips. 'I thought you mentioned it.'

Heap shook his head. 'We merely said it was an incident over the other side of the Downs.'

'I mentioned it randomly, then,' Rafferty said. 'Keymer is, after all, over the other side of the Downs.'

'So are many villages.'

Rafferty shrugged and tugged on his lower lip. 'Keymer is the one I happen to know best. I have written about it at length.'

'In which book?' Heap said.

Rafferty paused. 'Not just in books,' he said airily. 'In academic journals and specialist publications.'

'So not in any of your books?'

Rafferty tried for an indignant expression. It didn't really work. 'Of course, in my books. I've told you. It is probably the most important church in this area.'

Heap tilted his head. 'Really?'

Rafferty shot him a superior look. 'Yes. Really.'

'Sorry if I sounded surprised, sir. In your major work on Sussex churchyards two years ago you give that honour to the small church of St Michael beside Plumpton College. Second was its sister church at Plumpton itself; then Clayton parish church. Ditchling gets quite a lengthy entry. Keymer gets a mention only in a foot-note. In passing.'

Rafferty gave Heap a long look then glanced into the kitchen. Gilchrist followed his glance. Roger was no longer there.

'Look,' Rafferty finally said. 'I wasn't in Keymer churchyard in the middle of the night.'

Gilchrist slowly let out her breath.

'We didn't say you were, Mr Rafferty,' Heap said. 'I merely asked why you mentioned Keymer. We haven't mentioned Keymer at all.'

Heap stood now and for the first time he seemed quite tall. He began to tilt his head backwards then seemed to think better of it.

'However, a car matching the description of your car was identi-fied in Keymer at three this morning,' Gilchrist said. 'The driver was acting strangely in the graveyard. He then assaulted a police officer and ran away. It's an intriguing coincidence that you seem to have Keymer on your mind.'

Heap took a step nearer to Rafferty.

'Is there anything you want to say, sir?'

Rafferty held his look then cleared his throat.

'I wish to contact my lawyer.'

# THREE

I t is brightly coloured, single storey, with rooms down six
corridors radiating off the swimming pool in the central courtyard. Incense sticks burn everywhere. People, mostly half your
age, lounge on piles of cushions in alcoves around the perimeter
of the pool.

At the back of your room you have your own private pool in a
small yard. It is little more than a plunge bath. The water is deep
and cold.

You swim lengths in the main pool, aware of the stitches in
your stomach when you do crawl and backstroke. The pool is
pleasantly warm but heavily chlorinated. You finish with two
lengths underwater, enjoying the play of sunlight across the tiles
beneath you.

There is a bar next door to the motel serving western food. You
love Cambodian food but your motel doesn't serve lunch and you
don't want to travel too far afield. You sit at a table by the door,
set out your cigarettes and lighter beside your right hand and order
pizza and a triple vodka.

You watch two overweight, sweaty western men monkeying
around with two petite, much younger Cambodian women. Every
time the men grab at their buttocks or breasts the women giggle
with pleasure but you see the looks that pass between them when
the men are focused on their drinks.

Your pizza is pretty ropey but you ordered it for energy, not for
taste. You approve of the fact that the vodka comes from the freezer.
It is viscous; you take your time. Although you know it's the
custom, you've never understood why anyone would want to down
vodka or any other drink in one.

In the days when things had meaning for you, you loved a Hart
Crane couplet: 'Some men take their liquor slow and count the
river's minute by the far brook's year'.

The two men are joined by two more, equally scuzzy, mean-
looking westerners. They shoo the women away and huddle round

a table. One of the new arrivals keeps his eyes on you. He looks handy. You focus on the television behind the bar. Or rather the mirror beside it through which you can watch the men.

It's depressing that these four men look such stereotypes of those who come to Cambodia for sex and drugs. Paedophiles, pimps and pushers. You have no doubt these men are all three. You wonder if they might lead you where you need to go.

Your plan is as yet ill-formed but before you head for Siem Reap you need to see how the land lies.

The two women are outside in the alley, talking quietly but rapidly, sucking on cocktails through straws, fiddling with their cheap-looking mobile phones. They are solemn-faced, unless they notice the men looking, in which case they break into big, false grins.

You don't speak Khmer, the main Cambodian language, but your French isn't bad and these women may have a smattering. You're not sure whether they are Cambodian or Vietnamese, but it doesn't matter as both countries were once *Indochine* and the French influence persists.

You pick up your cigarettes, lighter and vodka and step outside. You nod at the women. They give nervous smiles and glance at their men inside.

You ask in French how they are. They look anxious. A man is suddenly by your side. The handy one who was keeping his eye on you.

'Help you, mate?' he asks with an accent that belongs somewhere in Bermondsey, not here in a back alley in Phnom Penh. Though maybe in the global village there's not much to choose between them.

'Just passing the time of day with these ladies,' you say.

'Wrong *ladies* to pass the time of day with.' The man gives a simulacrum of a smile. 'They're spoken for.' He edges closer to you. 'Might be able to help you out if you're looking for other female company, though. To pass as much time with as you can afford.'

You offer him a cigarette with a tilt of the packet. He shakes his head, the non-smile now a rictus.

'You might be able to help me at that,' you say.

'What do you need, brother?'

'Paradise.'

He snorts. 'We could all do with a bit of that. But are you meaning drugs, girls, boys or congress with a hairy fucking gorilla to reach that particular destination?'

'Sal Paradise. I assume he still runs this town? I need to see him.'

The cockney's eyes are hooded so you can't read anything into his blank stare. However, you see the women exchange rapid glances then look down.

The man shrugs. 'Never heard of him, brother. Sorry.'

Sal Paradise. Nobody knows his real name – at least, you don't. Italian possibly. Maybe French. Maybe not Italian or French at all. Nobody knows why he chose the name Salvatore 'Sal' Paradise. You know it's the name French-Canadian Jack Kerouac gave to the narrator of *On The Road*, his one good novel. Though Jack's Italian wasn't up to making the last name 'Paradiso'. Maybe the Paradise you're interested in was a Dharma bum who ended up here on his hitchhiking trail.

There is no way this man has not heard of Sal Paradise. In Cambodia Paradise has been The Man for damn near forty years. Home-grown *criminales* have tried to take him over; the government has tried to shut him down; Vietnamese wise guys have tried to put the pinch on him. He's seen them all off.

A certain amount of myth has accrued around him. Colonel Kurtz madness; Rambo righteousness; Fu Manchu sneakiness. All stereotypes. All wide of the mark. You met him thirty-five years ago. You were pleading.

Paradise was in shadow. Of course. He gave you twenty seconds then cut you off.

'Stop, for Christ's sake,' he snarled. 'A grown man begging turns my stomach. You never get anything with begging.'

'The person I'm talking about is someone I care for very much.'

You couldn't see his face but you could hear the grimace in his voice.

'More fool you,' Paradise said. 'We're not going to get along if you carry on like this. First thing you need to learn is that emotion is pathetic and useless. Look around: the world belongs to those who feel nothing.'

'Just let me know the whereabouts,' you said. 'I'll do the rest.'

'It doesn't work like that in my country.'

'I'll pay.'

'That was a given.'

'A lot.'

'That's where we begin to diverge. What constitutes "a lot" for you and for me are, I fear, two quite different things.'

'Payment doesn't have to be in money,' you said.

'I don't want your arse, thanks very much.'

'I didn't mean that,' you said. 'I have skills you could use.'

Paradise was silent for a long moment.

Now the cockney outside the bar is looking you up and down. You can see behind him that his friends in the bar are huddled together.

'What's your name anyway?' he says.

You tell him.

He eases away.

'Well, brother, if I come upon this Mr Paradise I'll be sure to mention your name.' He glances around you. 'In the meantime, why don't you stick that glass up your arse?'

The two women aren't there any more. You point the glass at the cockney but not in a combative way.

'What's *your* name?' you say.

'Neal.'

'Cassady?'

He laughs so you know he understands the *On The Road* reference. And that means he is tipping you to the fact that he knows Paradise.

'Just help me get started with him,' you say. 'You can't do whatever it is you do without his say-so. Give me a number.'

Neal gives you the once-over again. Frowns.

'You look like a stiff wind would blow you down. Why do you want to mess with Paradise?'

'That's a long story,' you say.

You're aware that Neal has shifted a couple of feet away and changed the angle between you. His stance is casual but you know he's getting ready.

You've been having problems with your temper lately. A lot of stuff coming up that you can't always control. There's been a lot of yin and yang going on. Mostly yang, unfortunately. Yoga and deep breathing exercises on the one hand; wanting to pummel people to death with your bare hands on the other.

You have the glass of neat vodka in one hand and your lighter in the other. You're tempted to throw the vodka over his head and touch the lighter to his hair.

But you've also been trying hard to be mellow. You drain the vodka, acutely watchful for any move from him to ram the glass into your teeth.

He's focused on you but is still caught off guard when you swing the glass away from your mouth into his left eye socket.

He stumbles back, instinctively putting his hand to his eye. You put him down with an elbow driven hard into his collarbone and another whack of the vodka glass, this time to his temple.

You walk back inside. You approach the table where the three men are sitting having a desultory conversation.

'I'm looking for Sal Paradise,' you say.

In the sudden silence Neal shouts something groggily incoherent from outside. They jerk around to look towards the door. You hit the two overweight men first and enjoy doing it. The other guy, the one who arrived with Neal, sits back.

'What have you done to my friend?' he says, working his jaw and starting to do something under the table.

'Pretty much what I'm going to do to you unless you tell me where I can find Sal Paradise,' you say.

The other guy sits back in his seat. 'Don't know the man,' he says, his body still.

The two creeps are bleeding worse than they're hurt but they're not thinking about anything other than their injuries. The barman is standing perfectly still behind the bar but his hands are concealed. He's up to something.

You look at the guy sitting at the table and gesture to Neal outside. 'Wuss.'

There's a hint of a smile then the man hurls himself out from behind the table, a knife in his hand. The problem is the table is screwed to the floor so hurling is a difficult thing to do.

You have time to hit him in the face with the glass in a hammer blow before he can get near you with the knife. It's a tough little fucker of a glass.

It's weird to watch the man's forward momentum almost

immediately reverse. You wish you knew the physics. He falls back, a glass-rim size impression on his forehead.

You figure it's about time you paid attention to the barman. You look at him and whatever it is he's bringing out from below the counter. You wag your finger and step towards him.

'How do I get hold of Sal Paradise?'

Watts had polished off his seafood and was thinking about his first official meeting as the new PCC when an Asian woman in an expensive-looking cashmere coat came into the pub. Chinese? Korean? Vietnamese? He really couldn't tell and that embarrassed him. At the bar, she bought a pint of beer and carried it carefully over to a table in the corner. A table Watts always liked to imagine his father drank at, back in the day. She sat, a look of misery on her face. He turned away from her grief.

The meeting had been with a contractor looking to sell the force Incapacitating Flashlights.

'Which are what?' Watts said.

The man was slick-suited, mid-thirties, a military background overlaid with a salesman's spiel. He placed what appeared to be a bulky-looking torch on the edge of the desk. Watts reached for it but the man shook his head.

'Handle with care. This is the next generation Tasers. A better non-lethal weapon. Homeland Security in the US developed it. It flashes intense beams of light to blind targets and make them vomit.'

Watts nodded slowly. 'What happens if they close their eyes?'

The contractor laughed. 'Then you go old-fashioned and kick them in the goolies.'

Watts smiled. If he had to see the salesmen Hewitt was clearly intending to sick on him then those with a sense of humour would work best for him.

'It's part of a range of next generation law enforcement aides,' the man said. 'We also have the Active Denial System. That heats the skin of a target individual in two seconds to fifty-four degrees centigrade, causing intolerable pain. Our acoustic bazooka – a sonic cannon – delivers a pattern of sound that is excruciatingly painful and incapacitates the targets by making them vomit.'

'How are they with seagulls?'

The man looked puzzled. 'Police Commissioner?'

'Just kidding,' Watts said. 'Is vomiting a common factor with these new generation weapons?'

The salesman shrugged. 'Vomiting is certainly a disabler.' He started rooting in his bag. 'I'm going to leave you a sample to test.'

The Asian woman abruptly rose and hurried out of the pub, still looking miserable. The pint was untouched so Watts assumed she had gone out for a cigarette, but the barman started to clear the drink away.

'You're sure she's not going to come back,' Watts called.

The overweight man snorted. The barman turned to Watts and shook his head.

'I wish she would. Waste of a good pint. Plus it might do her good – she looks so miserable.'

'She's done it before?' Watts said.

'She's been doing it for months,' the barman said. 'Same day every week. She buys a pint, sits there for a bit muttering to herself, then leaves without touching it.'

'Same seat?'

'Exact same seat. If it's taken she loiters and puts the pint down on the table when she leaves.'

Watts frowned and thought about that. 'All sorts,' he finally said.

The barman gives you the name of a nightclub Sal Paradise may or may not own. He is occasionally seen there. In the evening you search it out. It's more bar than nightclub. The few bored women scattered around are there for business purposes only. Various desperadoes are sitting around the room, in groups or alone.

The women assess you as you walk to the bar, dismiss you as a potential client. The desperadoes watch for longer.

'Sal Paradise?' you say at the bar.

The barman looks at you but says nothing.

'Doesn't he own this place?' you say.

The barman shrugs thick shoulders.

You ask for a bottle of Polish vodka and examine the seal before you hand over your money. It's cold enough. You take it to a table in the corner by the window. For the next hour you drink steadily, watching the street outside and the action in the bar, trying to ignore the rattle of the old fan above your head as it makes its wobbly rotations.

The drinking is unwise. This is not like you when you're on an operation. But then you're not like you and you haven't been for a long time.

Sal Paradise always had his fingers in a lot of pies. Prostitution, of course. He brought in girls from Vietnam. Doubtless he is now into people trafficking in a much bigger way. You've heard he is in the illegal organ trade. His people are skilled at filleting for all saleable organs some dope they've drugged in a bar and left bleeding out in a cheap hotel room. He is also heavily involved in the heroin trade. The fact he smuggles antiquities, either fake or real, seems almost benign, except that he uses the same distribution routes.

The custom in bars in Cambodia is that the waiter doesn't remove the old bottles from the table when he brings the new because he will count them up when it comes time to pay the bill. He sticks a paper napkin in the dead ones. There is a table in your line of sight with probably twenty bottles on it.

A western man in a sweaty T-shirt and stained shorts, his thick, hairy legs stretched out into the aisle between the tables, has his tongue down the throat of the tiny local woman in a red polka dot dress sitting beside him. He is pawing at her breast none too gently.

You look away to check on the three men in the street who turned up ten minutes ago. One of them is Neal, the mean man you glassed yesterday. Here on his own account or doing a job for Sal Paradise?

The sour taste of vodka comes up in your mouth. For a moment you think you are going to vomit. You breathe heavily through your nostrils.

Neal is lounging directly opposite the bar, the other two are at either end of the street. But is there someone round the back too?

Your plan, such as it is, involves getting behind them, letting them think they've lost you then following them to Paradise. Of course, if Neal is here on his own account, they'll just lead you back to the bar where you first met him.

You're pretty certain you can beat the bejesus out of any of them one on one and with the advantage of surprise. You're pretty sure they'll be carrying, but whether it will be knives or guns you don't know. You've got your own little helper in your pocket.

As you get up to go to the bathroom you catch the slightest of movements at the bar. A tattooed, thick-set guy not exactly looking your way but, by some slight adjustment of his being, tying himself to your movement. The barman is busily and pointedly polishing glasses. A woman in a tight black dress looks at you hopefully.

You were thinking maybe they wanted to take you in the street but now you're wondering if they want to do it here.

Well, you're on your feet now. You have to do something. You don't look at the guy. You stumble a little as you head over to the door marked *Toilettes*. You're putting it on, but only by a fraction.

You push open the door. It leads into a short corridor with another door to the right. Through that is a small room with wash-basin and, facing you, two doors: one for women, one for men. You push open the one for women. It's a narrow cubicle with no window. You push open the men's door. The same.

You close both doors and squeeze behind the outer door. There's just about space between you and the side-wall. You're pretty sure that as the door opens, a pursuer won't be able to see you in the mirror above the washbasin on the opposite wall.

In your inside pocket you have a cosh. Sand in a leather pouch. It is about sixty years old but it still does the job it was intended for when your father made it. He had a set of brass knuckledusters too but they went missing years ago. Tough guy, your dad. Especially when it came to women.

Your problem is the confined space. There isn't going to be much room to get a good swing.

The door handle rattles and you raise the cosh to shoulder height. The door opens against you, obscuring the person coming in. A hand reaches round the door and pushes it closed just as you start your swing. You would normally go for behind the ear but you're not sure of your aim so intend just to whack him as hard as you can on the back of the skull.

Except it isn't the man who was sitting by the bar. It isn't a man at all. You grab the woman in the polka dot dress as she folds. You kick at the women's toilet door and drag her in, lowering her on to the toilet seat. She slumps to the side. You wedge her against the wall, trying not to notice the lump rising on the back of her head like a soufflé and the blood streaking her dyed blonde hair with red.

'Sorry, love,' you whisper as you pull the door closed behind you.

You are turning in the confined space in front of the sink when the outer door opens again. A bulky male edges through. You let him get the door partway open then, just as he sees you, you shoulder the door shut in his face. You have your full weight behind the door and you feel it hit him hard.

You pull the door open. The man who was sitting at the bar is coming off the opposite wall. You go for the nose, swinging the sap in a tight arc then flicking your wrist to bring it down hard on the bridge.

You hear the crack and feel the blood spurt across you. The man puts his hands up to his face as he slumps. You drag him in and leave him half in, half out of the men's cubicle. You close the bathroom door behind you.

You follow the corridor to the end. The fire exit is locked, double-locked and padlocked. You are going to have to leave by the front door now. You re-enter the bar and move as quickly as you can before people respond to the commotion. You see the barman coming out from behind his counter.

You are trying to be light on your feet but, given the amount you have drunk, you feel like a barrel rolling into the street.

The humidity hits you first and then Neal, standing to the side of the door.

He is aiming for your kidneys but by chance your elbow gets in the way. He has his own knuckleduster. You feel the pain shoot up to your shoulder as your whole arm goes dead. You stagger to the side.

You still have the cosh in your other hand and you swing it tight and fast and hit him across the side of his head.

You are aiming for his temple. You are doing it by reflex and not thinking about the fact that you might kill him. But you can't get enough swing so it is not a good blow. Even so, he totters.

There is an alley directly across from the restaurant. You huff and you puff and though you may not blow the house down you do get across the street and halfway down the alley before the two little piggies at either end of the street have started moving.

You abandon any idiotic thought of trailing them back to Sal Paradise. Instead you head back to your hotel and take to your bed, exhausted and drunk and cursing yourself for that drunkenness.

You are woken some time later by the sensation of drowning. You are drowning, in the plunge pool in your backyard.

Whilst Rafferty was on the telephone to his solicitor, Gilchrist and Heap huddled.

'You know we have to arrest him, ma'am, if we're to secure the car and the house,' Heap said. 'If we leave him here he can destroy evidence.'

'I know,' Gilchrist said, chewing on a nail. 'But, Bellamy, we're out on a limb here. We don't know for certain it was his car. If it is his car we don't know he was driving it. He could say someone stole it – because, actually, we don't know where his frigging car is.'

'With respect, ma'am, we haven't looked yet.' Heap gave a half-gesture. 'And it's him, ma'am. You know it is.'

'It seems probable but he's an important person in the town.'

Heap looked up at her. 'I didn't know you were the cautious type when it came to worries about a powerful person biting back.'

Gilchrist flared. 'Mind your bloody lip, Sergeant,' she hissed. 'We have to be seen to be acting properly.'

'Arrest them both and we will be,' Heap said.

'Easy enough for you to say,' Gilchrist almost snarled at him. 'The shit doesn't stop with you.'

Heap nodded slowly. 'You're right, ma'am. Nine times out of ten shit does flow downward to land on my head and the heads of people like me. But in an instance like this the shit flows upwards.' Unexpectedly, he grinned, his cheeks reddening. 'But it doesn't stop with you either. Isn't that why God created chief constables?'

You lie on the tiles by the pool, face down, spluttering up chlorinated water and vodka. Someone kicks you in the ribs, hard enough to lift you off the tiles. You retch again and curl into a ball, expecting further kicks.

Nothing happens.

You can see out of the corner of your eye a man standing in the doorway of your room. He is half in shadow, appropriately enough. You look behind you. Neal and two of his men are standing in a semi-circle, well within kicking distance, looking towards the shadowy figure. He leans out of the shadow. He jabs a finger at you though his voice is low and calm. Hoarse, exactly as you remember it.

'If you want to speak to somebody, what's wrong with just picking up the bloody telephone, asshole?' He shakes his head. 'Jesus. Coming on like gangbusters in one of my bars.'

Sal Paradise. You recognize the voice but you've never seen his face before. You're not sure how you expected him to look. Mean-faced like Neal? Barbaric? You've met enough bad people not to expect him to be wreathed in sulphur or breathing fire from his nostrils.

Of course, he just looks ordinary. A bit jowly, bags under his eyes. He looks down at you. He has your passport in his hand. He scrutinizes it then looks at you, frowning.

'We know each other?'

'From a long time ago,' you say.

'And you've come for payback? Because, let me tell you, that ain't going to happen. Better men than you have tried, Gunga Din.'

'I came to you for help,' you say.

'I ain't in the helping business, friend.'

'That's what you said then.'

'What – and that has rankled with you all these years? Now that's what I call a slow burn.'

'I've got no beef with you. I'm looking for men you had deal-ings with thirty-five years ago – men you may still have dealings with. Men you told me were dead.'

'Most men I had dealings with thirty-five years ago are dead. Nature of the business. I'm the exception.'

'I know one of them is alive,' you say. 'I don't know if you still have dealings with him and the others.'

'If the others are still alive. You say I told you they were dead back then?'

'You did. An ambush, you said.'

Paradise shrugs. 'Then they're dead.' He peers at you. 'But if they are still alive you want me to welch on someone I do business with?'

'I just need to be sure there won't be a problem with you when I go after them.'

Paradise grimaces. '*When* not *if* you go after them, you say. Sounds like you've already made your mind up, whether I give you permission or not.'

You say nothing.

'That's all you want?' he says. 'My permission?'

'Current whereabouts would also be useful.'

Paradise shows his teeth. 'If I were you I'd be contemplating your own whereabouts in about ten minutes' time.'

You take a gamble. 'They ripped you off thirty-five years ago and I bet they just pissed themselves laughing at what a dumb fuck you were.'

Paradise clenches his big fists.

'You're about a spider's fart away from having your back broken. How do you feel about spending the rest of your life as a head on a stick?'

'Do you mind if I sit up?' you say.

'Go ahead – it makes it easier for me to kick your teeth in.'

You roll on to your side, trying not to grimace at the pain in your ribs. You're hoping they're only bruised, not broken, though it actually makes little difference. Your throat and chest burn from the forced ingestion of water. You sit up, cross your legs loosely.

'Thirty-five years ago you did a bit of business with four men: Rogers, Cartwright, Howe and Bartram. You told me at the time they were dead but I'm guessing in fact they ripped you off.'

'And pissed themselves laughing – yes, I got that. Why do you care?'

'That's a long story.'

'And you don't have much time left, so why don't you give me the SparkNotes version?'

'They took something precious away from me.'

'Thirty-five years ago?'

You nod. He laughs but it's not much of a laugh.

'And only now you're pissed about it?'

You cough up some more water. 'I've only just realized,' you say hoarsely.

'And what do you want with these guys? You're going to kill them?'

Your lungs are hurting now as well as your ribs. 'Probably.'

'No offence, but don't you think you're getting a bit old for that shit?'

You say nothing. Paradise shakes his head.

'And you want me to facilitate that? I don't think so.'

'Why?'

Paradise leans forward again. He has a vein throbbing in his forehead. You watch it, trying to calculate his heart rate. It's low. As if to explain why it's low he says: 'I never let emotion get in the way of business.' He sits back. 'Let me tell you something, pilgrim.' He works his jaw, preparing his pronouncement. Here it comes. 'The world belongs to those who feel nothing.'

You nod. 'I've heard. You think that's a good thing, do you?'

'I think it's a damned shame, but that is the world I live in so I have to acknowledge it.'

'Embrace it?'

'Deal with it.'

You look at the water in your pool for a moment. 'Don't you want to know how they ripped you off?'

Paradise shakes his head again and smiles. You think he's aiming for genial but he's forgotten how to be anything but ruthless. The smile is a grimace.

'That long ago? Couldn't give a fuck. I've done my share of shafting and been shafted since.'

'Do you still do business with them?'

Paradise stands. 'Leave them alone, pilgrim.'

'I know one of them is attached to an office in Siem Reap.'

'There you go then – you don't need me.'

'I'm paying that office a visit next.'

Paradise wags a finger at you. 'If you try that there may not be any *next* for you.'

Gilchrist told a constable to keep Rafferty and his house guest, now in a shirt and jeans, in the kitchen. She and Heap went into the hallway.

'We'll have the first look then let Don-Don and the rest do the thorough stuff when they get here,' Gilchrist said.

Don-Don was Detective Sergeant Donald Donaldson, who was a loose part of her team. Or perhaps a loose cannon part of her team was a better description.

'Ma'am,' Heap said.

'Obsessive-compulsive?' Gilchrist said to Heap, gesturing around the long ground-floor room.

'Extremely,' Heap agreed. 'Remarkable when it's so overstuffed with knick-knacks and all this fussy stuff.'

'No wonder he lives alone,' Gilchrist said. 'Who else could find shelf space? You live in Brighton, Heap?'

'Lewes, ma'am,' he said, leading the way up the steep staircase to the first floor. 'Brighton is too exciting for me.'

The front room on that floor was a library, lined with books from floor to ceiling. All hardbacks. The master bedroom was at the rear with long French windows looking out over the well-kept garden.

Neither these rooms nor the floor above held anything of immediate interest. The house was formidably tidy except for the guest room on the top floor scattered with Roger's clothes.

Gilchrist pulled the bedcover back. 'And?'

'He's been sleeping here,' Heap said. 'Whether he was last night I wouldn't know.'

They descended to the basement, which had been fitted out as a self-contained flat.

A room at the front was locked and bolted on the outside. The key was in the door. Heap and Gilchrist exchanged looks. Somebody locked in here?

There was and there wasn't. When they walked in both stopped dead. It was a big sitting room with sofas and armchairs and, over against one wall, a dining table and chairs. And on every available seat were placed oversized dolls, in skirts and stockings, aprons and Bo-Peep hats.

'Has he been nicking the museum stock . . .?' Gilchrist started to say when she realized something.

Heap must have realized it at the same time because he suddenly clutched at her. 'Christ,' he said.

'My sentiments exactly,' Gilchrist whispered, gently disengaging Heap's hand from her arm.

He looked down at what she was doing and the second

realization dawned. He jerked his hand away from her and flushed bright red. 'Sorry, ma'am,' he said.

'It's all right, Bellamy,' she whispered, unsure why she wasn't speaking in her normal voice. 'We all get taken by surprise.' She surveyed the room. 'I'd say Keymer isn't the first graveyard Mr Rafferty has robbed.'

Bob Watts looked down on the promenade from his balcony. The seafront was busy in the sunshine but hardly anyone was actually promenading. Scarcely a walker to be seen. Jostling together were cyclists, joggers, then grown men and women on scooters or roller-blades or skateboards. There was also a new breed: people on skis with little wheels attached, propelling themselves along with ski sticks.

One of the few people walking was a man with a huge cluster of balloons battling with the wind. Dirigibles really, shaped as Dalmatians, dolphins, whales and tigers. A big gust of wind almost lifted him off his feet as it caught the balloons. Watts smiled but the man didn't. There seemed something wrong about a man selling such happy, silly things being so churlish.

Damn if the middle-aged Asian woman from the pub wasn't standing against the railings, holding a carrier bag. She scowled at the balloons as they bobbed towards her. Watts watched her for a moment then went to his telescope.

He had bought it when he moved in. He'd decided that of a sleepless night, of which he'd been having many, he would star-gaze, light pollution permitting. He'd always been vaguely interested in astronomy and he'd read there would be two comets to watch this year.

Since he'd started living in the flat, however, he'd slept like a log and the nightly sea frets had obscured even the moon.

He trained the telescope now on a boat on the horizon that looked familiar. It was the elegant rum-runner from the Great Escape heading back to Brighton. Smoke puffed out of the central funnel. He scanned the length of the boat but could see no one on deck.

# FOUR

Gilchrist left Heap at Rafferty's house questioning Roger the house guest whilst she escorted Rafferty to the station. She handed him over to the desk sergeant to process and went to her office to call Legal for advice about what he might actually be charged with. Whilst she was waiting for a call back she googled 'contemporary grave robbing' and found a case of a man in Russia, an academic, who had done a horribly similar thing, even down to the tea party.

She was mulling over the fact that two minds thousands of miles apart had been having the same sick thoughts when her phone rang. Tracey, the chief constable's secretary.

Within the limits of her Botox, Hewitt was looking fraught.

'Sit down, Gilchrist. Bernard Rafferty is no friend of mine but he's a big cheese in our town. What is he doing in our cells without a lawyer in attendance?'

'Bernard Rafferty was interrupted digging up a body in Keymer graveyard,' Gilchrist said.

'Which is not a sentence I thought I'd ever hear,' Hewitt said.

'Indeed, ma'am,' Gilchrist said. 'His lawyer is on his way.'

Hewitt looked up at the ceiling. 'Maybe he was doing research for a new book.'

'With respect, ma'am: at four in the morning, by torchlight?'

'Don't ask me – academics are a law unto themselves.' Hewitt sighed. 'An actual body? Recently buried?'

'Not a body,' Gilchrist said. 'Bones – a skeleton, as far as we can tell.'

'Isn't that more grave robbing than bodysnatching?'

'I don't know, ma'am – I'm afraid I'm not up on this aspect of the law. Burke and Hare were a bit before both our times.'

Hewitt sniffed. 'I'm glad you included me in that comment. Had he actually dug up the skeleton or bones or whatever it was?'

'No, ma'am. Our officers stopped him before he had got that far.'

Hewitt clasped her hands. 'So in fact he's only guilty of something like disturbing or maybe desecrating a grave.'

Gilchrist tried not to stare at Hewitt's smooth forehead. 'Probably.'

'How old was this grave?'

'One hundred and fifty years or so.'

Hewitt slapped the palm of her hand lightly on the desk.

Gilchrist looked at the desk. She was bemused by the fact there was never anything on Hewitt's desk. Anything. The chief constable's computer was at a station behind Hewitt's chair and Hewitt would take her tablet out of her drawer at the start of any meeting.

Gilchrist assumed that at some stage Hewitt had been on the same in-house course that she had done a few weeks ago about an uncluttered desk equalling an uncluttered mind. She wondered impishly if Hewitt's implementation of the course's recommendations was the same as hers. Gilchrist's desk was also bare. But that was because she'd crammed everything into her drawers and now couldn't find anything.

'Oh Christ,' Hewitt said. 'Then he *was* doing a bit of amateur archaeology.'

'In the middle of the night?'

'But cemeteries are his thing, aren't they? He could argue he didn't want to upset the locals.'

'There's more, ma'am. I've just come from his house.'

'And you found?'

'He was living with the mummified bodies or skeletons of possibly twenty-five other women. He dressed them like dolls and kept them round his house.'

Hewitt looked intently at her bare desk. 'Run that by me again?'

'The women's skeletal or mummified remains have been dressed in knee and ankle socks, dresses, aprons, ribbons. Some have Little Bo-Peep hats on. In the basement one group of dolls were sitting at a dinner table set for afternoon tea. One chair was empty at the end. Presumably his. On closer examination of the house we found other remains stuffed under beds and in cupboards. There were two up a chimney.'

'Jesus.'

'I don't think Jesus had anything to do with it.'

'But none recently dead?'

Gilchrist shook her head. 'All look like they've been in the ground decades before he got at them.'

Hewitt made a quick sign of the cross. Gilchrist was surprised. She'd never thought of her boss as religious. She'd given no indication a few months earlier when fundamentalist Christianity and the occult collided in Brighton.

'What are people like?' Hewitt said. She looked as sour as her new face would allow. 'You never really know, do you? Rafferty? The man is insufferable but he is also very bright. He's on TV. He writes newspaper columns from time to time. He's a historian and a journalist. He speaks four languages.'

Gilchrist was surprised at Hewitt's naïvety. 'All except human, ma'am?'

Hewitt looked at the ceiling. 'So what are we going to charge him with?'

'I have no idea. Grave robbing?'

Hewitt leaned towards Gilchrist. 'Is this more of that black magic nonsense you dealt with a few months ago? Is he a black magician?'

Gilchrist grimaced. 'There are no black magicians, ma'am. Just people who think they are. But, no, on the surface this doesn't seem to have anything to do with black magic.'

Hewitt stood and leaned forward, pressing her palms into her desk. 'OK then, Sarah. I want to be sure this doesn't get into the papers. So long as it doesn't we can handle it discreetly. If it does it will be massive.'

'Yes, ma'am,' Gilchrist said, remembering Constable Stanford's parting expression. Thinking: that bird has probably already flown.

You take the coach from Phnom Penh north-east to Siem Reap. The journey takes all day but is not unpleasant. You have a bench seat to yourself. You sleep in the morning and at a stop in a village around lunchtime try a plate of fried locusts from a street vendor. You've had them before as a delicacy. They taste of nothing much but the salt on the crunchy carapace and evoke for you not Cambodia but the first occasion you had them on the other side of the world.

It was in Oaxaca, Mexico, in a restaurant on a balcony overlooking a square that was occupied by government tanks recently

involved in putting down an insurrection. A teacher's strike that
had got out of hand. Judging from reports a few months ago it
happened all the time in Mexico. Who knew teachers could be so
vicious? Actually, you did. Catholic upbringing.

Calm had now been restored but people were staying off the
streets. The fish and meat market housed in an old Spanish colonial
building behind the square was bare of food, the mongers slouched
behind their counters, listening to dance music on tinny radios,
waiting for the latest official statement.

You came up from Colombia where you were employed as a
mercenary on a special op in Bogota – another city with tanks on
the street. Not against the drug cartels, unusually, but against a
communist cell operating covertly there, giving tactical support
and advice to FARC and other communist guerrillas.

'First thing you've got to recognize is that these fucking FARC
bastards aren't propelled by ideology,' your friend 'Will' Rogers
was saying. Big man, good looking, bit of a swagger. 'They're
criminals, plain and simple. Kidnappers, human traffickers,
dabblers in the drug business. They cloak their criminal activities
in rhetoric but they are no better than some street-corner hustler
with a switchblade or a flashy handgun.'

He drew the long antenna of a locust from his mouth and laid
it on the side of his plate. 'That's why I fucking despise them.
They're hypocrites. At least your everyday scumbag doesn't
pretend to be anything else.' He reached for a toothpick. 'Still,
who are we to judge, eh? We're not exactly untarnished.'

He pointed at you with the toothpick.

'Well, except for Captain America here. Cryogenically frozen
in a time when you could tell good from bad, black from white.
Brought back to life in the here and now, shield unblemished,
outmoded morality intact.'

Cartwright, Howe and Bartram laughed wolfishly at your
discomfort. All moustached, all brawnier than you. These four had
known each other a long time and sometimes you felt excluded.
They seemed to have something else going on outside of each
operation but you turned a blind eye to that. In consequence, you
five were a team, knitting well. This was your third operation with
them.

'I don't have a shield,' was all you could think of to say. Quietly.

Rogers prodded at the carapace of one of the locusts. 'You've got a shell, though, laddie. That's for sure.'

Now you buy a big bottle of cola as you can't find a bottle of water with an unbroken seal. You hate cola but it does seem to work as a stomach-settler and you need that. You have a flask of vodka in your hip pocket and the rest of the bottle in your duffel. You leave that alone: you're trying to stay focused.

Your bruised ribs are constricting your breathing so you've been trying to stay still in the coach. You adjust the strap on the satchel on your lap. Paradise's men looted your safe but the stuff in there was all decoy. You know how easy it is to break into a battery-operated safe simply by removing the batteries so you'd factored that in. Most of your money and your real passport were in a waterproof bag buried in the little bamboo plantation in the corner of your yard.

You look out of the window at the passing landscape and think back to the first time you were here.

When Heap returned to the station Gilchrist took him down to the cells. Gilchrist looked through the window. Bernard Rafferty was sitting upright and perfectly composed on the edge of the concrete bunk. He saw her and mouthed the word 'lawyer' then mimed a zip closing over his mouth.

'He's here,' she mouthed back. Not mouthing what she was thinking: asshole.

Gilchrist and Heap went to the interview room.

'Time for me to fess up, I suppose,' Rafferty said cheerfully, when he entered the room.

'It's usually best,' Gilchrist said, struggling to keep the distaste off her face.

The Royal Pavilion director pointed at Gilchrist. 'Don't patronize me, young lady – I know exactly who you are and what you get up to with your chief constables.'

'Bernard,' his lawyer said quickly.

Rafferty sat beside his lawyer and shook his hand heartily. Rafferty's lawyer tried for expressionless but Gilchrist could see he was having trouble concealing his discomfort. Gilchrist gave the lawyer a look. He held it for a moment then looked down.

'Tell me about you and graveyards,' Gilchrist said to Rafferty.

'Graveyards fascinate me,' Rafferty said. 'I know more about them than almost any living person. I should – I've been studying them for around twenty-five years.'

'Studying them?' Gilchrist said.

'For years now I've been visiting cemeteries around Brighton and churchyards on the Downs to dig up women. I like them to be aged between fifteen and twenty-five.'

Gilchrist looked at Heap.

'How did you get the remains home?' Heap said.

'Bin bags. Those thick ones for the garden? Sometimes I'd dig up two in a night.'

'And put them in separate bags?'

'Not necessarily. It didn't matter anyway. Part of the fun was taking the skeletons apart and putting all the different bones of the women back together in new combinations.'

'So the skeletons we found in your basement—'

'That's right. Not all the bones in one skeleton are from one person.'

Gilchrist found herself gripping the edges of the table. 'Did you keep track of whose bones went where?'

He laughed. 'Heavens, no! Why would I do that? What mattered was the end result.'

'Why did you dress them up?'

'So they'd look nice at teatime.'

Gilchrist looked down at her hands. She was a big-boned woman but her hands, whilst long-fingered, were relatively neat and tapered. She lifted them off the table. Her knuckles were white. She wondered idly if they were too narrow to knock Rafferty out with one punch. She wouldn't mind trying one day. She had long despised Rafferty for the oleaginous creep he was but add this sick activity . . .

'You say you've been doing this for years,' she said, keeping her voice level. 'How many women have you dug up?'

Rafferty raised his scrawny shoulders. 'I didn't bother counting. And they are hardly women, are they, Detective Inspector? They're bags of bones. Corporeal life has left them – as has their spirit, if you think in those superstitious terms. Do *you* need to think in those superstitious terms?'

'How many?' Heap repeated.

The lawyer put his hand lightly on Rafferty's arm.

'Let me think,' Rafferty said. 'I've probably spent around seven hundred and fifty nights in cemeteries.'

'Seven hundred and fifty?' Gilchrist tried to make her voice expressionless.

'Over many years, that's probably about right.' Rafferty tried for a confiding expression. It came off as a leer. 'I like to sleep in them sometimes. Often in a coffin.'

She almost didn't notice that last remark as she was doing the maths on the first.

'You've dug up seven hundred and fifty women?'

Although she tried, Gilchrist failed to keep the high pitch of shock out of her voice.

'Calm down, dear,' Rafferty said. 'No, no, no – though that would be quite something, wouldn't it? But where would I put so many house guests? No – I didn't dig them up every time I was in a cemetery.'

'How often?'

'Maybe one in three visits.'

'Two hundred and fifty women,' Gilchrist stated, her voice only a little lower down the register.

'Is it? Goodness, that's quite a lot of digging. No wonder I have trouble with my back.'

'So where are they all?' Heap said, all business-like.

Rafferty yawned. He actually yawned. Gilchrist had the urge to reach over and slap it off his face. 'Oh, they're stashed away here and there. Some are still in bin bags. You know what it's like – sometimes if you don't do something straight away the moment has gone.'

'You desecrated two hundred fifty graves to satisfy your, your . . .'

'My what? There's nothing improper about the fact they are all women. Far from it – my interests lie elsewhere. Always have.' He looked peevish. 'Anyone would think I'd murdered them or something. Nobody cared about them after all this time.'

He leaned towards them over the table and it was all Gilchrist could do not to shrink back.

'Listen. They all died a long time ago. I didn't mummify any, you know – some of the bodies had simply dried out completely in the grave. Soil composition, I suppose. I dressed them up nicely.

Have you any idea what has always happened in the past when a graveyard's contents have needed to be moved? You think the contractors don't just dump them all together in a new mass grave? Every medieval cathedral has an ossuary with stacks of bones and skulls sorted by size.' He pointed at Gilchrist. 'You might be disgusted but I haven't really done anything wrong.' He looked at his lawyer. 'And now I'd like to go home.'

'You need to tell us where they all are,' Gilchrist said.

'If I can remember.' He turned to his lawyer. 'Get me out of here. I'm tired. I didn't get much sleep last night.' He looked back at Gilchrist. 'Well?'

Late 1978. You flew from London to Saigon with ten men. Your fourth mission with Rogers, Howe, Cartwright and Bartram, but this one was different.

You drove across country to Chau Doc then, next day, on to a riverfront hotel in Can Tho. There the ten of you picked up a boat to take you into the insane, collapsing world of Pol Pot and the Khmer Rouge.

You were an extraction team. Officially you were there to rescue three English yachtsmen from an interrogation camp in the centre of Phnom Penh. They had strayed into Cambodian waters and been accused of espionage. You were tasked with getting them out before interrogation and torture turned to execution. But you were planning to rescue a fourth person too.

Your journey up the Mekong at night had taken a stealthy seven hours. Patrol boats crisscrossed the river but not as many as you expected given that Cambodia was in an unofficial war with its neighbour, Vietnam, and expected an invasion imminently.

You were tense. Rogers was cracking weak jokes but you weren't in the mood. You didn't take your eyes off each floating village you passed, houseboats bobbing gently on the wash of your vessel. Rogers nudged you after some particularly fatuous joke and you flashed him a quick smile then went back to watching the swirling river as it brought you ever closer to the ghost city of Phnom Penh.

Pol Pot's genocidal Khmer Rouge regime was imploding. The Khmer Rouge, it was estimated later, had killed about three million of its own people. Most of those still alive were starving. In addition, the Khmer Rouge had been waging this suicidal unofficial war with its Vietnamese neighbour for three years, convinced the communist government was going to absorb Cambodia into a new Vietnamese empire.

In January 1978 a retaliatory Vietnamese force had got within twenty miles of Phnom Penh but decided for some reason not to finish the job. If they hoped their successful advance would be enough to damp down the Khmer Rouge they were wrong. Despite enormous losses against a better-armed and better-trained Vietnam (its crack troops seasoned in their long war with the US), the Khmer Rouge continued with cross-border raids.

These raids culminated, in April 1978, in two Cambodian regular army divisions advancing two kilometres into South Vietnam and massacring pretty much the entire village of Ba Chuc. Only two out of a village population of over 3,000 survived.

In response, in June the Vietnamese Air Force made some thirty bombing sorties a day along the Cambodian border. Now the Vietnamese army was massing along the border for a full-scale invasion.

It was only a matter of weeks before the Khmer Rouge was toppled. Although only twenty, you knew enough to know a regime in its death throes is at its most dangerous.

Unlike your colleagues, before this mission you already knew quite a lot about Cambodia – or Kampuchea as Pol Pot had renamed it when he took over in 1976. You knew that Pol Pot had immediately declared Year Zero and tried to turn back time by returning the country to a peasant society and economy. Any educated person was regarded as an enemy of the state.

Since 1976 the Khmer Rouge had forcibly depopulated both large and small urban areas. It also controlled food sources to control the people. It forbade fishing and rice planting and cut down fruit trees. The food that was produced was exported to pay for bullets for the unofficial war with Vietnam. The people starved but the Khmer Rouge refused offers of humanitarian aid from other countries because it wished to demonstrate national self-reliance.

Chillingly, Pol Pot had declared the country only needed a couple of million people to create his agrarian utopia. The attitude towards the surplus millions was: 'To keep you is no benefit, to destroy you is no loss.'

However, it was too expensive to use bullets to kill so many so the Khmer Rouge beat people to death with iron bars and wooden staves or hacked them to death with machetes. Thousands of people from the capital and elsewhere were taken to what became known as the Killing Fields – the Choueng Ek extermination centre – to dig their own mass graves. Often batches of up to a hundred were buried alive.

Many of those whose lives had ended in the butchery of the Killing Fields had first been imprisoned in the Security Prison-21 interrogation camp in the converted school in the centre of Phnom Penh. Your destination.

Sarah Gilchrist and Kate Simpson met for an early dinner in a French brasserie in what had once been Brighton's music library. There were people sitting at tables outside in the sunshine but they took a table in a quiet corner, deep inside.

Gilchrist was used to towering over other women – not to mention Bellamy Heap – but Kate was wearing flat shoes so Gilchrist felt even more Amazonian. She also felt slightly awkward. She liked Kate but they had been thrown together originally by circumstances and become flatmates almost by accident. Kate was ten years or so younger and they didn't have that much in common.

They ordered a bottle of house white and fizzy water.

'How's the flat?' Gilchrist asked.

'It's great.' Kate grinned. 'I bet yours is feeling spacious.'

Gilchrist smiled. 'I've spread out a bit,' she admitted.

'And now you can have a string of men back without worrying about the girl on the sofa bed.'

'Hardly,' Gilchrist said, curiously embarrassed. There was a moment's awkward silence.

'What's happening at work?' Kate said, too brightly.

'Usual organized chaos. You?'

Kate produced Southern Shores Radio's morning show, *Simon Says*. 'Why is every man in Brighton called Simon a prat?' she said.

'That bad, huh?' Gilchrist said. 'But how many Simons do you know?'

Kate swirled the wine in her glass. 'Two?'

Gilchrist laughed. 'Remind me not to ask you for statistical advice. I thought you liked producing Simon's show.'

'I like producing per se but producing Simon's show has one main drawback.'

'Simon?'

Kate grinned and nodded.

'I thought you got on really well,' Gilchrist said. 'You sound as if you do during the show.'

'The badinage? That's acting. The minute the microphones are turned off he's a total, self-absorbed pain in the bum. He'd treat me like dirt if I let him.'

'So you're not happy being a media star?'

'Happy and Southern Shores Radio do not usually coexist in the same sentence.'

They tucked into their food. They'd both gone for the grilled salmon salad on the understanding they'd make up for their healthy choice with a dessert after. Kate said between mouthfuls: 'Tell me about Bellamy Heap.'

Gilchrist was surprised. 'Bellamy? What's to say? He's a boy-policeman. Eager, far more intelligent than I am – though that's not saying much. He's the butt of a lot of jokes because of his height and his shyness—'

'I don't think he's shy.'

Gilchrist examined Kate's face. 'I don't think he is either.'

Kate picked up her glass. 'And, actually, though he's short, he looks as if he's perfectly formed.'

Gilchrist smiled and chinked her glass. 'That he does, Katie.' She took a sip of her wine. 'That he does.'

Katie looked a bit embarrassed at what she probably perceived as her forwardness. 'I phoned the cemetery today to see about exhuming the Trunk Murder victim's remains for DNA analysis,' she said abruptly.

'Really?'

'But I'm too late.'

Gilchrist frowned and put her drink down. 'What do you mean?'

'Someone has despoiled the grave and taken the bones.' Kate put down her fork. 'It's that bloody documentary I did. I gave too much information about where she's buried.'

Gilchrist thought for a moment. 'Maybe. But I can think of

someone else who might have done it.' She leaned forward and lowered her voice. 'Look, keep this to yourself . . .'

When Gilchrist had finished outlining the gruesome find at Rafferty's house, Kate said: 'But if he did dig up the murder victim, that's great. The woman's remains are at least out of the ground so they can be analysed.'

Gilchrist shook her head. 'I think you have to accept they are lost.'

'Lost how? Her bones are in his house somewhere.'

'But they might as well still be in the ground. We don't know which are her bones and we can't be doing DNA tests on every single bone in his house. It would cost an arm and a leg.'

'So to speak,' Kate said. 'I see that. But how frustrating.'

'Why?' Gilchrist said. 'We'd need familial matches for it to make any sense.'

'Well, not just that. You know they can figure out where your mother was living when she was pregnant with you? We can find out all sorts of stuff.'

'I know, Kate. But we've recovered the remains of at least thirty women. Do you know how many bones that means? We would need to take samples from every bone; that's the only way to be sure we've covered everybody.'

'Small price to pay for closure,' Kate said.

Gilchrist looked at her over her wine glass. 'Closure is over-rated,' she said finally.

# FIVE

You disembarked beyond the harbour three miles from Security Prison-21. There were two trucks waiting, provided by your local collaborators. Howe and Rogers huddled with their leader before you boarded. They drove you through the deserted streets. There were no other vehicles moving.

Your mission was hazardous but straightforward. 'A simple smash and grab,' Rogers had called it. Break into SP-21, release the three Englishmen and get them out of the country. But as you made your way from the dock through the ravaged capital, past packs of dogs tugging at corpses abandoned in the streets and rotting bodies hanging from lampposts, you also burned to kill every Khmer Rouge soldier or official you came across.

You knew that the prison was heavily guarded but the guards usually faced inwards, watching the compound. The guards were mostly teenagers armed with old carbines with only a few bullets between them. They were terrified of making mistakes since to do so would result in their own arrest, torture and death.

They were not allowed to take naps, sit down or lean against walls whilst on duty. They were fed poorly. In consequence, at night, whether on duty or off duty, all were exhausted.

What you didn't know for certain was where the fourth person was in the camp.

Aside from searchlights anchored at each corner of the compound, there was little in the way of electric light. There was what looked like a cook-fire dug into the earth by the front gates. Oil-lamps hung from posts and balconies.

You isolated the electric cable at one small section of the razor wire at the rear of the main building and cut through. You left two men on guard and you led the way in a crouching run to the single cells in building C that housed the foreign prisoners.

You had lightweight ladders. You climbed to the top floor on the outside wall a little shakily. You looked through the window of the stairwell. There was a guard at the opposite window looking into the compound. Rogers went through the window and slit his throat. Bob Cartwright took the guard's place whilst two others went down the corridor to deal with the guard at the other end. You then moved down to secure the next floor. And the next.

You left the ground floor until it was time for your exit.

It was a hot night and mosquitoes were everywhere. You looked out into the compound and looked again when you saw three men hanging from what looked like a set of soccer goalposts. They looked like they had been crucified since they were hanging from their hands with their arms racked up behind them. The weight of their bodies would eventually tear their arms out of their sockets. Their shoulders would already be horribly dislocated but you could not hear them making any noise. You didn't know if they were dead, unconscious or simply suffering in silence.

The single cells all had heavy, ill-fitting wooden doors that were secured from the outside only by bolts. You oiled the bolts and drew them slowly, conscious they still scraped and screeched. Most people were awake but remained silent. As prisoners, they were forbidden to speak or utter any noise. Unable to see who was behind the torch shining on them, they assumed you were a guard. They cringed in terror.

It upset you to lock them in again. You wondered about leaving their doors open so that they could try to escape if they wished. But the Englishmen came first. You couldn't afford to have your mission jeopardised by other escaping prisoners alerting the guards.

You found the three sailors in adjacent cells. Gaunt, semi-naked and filthy. You warned them to be silent. You squatted down beside the oldest of the three. He'd been badly knocked about.

'Where's Michelle?' you whispered.

'Michelle?' he croaked.

'Your daughter.'

The man – you knew his name was Westbrook – looked at you with sudden alertness. You broke open his crude shackles.

'You'll never find her,' he hissed. 'There are hundreds of people here.'

You could hear stirring in the other cells. You did not want anyone crying out.

'Where is she?' you repeated. 'Is she somewhere in this room?'

You started to move him out of the cell.

Westbrook pulled back. 'Who are you?'

'I'm a man who has come to rescue you and your daughter from your madness.'

'She'll be on the top floor in the main cells.' Westbrook's eyes were cloudy. He peered at you. 'But we may never find her.'

You pulled him towards the door. You checked your watch. Seven minutes before the diversions started.

'Show me where she is.'

Gilchrist didn't see Bob Watts when she did her morning run. It rained but not the kind of downpour that had drowned Brighton a few months earlier. It was cooling against her face and smelled fresh and tangy. It had stopped by the time she got back to her flat. She dried off the chairs and table on her balcony and plonked down, a glass of juice and her tablet by her side.

She went online for the papers and groaned when she saw the headlines in the redtops. One of the posher papers had the headline: 'Brighton's Burke – But Where's Hare?'

She read the article aloud under her breath: 'The Director of Brighton's Royal Pavilion, the second most popular tourist attraction in the UK, was arrested yesterday on suspicion of attempted grave robbery. Bernard Rafferty, 63, was released after several hours in custody without immediate charge.

'The question must be asked whether this is an isolated incident for Rafferty, who has written widely on cemeteries and has been, in consequence, a regular visitor to Sussex's churchyards over the years.

'Over those same years, there have been reports of a number of graves being disturbed in the area and floods some months ago revealed a number of empty graves around the county.

'Southern Police, who have made Rafferty's house a crime scene, have made no official comment but one unnamed policeman said: "Think Fred West's house without the murders." Mr Rafferty, who did not return home on his release nor go to his job at the Royal Pavilion, could not be reached for comment. Perhaps he's gone underground. Again.'

On his balcony, Bob Watts was reading the same report. Bernard Rafferty. He'd always loathed the creep but he was out of his depth when it came to an objective response to what Rafferty had been up to. His liberal side was saying: it takes all kinds. His Mail Online side was saying . . . actually, he didn't want to go there.

Watts put his tablet down and looked out to sea. He hoped the job of PCC was going to give some meaning to his life. He was officially a millionaire as he'd inherited a third of his father's net worth. Not that a million was much these days – certainly not enough to buy that beautiful schooner he now coveted.

And anyway: money. That had never been a goal in his life. Other things mattered more. His wife had left him for a man in Canada, his children didn't speak to him and he'd no idea what he wanted to do. All he had left was energy: too much energy to retire.

His phone beeped. A text from Karen Hewitt. 'Have you seen the papers? Do you want to make the public statements when that time comes?'

The other two rescued sailors were waiting in the doorway to the room. They had been hurriedly dressed and given flip-flops for their feet. They looked weak and haggard. You pulled trousers and a tunic on to Westbrook. He stank.

Howe, in nominal charge, gave you the thumbs up. You gave the thumbs down.

'There's one more,' you hissed in his ear. 'We can't go without her.'

'Impossible,' he said. He glanced at Rogers as if for agreement. 'We're here to get three.'

You gestured at Westbrook. 'His daughter. Impossible to go without her.'

Howe sighed. 'The diversion starts in five minutes.' He nodded at Rogers. 'Go with them.' He pointed at you. 'But when the diversion starts, we leave, whether you're with us or not.'

'What happened to "never leave anyone behind"?' you hissed.

He shrugged. 'All arrangements are fluid in a combat situation – you know that.'

You nodded at Westbrook and led him upstairs with you. He ran out of breath by step three so you and Rogers half carried, half dragged him up the remaining steps, closely watched by Cartwright guarding the top stair.

'What are you trying to pull here?' Rogers whispered. 'You've got your own little side-arrangement going on?'

You glanced at him. 'The same way you have, you mean?'

You knew his team were up to other stuff on operations you'd been involved with. You just didn't know what – partly because you had no real interest in finding out.

The door to the communal cell was only bolted. You slid the bolts, stepped carefully in and when your man was inside closed the door behind him. You tried to ignore the stench of faeces, urine and blood. There was heavy breathing and snoring and snuffles and gasps.

You shone your torch low on the floor. As you ran the light from front to back you were startled by what you saw. Once, as a schoolboy, you had seen an exhibition about slavery and the conditions in which slaves were transported from Africa to the Americas. The slaves were packed into the holds of the ships side by side, head to toe, with no space between them.

It was the same here. Four rows of people, two rows either side of a narrow central aisle, lying so that the feet of the people in the two rows faced each other. All were lying flat on their backs, naked except for filthy loincloths or underwear. Those woken by the torchlight turned their heads away.

Rogers stayed at the door and you took Westbrook's hand to lead him down the narrow aisle. He cried out. You shushed him and shone your torch on his hand. The ends of his fingers were a swollen, bloody mess where his fingernails had been torn out.

The cry had woken a number of people in the room. You led the way down the middle, moving the torch-beam along the rows one by one. These were all men.

At the far end of the room, a tall, narrow doorway had been crudely hacked through into the next classroom. You glanced at your watch. Two minutes before the diversion. Westbrook saw your look and pushed past you into the next room. You followed. A room of women pinned to the concrete floor, all virtually naked.

You could not find her as you listened for the dull whump of the explosion two blocks away. Westbrook called out her name. You shushed him again. Women cried out. The despair was unbearable.

Rogers was suddenly beside you. 'We have to go,' he hissed.

'Not without her,' you said. 'She must be on another floor.'

You and Rogers dragged Westbrook stumbling through the men's cell and out of the door you entered. The diversion had begun. Flames were leaping into the sky behind the building across from the prison compound. The hope was that the fire would distract the night guards around the prison but not waken the rest of the garrison.

You set off down to the next floor, Rogers virtually carrying the man behind you.

Two guards lay dead on the ground floor. Otherwise the corridor was deserted. Your unit had left.

Gilchrist wondered if Rafferty had stashed some human remains in the Royal Pavilion. She remembered that Rafferty had personally found the police files relating to the unsolved Brighton Trunk Murder of 1934 in the basement. Those files had formed the basis of her friend Kate's radio documentary about the case and had involved Bob Watts' father, the late writer Victor Tempest.

She'd heard Rafferty was a pretty hands-off director of the Pavilion so wondered what he was doing rooting around in the basement to be able to find the files. Had he stumbled upon them when he had been stashing other things there?

A young woman in a black skirt and shirt was waiting for Gilchrist and Heap in the portico of the Pavilion. She introduced herself as Rachel, from marketing.

'I remember you,' Heap said.

She looked at him and nodded. 'I remember you too.'

Heap turned to Gilchrist. 'This young woman was working in the shop at the Art Gallery when that Gluck painting was stolen a few months ago.' He gestured vaguely around the hallway. 'Promotion?'

She smiled and pointed at his warrant card. 'It is. For you too, I think? Weren't you a constable then?'

Heap flushed.

Rachel turned to Gilchrist. 'I understand you want to see the tunnel.'

'Tunnel?' Gilchrist said. 'We want to see the basement.'

'That too, but there's a store where Mr Rafferty deposited stuff halfway along the tunnel.'

'Lead us to it,' Gilchrist said.

'The tunnel is usually out of bounds because of asbestos so you'll have to be careful.'

She led them down a short flight of steps and passed over hard hats and masks. A long corridor led off to their left with, at intervals, solid wooden doors.

'We use some of these as workshops and others as storage space.'

'And you know what is in each of them?' Gilchrist said, her voice slightly muffled by the mask.

'Only that there is nothing of real value. It's a bit damp down here so we don't store museum pieces. It's mostly lumber, old files, that kind of thing.'

'Where did Mr Rafferty find the police files some months ago?'

The woman gestured to her right. 'In the old tunnel.'

'What was the tunnel for?' Gilchrist said.

'How much do you know about the history of the Pavilion?' Rachel asked with a smile.

'Clearly not enough,' Gilchrist said. She gestured to Heap. 'I bet my sergeant will know, though.'

Heap reddened a little. 'It's a tunnel connecting the Pavilion with the Dome complex a couple of hundred yards away. The story goes that the Prince of Wales had his women smuggled in and out of the Pavilion in secrecy via this route.'

Rachel nodded. 'A story that is total rubbish, of course,' she said with a laugh. 'Women like Mrs Fitzherbert would have gone through the front door.'

'Shame,' Gilchrist said. 'It's a good story.'

Rachel led them to the right then turned left. She flicked a light switch and Gilchrist and Heap were looking down a long, slightly curved tunnel with a brick floor and plastered ceiling and walls. Utility cables and pipes ran at head height down each side of the vaulted ceiling and a bigger pipe, presumably for sewage, ran along the left-hand wall at floor level. There were electric wall-lights every twenty yards or so.

'This was in use when the Pavilion was being used as council offices. Then asbestos was discovered all down here and down the other tunnel back there, so it's been closed to the public ever since. We're planning to refurbish and reopen it soon, though.'

'What was its purpose, then, if not to shuttle the Prince's totties to and fro?' Gilchrist said.

Rachel frowned. 'Just a convenient way to get between here and the Dome, I suppose.'

'Why would you want to?' Heap said. 'The Dome was just stables, wasn't it?'

Rachel shrugged. 'Maybe they didn't want to track horse-poo on the carpets upstairs.'

They all smiled.

Rachel pointed. 'See that window bay down on the left there? The files were piled there with a lot of other stuff. And there's a storeroom on the other side a bit further along. But I think both spaces are empty now.'

Heap went first with the bolt-cutters. Gilchrist instinctively ducked, although the curved roof of the tunnel was a good foot above her head.

The window bay looked out on to a brick footway. It was empty. Heap walked on to a solid-looking wooden door on the opposite wall. A large padlock hung from it. He looked back down the corridor to where Rachel was waiting.

'Sure you don't have a key?' he called, brandishing the cutters.

She grinned. 'Afraid not,' she shouted back. 'Do your worst.'

It was fiddly getting the blades of the cutter in the right position around the shackle but once Heap had done so he cut through without any difficulty. So easily, in fact, that the lock clattered to the floor before Gilchrist, who was standing beside him, had a chance to catch it.

They looked at each other.

'After you, Detective Sergeant,' Gilchrist said.

Heap undid the hasp and pulled open the door. The daylight coming through the window behind them illuminated the storeroom enough for them to see that there were things in it, but both turned on their torches to see what those things were.

Mostly they were green bin bags.

They exchanged looks again.

'Seniority, ma'am – you should go first.'

Gilchrist approached the pile of bags cautiously. They were knotted at the top but she used her Swiss army knife to make a small slit in the side of the first one. She pulled on the sides of the incision to make a hole. Heap stepped forward to shine his torch inside. He didn't need to: they could both see the end of a bone protruding from the hole in the bag.

'And that's just the first bag,' Gilchrist murmured. She played her own torch on the rear of the store. 'There are packing cases here too.'

She shouted back at Rachel hovering a few yards into the tunnel. 'We're going to have to get more people down here. This tunnel is now off-limits.'

You looked across the compound. The other guards were still gathered at the gate, alarmed by the flames shooting into the night sky.

Westbrook pointed into the yard. 'There.'

You saw now that one of the people hanging from the goalposts was a woman, her small breasts exposed, long hair falling down over her face.

Rogers exchanged a glance with you. 'The guards won't be diverted by the fire much longer.' You nodded. 'Going out there to cut the woman down is very risky.' You nodded again. 'You'll be totally exposed – especially if the guards on the landings of the other buildings turn on the searchlights.'

You nodded and walked out on to the courtyard, trying to make yourself inconspicuous. The guards at the gate were still looking outwards. Twenty yards. The woman was unmoving. She might well be dead. Ten yards. A couple of the guards started to drift away from the gate. Five yards. Several others turned away from the conflagration.

She was alive. Her eyes moved as she watched you reach behind her to cut the rope. Her face contorted in agony but she made no sound as she started to fall. You caught her and hoisted her over one shoulder. You took a firmer grip on the weapon in your other hand. She too smelt of sweat and shit and vomit. She weighed scarcely anything.

You started to reverse your steps. You couldn't see Rogers but you knew he was there. Thirty yards to go.

A shout off to the left. A clatter of movement by the gate. More shouts. A rattle of gunfire from Rogers aimed at the tower away to your right. Single shots whizzed by you. None close enough to worry about.

Twenty yards. A searchlight burst on to you.

You moved to the right and Rogers turned his fire on the guards at the gate. You ran the last few yards, conscious of the woman gasping as her body jogged on your shoulder.

Rogers shot out the searchlight.

You kept going to the gap in the barbed wire and ducked through. You'd thought your unit might leave one of the lorries. Both had gone.

'Fuck,' Rogers said from behind you.

'We're on our own,' you said.

'Let's get the hell out of Dodge.' Rogers pointed towards a block of flats about fifty yards away. 'Let's get there.'

Rogers was big, much bigger than you. He hoisted Westbrook over his shoulder. He set off at a staggering run. You followed. The woman was making odd mewling noises now.

'Sorry, love,' you whispered.

You were aware of single shots pocking the ground pretty randomly around you. They came from the guard in the tower who had been firing at you earlier. He couldn't shoot for shit.

The block of flats was built on concrete stilts with a kind of through road running between the stilts to the street on the other side. You ran beneath the building. Rogers leaned the man against the wall. You kept the woman on your shoulder.

Rogers looked back at the prison and shook his head.

'I can't believe they've fucking left us.'

'They were on a schedule,' you said.

'Yeah, but the job was to get three people. They're one short.'

'It's me they've left, not you,' the man croaked.

'I never asked about these three people we were rescuing,' Rogers said. 'But, of course, I had my suspicions. Sailors drifting into Kampuchean waters? Only three kinds of sailor would go anywhere near this nuthouse country: drug traffickers, smugglers or spies.'

Rogers looked across at the rangy man leaning against the wall. 'Which are you?' Rogers stepped in front of Westbrook. 'Looking into your eyes and seeing how alert you are I'm going with spy. But then I'd always kind of assumed that. The British government wouldn't sanction an illegal mission just to get back some tourists.'

'But what interest would Britain have in Cambodia?' you said. 'How are Britain's interests affected by what's going on in Cambodia? Is it a Pacific thing? Australia? An Indian sub-continent thing?'

Rogers stepped back. 'Above my pay grade, that kind of information.' He turned to you and gestured towards Michelle. 'And then there's you and Mata Hari here, sonny boy.'

You ignored him and turned to watch the street between the prison and the block of flats. A dozen or so soldiers were milling around the broken wire, looking out into the street but with no clear focus.

'They have no idea what to do,' you said.

'And we do?' Rogers said.

'We just head back to the harbour.'

'On foot with two banged up people?'

You hefted your machine gun. 'Sure.'

Rogers shook his head. 'I think we make a stop and wait until it quietens down.'

You thought he might say that. 'It's three miles maximum,' you said. 'And unless we meet a tank we're better armed by far than anyone we're going to come across.'

'It's not about being better armed,' he said. 'It's about numbers. They have a whole bloody army in the city.'

'You know that how? What's left of their army is on the border with Vietnam. What's left in this city is their equivalent of the Home Guard. I think even you can handle Private Pike, can't you?'

Rogers looked at the woman. 'We need to get her arms back in their sockets.' He shook his head. 'She must be in bloody agony. I don't understand why she's not screaming non-stop.'

You looked out into the street. The guards were fanning out along the pavement. A number of them were looking your way.

'I think we need to move from here first,' you said. 'At least a couple of blocks.'

You glanced towards Westbrook, who was watching you intently.

'I can walk,' he croaked. He reached behind you and stroked Michelle's head, murmuring something in French. You didn't hear her respond. He looked at you. 'Thank you.'

You led the way to the back of the block of flats. There was an alley directly across from you. You navigated between three decaying bodies at the entrance.

'The City of Death,' Westbrook croaked, his legs flexing awkwardly as he jerked along almost robotically, his joints stiff and inarticulate.

'How did they get you?' you said, aware that the woman was moaning constantly now. 'What were you even doing here?'

Westbrook glanced across. 'That's a long story.'

'That may be. But is there stuff you need to be telling me in case we split up and you don't make it?' No point sugaring the pill.

The man grimaced. You thought he was trying to smile.

'What I know about anything I could write on the back of a postage stamp.' He raised his bloody hand. 'Were I able to hold a pen, that is.'

'Michelle?'

You were reaching the end of the alley now. It was dark down here so you paused for a moment.

'Long story,' he said. 'We were in Angkor Wat.'

'She has information?'

'Long story,' he repeated, touching her hair again.

You knew Rogers was listening as he watched the street. He seemed to sense you watching him.

'They'll be sending out patrols by now,' he said. 'This place will be humming. We've got to get going before the whole city goes into lockdown.

You looked at your watch. Still a few hours of daylight. 'We need to circle round to get back to the harbour.'

'Lead on, Big Mac,' Rogers said.

'I think you mean Macduff,' you said.

'Whatever,' Rogers said. 'As long as dill pickle features.'

# SIX

Gilchrist had arranged an urgent appointment with a psychologist called Mike Simeon at Sussex University to see if he would do a psych evaluation of Rafferty before they decided how to proceed.

She and Heap got lost on campus. They were eventually directed to an office block set against a steep slope. There was no reception so they just followed signs to Simeon's door, which was open, as was his window. Papers fluttered on his desk from the through breeze.

Dr Simeon was a lanky man with a three-day growth and untidy hair. He was wearing jeans and a denim shirt poorly tucked into his waistband. He sat with them at a table by the window, in the cooling breeze.

Gilchrist had filled him in on Rafferty on the telephone.

'He sounds like he might be the kind of person I'm studying,' Simeon said now. He had a quiet, calm voice that Gilchrist found soothing.

'And what kind of person is that?' she said, conscious she had lowered her voice in response.

'People born without empathy.'

'Empathy,' Gilchrist repeated.

Simeon cleared his throat. 'Empathy is the urge to respond with an appropriate emotion to another person's thoughts and feelings. But there are those people who feel nothing. People who don't give a damn about the rest of us.'

Gilchrist gave a little snort. She'd known a few of those in her time.

'Born without it or had it destroyed in them?' Heap said.

Simeon chuckled. 'Ah – the old nature versus nurture argument. I believe these people are fundamentally born without empathy but, yes, a bad environment would make them worse or paralyse empathy in someone. Child soldiers in Africa, for instance. Those involved in genocide in Rwanda or, before that, Cambodia, say, under Pol Pot. Terrorists who plant bombs in crowded markets or on planes.'

'Although Rafferty's interest is in the long-dead,' Gilchrist said. 'Can any of us be expected to have empathy with a skeleton?'

'Of course – if only as a memento mori,' Simeon said.

Gilchrist glanced at Heap, her walking encyclopaedia. He didn't disappoint.

'As a reminder of our own mortality,' he murmured.

Simeon looked from one to the other of them and smiled. 'Simon Baron-Cohen is *the* expert on autism. He reckons an autistic child can't grasp either their own or other people's thoughts and feelings. Feelings are like an alien language to them. That's why they are so socially inept. Baron-Cohen calls it mind-blindness. He's also come up with the idea of the Extreme Male Brain.'

'He must have met Detective Sergeant Donaldson,' Heap blurted, then flushed.

The psychologist smiled but shook his head. 'Extreme male doesn't mean macho, if that's what you're thinking,' he said.

'What does it mean?' Gilchrist said.

'Baron-Cohen – he's related in some way to that *Borat* guy, by the way – thinks people are all somewhere on a spectrum between empathy and systemizing.'

'Systemizing?' Gilchrist said.

'Yes – you know: organized, interested in how things function or making sense of things by identifying or creating a system around them. You might say that's what founders of religions have done to make sense of the world. But you're mostly talking scientists, technologists, engineers and maths geeks.'

'This is the Extreme Male Brain?'

'It is primarily a male thing, yes.' Simeon gave a little shrug. 'On the whole women empathise, men systemize. But the Extreme Male Brain is at the extreme systemizing end of the spectrum. No empathy at all.'

'Most women are more empathetic,' Gilchrist said. 'That's clearly true. But you're saying autism is an extreme form of maleness?'

'In this narrow context, yes.'

Heap leaned forward. 'Sociopaths feel nothing – does that make them autistic?'

'Good question – but no, Baron-Cohen identified two kinds of empathy. Cognitive and affective.'

Gilchrist sat back. 'I was doing so well too. Speak as if to a child, doctor. I'm just a Plod.'

He seemed to take Gilchrist at her word, which miffed her a bit.

'OK, cognitive empathy is where you're trying to figure out what a person's feeling and thinking. Affective empathy is the way you respond when you do figure it out.

'So, autistic people and people with Asperger syndrome have no clue what mental shape another person is in. They get a zero for cognitive empathy. But, often, once they are told about someone's state of mind they know how to respond in an appropriate way. Now this response is most likely learned but it means that, after a fashion, they can operate in society.'

'Sounds like a sociopath to me,' Heap said.

Simeon shook his head. 'A sociopath is the other way round. They have cognitive empathy but no affective empathy. Sociopaths can figure out what a person is feeling and thinking but they don't use that information to respond empathetically, they use it to manipulate them. Further, autistic people aren't cruel – not deliberately, at least – although they might be cruel by default. Sociopaths are manipulative and use their cognitive empathy just so they can hurt others.'

'Which is Rafferty?'

'Well, I'm not sure I know how to answer that because, as you said, detective inspector, he's not trying to relate to living people. He's dealing with bones – so he doesn't have to worry about what they're feeling. But in his puzzlement at how other people react I'm guessing he's not got much cognitive empathy.'

'Except that he did this activity in secret, at night,' Heap said. 'As if he knew it was wrong.'

Simeon looked at him for a moment. 'Surely that was just so he wouldn't be caught.'

The ensuing silence was interrupted by Gilchrist. 'So in this theory it's definitely nature over nurture?'

'Sure – except for what autistic people can learn. It's also averaging out – it doesn't mean that any individual man or woman is typical. And it doesn't mean every autistic person is going to be great at taking a bike apart and putting it back together.'

'Even in Brighton?'

Simeon gave an unexpectedly broad grin. 'Maybe here.'

You spent the next hour dodging foot and vehicle patrols as you made your slow way back to the waterfront. You'd dosed Michelle with morphine and she was out cold.

You gave Westbrook sugar solution and water. He got stomach cramps and he squatted in a corner for a while, afterwards casting around for something to wipe himself with. When he started moving again, he seemed a little stronger.

He walked with Rogers as you carried Michelle. The two men carried on a low conversation.

When you'd come up the Mekong you had disembarked some kilometres down the coast then done a loop round the back of the city. Now your plan was to go directly to the port and steal a boat.

You were better armed and better trained than anybody you were going to come across but you knew the enemy could strike lucky. Even so, you felt your chances were good if you kept your wits about you. You were forgetting the state of undeclared war with Vietnam.

You estimated you were within six blocks of the harbour when your way was blocked by a much bigger patrol than you had yet encountered. You scurried down an alley to the right. There was another patrol on the next street. On the next street it was the same story.

You and Rogers exchanged glances.

'I don't know if they're looking for us,' Rogers said.

'Makes no difference,' you said. 'We don't want them to find us.'

You were on Street 178, near the junction with Street 13. To your left there was a dilapidated, once imposing building built in mock-traditional Khmer style.

'The National Museum,' Westbrook said. 'Long abandoned and probably looted.'

Rogers led the way towards a long, broken window. You stepped inside. The moon shone through huge holes in the roof. You could see the movement and hear the flittering of bats all around you. Hundreds of bats.

'Great – we've found the bat cave,' Rogers said. He nudged you. 'You can be Robin.'

'If they're vampire bats, we're fucked,' you said.

'Vampire bats are only to be found in the New World,' Westbrook said. 'But you might want to avoid the guano.'

Rogers frowned at him.

'Watch out for the bat shit,' you explained.

Rogers grunted. 'Let's find somewhere to hunker down.'

The floor was littered with broken fragments of statuary and piles of rubbish. There was a reception desk near the main entrance with an office behind. You laid the woman down on the floor in the office and settled down.

'I'll take first watch,' Rogers said.

'I'll let you,' you said.


Detective Sergeant Donald Donaldson was sitting in Bellamy Heap's chair when Gilchrist and her DS got back to their office. Sitting didn't accurately describe it. He was overwhelming the chair. Gilchrist wouldn't have been surprised if it simply crumbled beneath his weight. Donaldson was a solid, ungiving block of concrete.

He was playing with a bulky-looking torch, pointing it at the wall and switching it off and on. It seemed to give an unusually intense light.

Gilchrist and Heap exchanged glances.

'Extreme male brain,' Heap muttered. Gilchrist kept a straight face.

'Did you get everything out of the storeroom, Don-Don?' Gilchrist said.

He put the torch down and nodded. 'Fifteen sacks. I'll let the pathologist figure out how many bodies that represents.'

'What about those packing cases at the back?'

Donaldson shrugged his beefy shoulders. 'We had a quick shufti. Museum stuff. Indian and Chinese, they reckon. Guy with an elephant's head seems popular. Buddha too. I left it all with the museum boffins to examine – they're the experts. There was an iron door back there too but we couldn't get it open. We'll keep trying.'

'Two different religions,' Heap murmured. He looked thoughtful.

'But then the Pavilion can't decide whether it's Indian or Chinese. Not sure how Buddha fits in, though.'

Donaldson raised an eyebrow. 'I'm more of a Nietzsche man myself.'

Heap looked at him but said nothing.

'And I'm more of a George Clooney girl,' Gilchrist said.

Both men looked baffled.

'What are we going to charge him with anyway?' Donaldson said. 'Aside from being a scumbag.'

'Under the Anatomy Laws stealing a corpse is not in itself illegal as the corpse has no legal standing and is not owned by anybody,' Heap said. 'Dissection of the corpse and theft of items other than the corpse is illegal.'

'But these weren't corpses,' Gilchrist said. 'They were bags of bones.'

'Exactly,' Donaldson said. 'So what do we charge him with?'

'Desecration?' Gilchrist said.

'Burning or otherwise desecrating the US flag will get you in deep shit in the States but that's nothing like this,' Heap said. 'And we can't do him for trespassing because churchyards are open to everyone.'

'What then – making a public nuisance?' Gilchrist said.

Donaldson snorted. 'Yeah – let's give him an ASBO.'

'Even if we can't get him for anything substantive,' Heap said, 'public opprobrium will dog him for the rest of his life.'

'*Substantive?*' Donaldson snarled. '*Opprobium?* Jesus, Heap, don't you know any normal words?'

Donaldson picked up the folded newspaper on Heap's desk and pointed at the crossword in the bottom corner of the page. Nothing had been filled in.

'Is that why you can't do the quick crossword? Words too short for you?'

Heap blushed. 'I've done it.'

Donaldson looked back at the empty crossword and threw the paper on the desk. 'Police issuing invisible ink these days, are they? Do you think I'm an idiot?'

'Do I have to answer that?' Heap murmured.

'What?' Donaldson was out of the chair, heaving chest straining at his shirt. 'What did you fucking say?'

'Sergeant Donaldson!' Gilchrist gestured for him to resume his seat. After a long moment, he did.

'It's a blind crossword,' Heap said.

'Is it?' Donaldson said. 'And what's a blind crossword when it's at home?'

'They used to use them as a test when interviewing potential code-breakers at Bletchley during the war.'

'Did they? Well why don't you fuck off to GCHQ and do us all a favour?'

'Sergeant!' Gilchrist said again.

'Well, Lord Snooty here thinks he's a cut above the rest of us. A blind crossword, for God's sake. He must think I'm born yesterday.'

'You haven't actually explained what one is,' Gilchrist said to Heap.

'You do it in your head,' Heap said.

'Just the quick one though?' Gilchrist said.

'I usually do the main *Times* crossword,' Heap said.

'What – and you keep it all in your head?' Donaldson sneered. 'Bullshit.'

Gilchrist believed Heap. He was the brightest man she'd ever met.

'Boys, boys,' Gilchrist said. 'Detective sergeants should show respect for each other.'

'Oh, yeah,' Donaldson sneered. 'I forgot. Wonder Boy here is a detective sergeant after five minutes in the service.' He jabbed his finger at Heap. 'Took me fifteen years, sonny boy.'

Gilchrist could guess what Heap was about to say, which would only inflame the situation more. She caught his eye.

Heap pursed his lips. 'Anyway,' he said. 'DS Donaldson's mention of an ASBO is correct. It's probably all we can give Rafferty, repugnant though his crime is.'

Donaldson fixed Heap with a gleaming eye that put Gilchrist on the alert.

She interrupted. 'We need to question him again about where else he might have stashed these poor women's remains.'

'But if he's not going to be charged he has no incentive to help us,' Heap said.

Donaldson turned to Gilchrist. 'Maybe, while I question

Rafferty, Boy Wonder could do the grunt work, being new to the job? I thought my years of service might entitle me to be put on something a bit more demanding.'

Gilchrist was pretty sure Don-Don took steroids to bulk himself up but maybe that look in his eye meant he took something else too.

She held his fierce look. 'I decide who does what, Detective Sergeant Donaldson. The task I've given you is far more important, believe me, than Detective Sergeant Heap acting as my chauffeur.'

'And you're the big expert on investigations suddenly, are you, Sarah? I think we have about the same amount of time in.'

'But I have the rank,' Gilchrist said coldly. 'Is there anything else?'

Donaldson glowered up at her. 'Nothing at all, *Detective Inspector.* Except my motto becomes more and more relevant.'

'And that is?' Gilchrist said cautiously.

Don-Don showed his teeth. 'Life is a blank canvas: you can either paint on it or shit on it.'

'It's a good one,' Heap said.

Donaldson swung the chair towards him, scowling. 'Why thank you, Constable Heap. What's yours?'

'Detective Sergeant Heap,' Heap said. 'It's *festina lente*, actually.'

Donaldson barked a laugh. 'Well, *actually*, it would be some fucking Greek thing you got at your public school.'

Gilchrist leaned in from the other side of the desk. 'Don-Don – are you OK?'

'It's Latin, not Greek,' Heap said.

'It's fucking Greek to me,' Donaldson said. He shot a look at Gilchrist. 'And I'm fine.'

There was definitely something odd about his eyes.

'I wasn't at public school,' Heap said.

'Wherever,' Donaldson said.

'What does it mean, Bellamy?' Gilchrist said.

Heap shrugged. 'It means: make haste slowly.'

Donaldson frowned as he thought for a moment, then bared his teeth. 'Bloody typical. You never do make sense.'

Make haste slowly. Gilchrist kind of liked it. They were all quiet for a moment.

Gilchrist gestured to Donaldson. 'A word, Detective Sergeant.'

Donaldson's chair rocked as he stood. 'Ma'am.'

She led him out into the corridor. She looked into his unfocused eyes. 'What's going on, Don-Don?'

He curled his lip. 'Nothing, ma'am. I'm merely impressed by Constable Heap's rapid rise. Constable to detective constable to detective sergeant in about a week . . .'

'Longer than that,' Gilchrist said.

'Took me fifteen years,' Donaldson said.

'As you've said. Maybe you need to ask yourself why.'

'Do you have the answer, ma'am?'

She nodded. 'If I had to hazard a guess I'd say it's because you're old style. Drag your heels, take the piss when you have a chance but get results when you're so inclined. A lazy sod.'

'And Boy Wonder is different? No offence, *ma'am,* but he's so far up your arse – well, maybe you like that, maybe that's your thing.'

Gilchrist's open hand caught Donaldson so hard on his cheek he actually rocked on his feet. His eyes narrowed but he didn't move to retaliate.

'Striking a subordinate, *ma'am*? Not good. Not good at all.' Then he forced a smile. 'But it's not the first time a pretty woman has slapped my face and I'm sure it won't be the last. And it's never stopped me getting what I want.' He gave her a hard look. 'Ever.'

Gilchrist wanted to slap herself. She ground her teeth. 'Report me if you want,' she said. 'I won't deny it. But if I find you're not pulling your weight in this investigation—'

'You'll never find anything like that,' he said, his voice low.

'Everything OK here?'

Bellamy Heap was standing in the doorway of their office.

'Fine, Bellamy, thanks,' Gilchrist said.

Donaldson scowled. 'Hunky dory, Bell-ender.'

'You need to watch your language, Detective Sergeant Donaldson,' Heap said quietly.

'You going to make me?'

'Jesus, you two,' Gilchrist said. 'Stop this right now. You're serving police officers.'

Donaldson rubbed the red mark on his face left by Gilchrist's

slap. 'Don't think you're in a position to talk, Sarah. And sometimes men need to settle their differences like men, even if one of
them is a boy trying to be a man.'

'That's a bit wordy,' Heap said. 'Why don't you just grunt?'

Gilchrist stepped between them. 'We've got an investigation to
get on with,' she said, holding up a finger in warning.

Donaldson drew in his breath, almost popping his shirt buttons
again. Gilchrist had an image of the Incredible Hulk. There was
definitely something off about Don-Don's wild eyes.

Heap squared off. Donaldson saw it and sniggered. Though he
was only about six inches taller than Heap, Donaldson was about
three times the bulk. He dwarfed him.

'What – you're going to hit me with some of that kung fu shit
you do?' Donaldson said. 'You know the truth about the martial
arts, Heap? The bigger your opponent, the bigger the beating he's
going to give you.'

Somebody had told Gilchrist once that if you're small getting
in fast is the only way to go. Heap was very fast. He stepped
round her and moved in on Donaldson with a flurry of blows to
head and neck and belly. He kicked at Donaldson's shins and
knees, twisting round him and getting his elbows into Donaldson's
kidneys.

Donaldson didn't budge. He just stood there and absorbed it.
But Heap was relentless. His barrage of blows continued. Then
he kicked the bigger man's legs away from under him.

Donaldson fell like a tree. Gilchrist was sure she felt the floor
shake. Heap was shaking his left hand and grimacing. One of his
blows had hit bone. Gilchrist smiled to herself. She'd always
thought Donaldson a knucklehead.

Heap caught his breath. He glanced at Gilchrist. She stepped
between him and Donaldson, lying on the floor.

'OK. This is over now. What happens here stays here.'

She looked down at Donaldson.

'OK?'

No response.

'OK?'

Donaldson nodded slowly.

Gilchrist looked at Heap. 'Tenacious little sod, aren't you?'

He was still shaking his left hand. 'Ma'am,' he said.

Donaldson gathered himself together and got to his feet. Gilchrist saw the expression on his face. She was pretty sure he wasn't going to let this go.

When you woke it was light. Westbrook was sitting propped up beside Michelle but he was watching you. You looked round for Rogers.

'Doing a recce,' Westbrook said. His voice was stronger now but he kept it low. 'How did you know about Michelle, by the way?'

You didn't respond. He gave a little smile and gestured round, wincing.

'Pol Pot killed most of the museum workers and closed this down three years ago. Let the building go to shit. I would think three years of bat guano hasn't helped the health of the collection. In fact it's not too healthy for us.'

You said nothing.

'How long are you planning to stay here?' he said.

You shrugged.

'I'm guessing you don't have much food with you?' Westbrook said.

'You're guessing right.'

'It's OK – I'm used to doing without.' He gave you a long look. 'You'll never get out via the harbour.'

'We got in,' you said.

'That astounds me. They are expecting a full-scale Vietnamese invasion any day now. The Mekong is an obvious way into Cambodia from Ho Chi Minh City.'

'Saigon,' you said, without really thinking.

Westbrook gave a faint smile. 'The port is a high security area.'

'Our intelligence is that what is left of the Khmer Rouge army is deployed all along the eastern border with Vietnam,' you said. 'That's why there are so few patrols here in Phnom Penh. They don't really expect a sea invasion and if they do it's a big one coming in, not four people getting out.'

'You would still be wiser to head northwest and cross the Thai border. Scarcely any security there.'

'How do we get there?'

'There's a truck outside. Parked out of sight of the road.'

You looked at him. 'How do you know that? And even if there is, it isn't going to have any petrol in it.'

Westbrook shrugged. 'Looks in pretty good nick to me. Worth checking out anyway.'

You were scratching yourself.

'Lice,' he said. 'Sorry. We all had it. Have it. Better check Michelle for ringworm too.'

'And you?'

Westbrook shook his head. 'That's one good thing about isolation – you don't catch contagious things.'

'Except lice. I'm guessing you didn't bathe much.'

'We got hosed down every few days and lived in our own filth in between,' he said.

'They fed you?'

'Four spoons of rice at the start of the day and soup made from leaves later in the day.'

'Water?'

'Some,' he said. 'I saw a man beaten for drinking water without permission. Then he was forced to ingest a guard's urine and faeces.' He gave a wan smile. 'I quickly learned obedience.'

You were impressed there was no self-pity in his voice.

'There were rules we had to follow otherwise we were punished. We were warned not to cry out at all when getting lashes or being electrocuted. Any infraction of the rules, including that one, would get you ten lashes or five jolts of electricity.'

'You were interrogated?'

'Of course. There were three levels of interrogation. The first level was operated by the political unit. The unit wasn't allowed to use torture to obtain confessions. But since nobody had anything to confess pretty much everybody was handed over to the cruel unit. The torture unit. If the torturers there didn't get results you were handed over to the men graphically known as the chewing unit. They took torture to a higher level.'

'You got all these?'

He nodded. 'Michelle too,' he said, and looked down at her. 'You haven't said how you knew about Michelle.'

You said nothing.

'But I think I know.'

'Do you now?' you said cautiously.

He nodded. 'You're her soldier boy and she wrote to you before we left.'

You looked at him but said nothing.

He raised his battered and torn hands. 'You're going to have to set her shoulders, you know. I'm afraid I can't.'

'I can do that,' you said.

'I'm sure.'

You could see that both arms had popped out of their sockets. Michelle was so emaciated the end of the humerus bones bulged way out, stretching her skin so tightly it looked as if it was about to split.

You had dislocated your shoulder playing rugby a couple of times so you knew what agony she was in. The way to fix things was to manipulate the arms gently back into their sockets but that presupposed several things.

The first was the state of the humerus bones. You could check if they were broken but only an X-ray could tell you if either humerus was fractured.

The rotator cuff tendons were bands of tissue stretching over the tops of the shoulders. There was more tough tissue – the labrum – surrounding and supporting the shoulder joints. If any of this tissue was torn then she would need surgery to stitch the tendons back on the upper arm bone. After surgery, it would take three or four months for her to recover.

If nothing was torn or broken, she would be functioning again in a couple of weeks, fully recovered in six. You looked at her. Youth was on her side.

You gave her more morphine. She still winced as you gently touched the end of each bone. No apparent breaks.

You made a crude sling out of a shirt and bunched a blanket up beneath her left armpit to put her elbow at right angles. Then you gently manipulated the bone back into the shoulder joint. You heard a kind of wet click as it slotted back in. That probably meant the joint was still relatively healthy.

Even with the morphine you could see the pain flare in her eyes, which never left your face. You repeated the operation on her other arm. When you had finished she continued to stare at you until her eyelids fluttered and she slept.

You watched over her for ten minutes. As you did so you were aware that, leaning against the wall, Westbrook was still watching you.

You were wondering about Rogers – and that truck.

'I'm going to find Rogers,' you said.

You made your way through the rubble and rubbish, past colossal statues drenched in bat shit. Some of the objects were lying on their sides or were chipped and broken. There were a number of empty pedestals. You looked through the windows on three sides of the building. The streets were eerily empty. It was like some post-apocalyptic scene from a science fiction film. Or, worse still, a zombie film.

You could see the lorry parked down a narrow side road right next to the museum. It was one of those you had come in. Howe and Bartram were loading crates into the back.

'Seemed a shame to miss the opportunity whilst we're here,' said a voice behind you. You recognized it as that of Rogers just before he smashed his weapon over your head.

# SEVEN

'Sarah, it's Karen Hewitt.'

'Ma'am.'

'I've had an odd call from the Pavilion about some of the stuff you found there.'

'The bones?'

'The boxes.'

Gilchrist frowned. 'There are more bones in them?'

'No, thank God. There are ancient artefacts.'

'Well? It's a museum, isn't it?'

Hewitt sighed. 'Wrong period or something. Hang on.'

Gilchrist could hear a shuffling of papers. 'I'm not really into history, ma'am.'

'You think I am?'

'I wouldn't presume, ma'am.'

'Of course you wouldn't,' Hewitt said drily.

'Is it linked to our current investigation of Rafferty?' Gilchrist said.

'That's for you to decide,' Hewitt said.

Gilchrist stifled a yawn. She was tired today, for no good reason. 'Who do I call?'

Gilchrist shouted across to Heap as she dialled the number Hewitt had given her: 'Something else is happening at the Pavilion.' She turned back to the telephone. 'Hi there – is that Angelica Rutherford? This is DI Sarah Gilchrist. I understand there's a problem with some things you found in Mr Rafferty's storage boxes in the basement.'

'Major problems,' the woman on the other end of the line said. She had a kind of toned-down posh voice.

'Because?'

'We can't find any provenance for the goods.'

'Provenance?'

'Who they were bought from,' Rutherford said. 'How much they cost. Where they came from. The export certificates from wherever that was. Import certificates. We have none of that paperwork.'

'And that means?'

'They might be stolen or have been illegally exported from their country of origin.'

'Valuable stuff and you don't know where it's come from?'

'High-end stuff and, actually, we do know where it came from. That's the puzzling thing. I can't imagine why we have them or how we procured them.'

'What kind of stuff are we talking about?'

'Hindu relics, possibly from the world's biggest temple complex. Sandstone or brass heads and sculptures.'

'What does Mr Rafferty say?'

'Mr Rafferty isn't available at the moment,' Rutherford said. 'I assume he's keeping a low profile.'

'I assume he is,' Gilchrist said. 'But I heard Rafferty isn't very hands-on. Isn't there a curator of this collection?'

'As I said, we don't have this kind of collection. The nearest thing to a curator for these objects went off months ago to find herself at a yoga retreat in Kerala.'

'She's still out there?'

'Still looking, yes.'

Gilchrist laughed. She liked Angelica Rutherford. 'Hindu stuff, you say? I thought the Royal Pavilion had strong connections with India?'

'It did. In the Great War the Pavilion was used as a hospital for Indian Army soldiers wounded on the Western Front. But what's your point?'

'That it's understandable there should be Hindu things in the Royal Pavilion. Could they have been gifts from the Indian people after the Great War? They donated that ceremonial gate just outside the Pavilion and the Chattri up on the Downs, didn't they?'

'You're missing my point. The biggest Hindu temple in the world is not in India.'

Gilchrist thought for a moment. 'Sri Lanka?'

'No. Cambodia. Angkor Wat at Siem Reap in the north-east of the country. Huge palace and temple complex.'

'I thought they were Buddhists in Cambodia?' Gilchrist said. As if she knew anything about that kind of thing. And then remembered Heap being surprised there were some Buddhist relics in the boxes Donaldson had looked at cursorily.

'They are, but Angkor Wat is Hindu. Back in the twelfth century there was a great Hindu empire stretching across that part of Asia.'

Gilchrist frowned. 'And you're sure that doesn't fit the Pavilion?'

'Certain,' Rutherford said patiently. 'This stuff is about eight hundred years older than the Pavilion. It doesn't fit at all.'

Rutherford cleared her throat. 'I believe a lot of artefacts were looted by the Pol Pot regime in the seventies.'

Gilchrist had only vaguely heard of Pol Pot but what she'd heard wasn't good. 'So the Royal Pavilion could have bought these things from Pol Pot?' she asked, cautiously.

'Certainly, Pol Pot sold everything. The Tamil Tigers did the same twenty years later in the part of Sri Lanka they controlled. Pol Pot had no respect for human life so he wouldn't care a hoot about religious artefacts. He needed weapons and he needed bullets so I'm sure he looted his own country's heritage. I know the National Museum lost most of its most valuable pieces.'

'What is this stuff again?' Gilchrist said.

'Stone heads, wall art. Some brass.'

'Portable?'

Rutherford laughed. 'Everything is portable if you have the right equipment. These things are bulky but, yes, portable.'

'And valuable?'

'Not my field but I'd say yes. Not priceless but worth a bob or two. Cumulatively worth quite a lot.'

'But these things have just been sitting there?'

'They've never been displayed, if that's what you mean. No reason why they should be by us. I can't see where we would display these objects.'

'And Bernard Rafferty acquired them?'

Rutherford was silent. 'There is no one else who could have,' she finally said, almost reluctantly. Didn't want to land her boss in it, presumably.

Gilchrist thought some more. 'Any chance this stuff could have been in the Pavilion for decades and just been forgotten about?'

'That storeroom was empty when Mr Rafferty found the Brighton Trunk Murder files. We looked at the time in case there were any more files.'

Gilchrist frowned. 'So they've only been there a couple of years?'

'It would seem so.'

Gilchrist glanced across at Heap. 'We'll be right down.'

You vomited when you came round. You glanced at your watch. You'd only been out a few minutes. You made your way back to the office, slithering on bat shit more than once. You tried not to put your hands in it. Guano was full of nitrates, which, aside from being an essential component of fertiliser and gunpowder, burned like lime and could fuck up your lungs.

The office was empty. Westbrook and Michelle were nowhere to be seen. You hurried to the side of the building, where the lorry had been parked, slipping on guano as you went. The lorry was gone but you could hear its engine.

You went to the broken window you had entered through. The lorry was bumping away into the distance.

Rogers, Howe and Bartram had gone, taking Michelle and her father with them. And whatever they had stolen from the museum. You thought you knew why and where they were going. Unless they were making a big loop they were not heading for the harbour. They were heading north but not to the Thai border. They were going to Angkor Wat.

You found a bicycle in a storeroom at the back of the museum. It had a basket on the front. There was an overall and a lampshade hat hanging on a wall. You put them on. Not much of a disguise but it would have to do. You put your weaponry in the basket, tried to hide it with piles of paper. You set off after the lorry.

The streets were potholed and rubbish strewn but on you headed to the west and then north. You saw no patrols. You figured the lorry wouldn't be going faster than fifteen to twenty miles an hour until it got free of the city and then, given the state of the roads, probably wouldn't be able to go much faster. Maybe it would even be slower.

The bike had no gears and the tyres were almost flat but you calculated on the flat ground you could make eight miles an hour. For a while at least.

So every hour the lorry would gain between seven and twelve miles. By the end of the day it would be over a hundred miles ahead of you. It was a hopeless pursuit. You cycled on.

The lorry might run out of petrol. It stood out more than your bicycle so might be stopped – and more than once. You could keep going for as long as you had strength.

It was a hopeless pursuit. You cycled on.

On the edge of the city you found an abandoned petrol station. You poked around the back. In the far corner of a shed, under tarpaulin, you found another bicycle, this one with a crude motor on it. Within ten minutes you were chugging along the road, smoke trailing behind you. No faster but your leg muscles were getting a welcome break.

When you finally left Phnom Penh behind you entered a land of devastation and desolation. Unploughed fields. Fire-blackened crops and groves of trees. Entire villages burned down or simply abandoned. Dead bodies by the roadside, some hanging from trees. Carrion birds wheeling and shrieking.

You checked your compass occasionally. You needed to reach a decision soon. At some point the road would fork and you needed to be sure that Rogers wasn't just making a run for the border. That he was, in fact, taking Michelle and her father back to Angkor Wat.

Michelle and her father were archaeologists. Angkor Wat was her area of expertise. What you were puzzled about was how Rogers knew this. You were certain he did – you couldn't think of any other reason for him to take them. You wondered about the conversation Westbrook and Rogers had been having as you headed for the museum.

You'd been trying to figure out how Michelle and her father had been captured. They should have left Cambodia years earlier, when the French organized a convoy of lorries to take all French subjects over the Thai border. Westbrook, despite his cut-glass English accent, had dual nationality – his mother French, his father English. Michelle's mother was Cambodian.

The only reason they would be caught in Cambodian waters was if Michelle and her father had been doing something to secure the magnificent ruins at Angkor Wat. Perhaps they had been accused of looting as well as spying. Though you couldn't be sure that Westbrook wasn't a spy.

The motor on your bicycle started to falter. It missed strokes, belched smoke, hiccupped then died. You carried on pedalling but the bike was sluggish and it was hard work. Eventually you pulled up under a tree. You leaned the bike there and sat down beside it.

You were hungry and tired. You had a little water left and took small sips. Your stomach gurgled.

You'd been travelling for six hours. Maybe fifty miles. Rogers could have done as many as ninety.

You'd been resting under the tree for about fifteen minutes, weighing your options, when you heard an engine. A jeep bouncing along the road towards you. You watched it approach. A soldier was standing in the back, facing backwards, a machine gun on a tripod in front of him pointing back down the road. There was another soldier beside the driver. He was pointing at you, starting to stand in his seat. You looked beyond them. The road was empty.

It was brief and bloody. You shot the driver first and as the jeep twisted off the road you killed the machine-gunner. The soldier in the passenger seat – he had stripes on his shirtsleeves – was struggling to get his gun from his holster when you shot him.

You dragged the three bodies from the jeep and piled them behind the tree. The soldiers were little more than children. You tipped the machine gun and its tripod off the jeep and climbed in. You set off down the road in a cloud of dust. It was no longer a hopeless pursuit.


Anjelica Rutherford was an attractive woman in her fifties with her dark hair pulled back from an intelligent face. She shook hands with Gilchrist briskly and ushered her down a side corridor on the ground floor of the Pavilion into a spacious but cluttered office. As in the rest of the building the blinds at the long windows were down, presumably to prevent sun damage to the expensive-looking wallpaper. The soft light gave the room an air of tranquillity.

'Nice place,' Gilchrist said.

'Isn't it? This was the mayor's parlour for ages before Brighton and Hove merged and the Pavilion got it back.'

'We've been assuming Rafferty put those artefacts there,' Gilchrist said. 'But maybe it was someone else?'

'From the Pavilion?' Rutherford sounded sceptical.

'Or the Dome?'

Rutherford sucked in breath. 'Unlikely.'

'Why?'

'Not because I don't think my colleagues are capable of such iniquity but for strictly logistical reasons. They could never get that stuff in without anybody noticing.'

'You know we've found an iron door at the back of the store room. Where does it lead?'

Rutherford shrugged. 'That's been sealed for years, as far as I know.'

'So no ideas about where it might have led?'

'It could link to any number of tunnels – you know there are a lot under old Brighton.'

Gilchrist remembered doing the Brighton sewers tour one summer, getting in them near the Palace Pier and emerging from a manhole cover a few hundred yards north in the Old Steine. Parts of the tunnels had been cavernous.

'You mean the Victorian sewer tunnels?'

'Not just those. Do you remember the first City Reads, when we were all encouraged to revisit *Alice in Wonderland*?'

Gilchrist did. She'd liked the book when she was a kid.

'It was chosen for Brighton because Lewis Carroll was partly inspired by a visit to a friend in Kemp Town. There was a tunnel going down to the seafront in the corner of one of the squares.'

'Which inspired the rabbit hole,' Gilchrist murmured, wondering which square the tunnel was in.

'Then there are all the tunnels the smugglers used in the old days to get illegal merchandise up from the seafront to the Lanes. Don't forget that all those boutique shops in the Lanes were once a warren of fishermen's cottages. They all have cellars that are essentially sealed off sections of those tunnels.'

'I didn't know that,' Gilchrist said, ideas sparking.

'The pubs in the Lanes were once all serviced by a single brewery. It would deliver barrels via underground tunnels linking them all. It used to be the same in Covent Garden in the area around Seven Dials.'

'And these tunnels in Brighton used to link to the Dome and Pavilion?'

Rutherford sat back in her chair. 'There are lots of stories of women housed in the Lanes sneaking down through the tunnels so the Prince of Wales could have his wicked way with them.'

'Your colleague Rachel told us they were just stories,' Gilchrist said. 'She reckoned Mrs Fitzherbert would probably have gone in through the front door.'

'True enough. But the women I'm talking about were rather

lower in social status and probably up for anything that would please a jaded palate. Plus the Pavilion had a big staff – women would also be visiting men much lower down the social scale too.'

'Are there any maps of these tunnels?'

'Not that I know of,' Rutherford said. 'The local history unit on the top floor of the museum might well have something though.'

'I'll get my sergeant on it,' Gilchrist said. 'How are you getting on with the artefacts?'

'I've got an expert from the British Museum coming down later today – Charlotte Byng. She told me some of these things are on the Red List.'

'The Red List? Is that like a stolen property thing?'

'The Red List doesn't quite work like that.'

'How does it work?'

'There are a number of Red Lists, each for a different country. They are a series of booklets published by the International Council of Museums about antiquities that are at risk.' Rutherford glanced across at the shelves lining the opposite wall. 'I've probably got some buried among my books over there. In Cambodia the council works with a couple of government departments and the National Museum. There has been a lot of looting of Angkorian and post-Angkorian sites but there is also concern about prehistoric cemetery sites.'

More graveyards, Gilchrist thought, stifling a yawn. 'What kind of stuff?' she said.

'Sculpture, architectural elements, ancient religious documents, bronze, iron, wood and ceramics.'

'But it isn't a stolen property list?'

'No – the objects in the list aren't specifically stolen but they represent the category of objects that are sought after. However, there is one item that has been missing since the seventies. It may have been destroyed by the Khmer Rouge; it may have been sold. It's priceless and all we know is that it has disappeared along with some Fabergé eggs.'

'Fabergé – I thought he did Russian stuff?'

'His fame spread far and wide so he did some work for the king of Siam and the king of Cambodia.'

Gilchrist was doodling on her pad. 'I just don't see this as the kind of stuff Rafferty would get involved with.'

Rutherford nodded. 'I'm inclined to agree,' she said.

'Perhaps we could come over when you're meeting with Ms Byng and we could all take a look at the artefacts.'

Rutherford nodded agreement.

Gilchrist stood. 'I need to go and see a sociopath now.'

Rutherford was deadpan: 'I have colleagues like that too.'

Gilchrist laughed. 'I know – it's your boss I'm talking about.'

You reach Siem Reap and scarcely recognize it. You're staying in a hotel just over the bridge from the main part of town. It's expensive and swish, with a big pool with turquoise lights beneath the surface of the water. You track down the address on the card over the bridge at the edge of town. It's an office behind a shop. The shop is shuttered up. It doesn't look like it has been open for a while.

You return to the hotel and sit on the veranda outside your room, nursing a vodka, looking down at the turquoise ripples on the water below you. It's not too long before glugging replaces nursing the vodka.

You are remembering when you caught up with Rogers and the others.

The jeep had enough petrol in it to take you all the way to Siem Reap. The town looked deserted but even so you skirted it and took the road through the jungle to Angkor Wat.

The site was vast. You knew it had been constructed as a model of the universe in stone. And you had a pretty good idea where in this universe they might be.

You shone your torch on the crude map you'd taken from the information desk in the National Museum. You checked your compass. You stopped the jeep beside an enormous reservoir, now only half full. The Khmer empire's strength had lain in its talent for irrigation.

To your right was the temple complex you were looking for. You could see lights flickering in the trees. You walked down between crumbling buildings the jungle had grown through.

A huge tree with vast above-the-ground roots thrust through the main courtyard of the temple. Another was growing through the roof of a wing of the temple itself. Will Rogers was straddling one of the roots of the tree in the courtyard, leaning back against the tree, smoking a cigarette. You could hear the sound of hammer and chisel from the temple behind him.

'Well met by moonlight,' he growled.

'Shouldn't that be ill met?' you said.

'Why be pessimistic?'

Rogers pushed himself into a standing position.

You gestured around the courtyard. 'What is this, Will? What are Bartram and Howe up to?'

'Don't forget Cartwright.'

'He's in on this?'

'You should be too. This is the future.'

'What are they all doing?'

'What do you think they're doing? Asset-stripping, of course. This stuff is twelfth-century, rare art. Going to be worth a fortune.'

'But they're wrecking the place. Isn't this like tomb-robbing in Egypt?'

'No. It's like saving the Elgin Marbles from destruction. Enlightened action by people who care.'

'Doesn't look very enlightened to me.'

'What's underneath is not the art. What we're leaving behind doesn't need protecting.'

'The art is the art because of where it is,' you said. 'Ripping it out of there isn't going to make it more valuable.'

'Jesus, I didn't know I was taking part in the fucking *South Bank Show*. Anyway, tell that to the collectors. I'm a soldier turned entrepreneur. That's not indecent.'

'You're going to be smuggling this stuff out of the country and selling it illegally. That's not so decent.'

'Not for the first time. Got some great pre-Colombian shit when we were down in South America. We talked about cutting you in then but you were such a goddamm boy scout.'

You shrugged.

'Don't you want to be rich?' Rogers said.

'Not particularly. No worries would be nice.'

'Believe me, come in with us and you'll never have to worry again.'

'Why didn't you offer me the option in Phnom Penh instead of bashing me over the head?'

'Sorry about that. The others still thought you were too much of a boy scout.'

'Captain America.'

'Right. But I knew you'd turn up. Like a bad penny.'

'You're the bad penny, Will.' You gestured to the noise of the men hacking away at the stone façade. 'This is worrying.'

'This is archaeology.'

'You're the expert suddenly?'

'Are you? And, actually, Mr Westbrook is kindly providing the expertise.'

You didn't know what to do. You weren't big on history but you knew this was wrong. You looked at Will. Could you do what he wanted? Time to worry about that later. Your priority was Michelle. 'What does Michelle think?' you said.

Will looked solemn. 'We need to talk about Michelle.'

You were off balance when you tried to hit him. He had you on the ground in a second. You fell well but it still hurt like shit.

He looked down at you. 'I have to say you're losing your grip, son,' he said. 'A little more self-control would suit you well.'

'What has happened to Michelle?'

Will's voice was calm. 'Stay down.'

'What has happened to her?' you repeated, your voice equally calm.

You realized Will was sweating. 'She's gone.'

'I'm getting up and don't you fucking try to stop me,' you said.

Will showed his palms and stepped back. You got to your feet. Will responded to your stance.

'Listen,' he said. 'I'm not happy about this. Believe me. But you're going to blow everything if you're not careful.'

You looked at the sweat rolling down from his hairline, conscious of the wetness of your own face. 'Where's Michelle?'

Will leaned forward. His voice was quiet. 'I wish I knew.'

You were planning a complicated sequence of hits, depending on his responses. 'What happened?'

'Nothing that makes sense. One minute she's here, the next minute she's gone.' Will stepped back. 'Way of the modern world.'

You looked at him, grinding your teeth until your jaw ached. 'She's been unconscious for the past twenty-four hours. You can't just fucking say she's gone and that's the end of it.'

Will leaned forward again. 'Steady, mate. You've already landed on your arse once.'

'Where has she gone?'

Will stepped back. 'You know, you never really explained your relationship with the beautiful Michelle. This wasn't just some simple rescue mission, was it?'

You ignored that. 'Where is she?'

Will shrugged his big shoulders. 'She left us.'

You couldn't help yourself. 'Left *you*? I repeat, she wasn't in any condition to leave anybody.'

'Apparently she was. She left, and how would I know why? You know why anybody does anything?'

'I know why *I* do things,' you said, brain racing.

'Do you? Do you really?' Rogers spat on the floor. Thick phlegm. 'I somehow doubt that.'

'What about her father? Isn't Westbrook tearing his hair out?'

'He is, he is.'

You hit him again. A better blow than before. You caught him on the temple and he reeled, stumbled. You went for the follow-up but he curled away, hugging himself to the floor. You weren't expecting that. You looked down on him.

Then something happened to your head you weren't expecting either but you recognized only too well. You twisted to see who had clobbered you as your brain bounced around in your skull for the second time in a day. An arcing arm withdrawn. A club of some sort in the hand. A familiar face.

You whispered a single word – or maybe you didn't – before you lost consciousness. That face.

'Westbrook?'


On Marine Parade, the light was biblical. Lowering black clouds, a single beam of sunlight looking like a funnel between sea and sky. Sarah Gilchrist half expected someone to be drawn up from the sea into it or to descend from the sky.

Rafferty was holed up in East Preston, in the opposite direction, but the detour was to pick up some documents the club owner had promised on pain of having his premises closed down.

Gilchrist watched as the clouds coiled around each other and the beam of light vanished as abruptly as it had appeared. There were a handful of runners and dog walkers. A young woman was scattering bread for the seagulls and pigeons. A benign thing to do. Except that as the bread attracted the birds, her son was rushing among them trying to kick them and stamp on their heads.

Gilchrist had never had the mothering instinct. She was almost Victorian in her belief that kids should be seen and not heard – especially in cafés, and extra especially in pubs. A 'family friendly' pub was a contradiction in terms as far as she was concerned. You want kids? Stay home and look after them until they are old enough to behave properly. Leave the going out to grown-ups who want to stay grown up and not spend half their lives doing baby talk.

Gilchrist drew her breath in sharply. Where had that little internal rant come from?

Further down the beach she could see a gang of visiting football supporters in a conga line, all naked but yoked together by their football scarves around their necks. Every other step they thrust their hips forward and their penises flew out in front of them and flopped back. Well, the bigger ones did. She could hear the raucous laughter of the group even with the window up.

Gilchrist shook her head wearily. 'You know the word I hate most, Bellamy?'

'No, ma'am.'

'Tribe.'

Heap nodded. 'I'm assuming you've seen football supporters.'

'Didn't you?'

'I'm the driver, ma'am.'

'You mean you don't have the luxury of gazing out of the window watching the world go by.'

'Your words, ma'am, not mine.'

'What do you make of this antiquities thing?'

'It's always been a big criminal business in Brighton. Stealing stuff from all the big houses in the area then getting it across the Channel before the theft is even reported.'

Gilchrist nodded. 'But that market has been in decline for years. That's why we got rid of our special antiques unit. Maybe there is more of a market for this Asian stuff, given all the New Age, Buddhist stuff around here. Every other garden seems to have a Buddha sitting underneath its wind-chimes.'

'True, ma'am, but how many people could tell the difference between a twelfth-century Buddha and one cast last week? I mean,

I don't think I'm being racist when I say that with the same little smile on them, all the Buddha look the same.'

Gilchrist laughed, watching the football supporters in her side mirror. There had been a near-riot in town the previous evening when the visiting team's supporters had taken defeat badly. During the match one footballer had also almost bitten off the ear of another.

'Ear-biting – is that a gay thing?' she said. 'And all that pulling on shirts and shorts. Same deal, surely?'

'You're back to football. Why would a gay person particularly ear-bite, ma'am?'

'You're right – I'm getting into deep waters there. Let's just stay with football fans as moronic. Not as individuals but as part of crowd dynamics. They work each other up so much and are so hostile to the supporters of rival teams. Makes absolutely no bloody sense.'

'Absolutely, ma'am,' Heap said, giving her a quick glance. Gilchrist decided to shut up.

They drove past the Volk's railway. Both of them looked off to their right. An almost naked man was sitting with his back to a lamppost, knees up, one arm raised above his head, a large pool of vomit by his side. He was secured to the lamppost by plastic cable around his wrist.

'Stag night rather than football supporter, ma'am,' Heap said, stopping the car. He rummaged in the glove compartment and took out a pair of clippers.

The man was half-awake, one eye open, head tilted. He watched Heap and Gilchrist approach. They stepped round the vomit, noticing he had more down his bare chest and on his underpants – those and socks the only clothes he wore.

'That is some serious puke,' Gilchrist muttered. 'What has this man eaten?'

'A horse was stolen from Lewes Stables yesterday,' Heap murmured as he snipped the plastic cable. Gilchrist laughed. The man's arm dropped abruptly.

'What time's the wedding?' Heap said.

'Two o'clock,' the man mumbled.

Heap looked at his watch. 'You've missed it.'

The man tried to focus. 'What?'

'Two o'clock today?' Heap said.

'Tomorrow. Tomorrow. Is today tomorrow?'

Heap looked at Gilchrist. 'Questions like that can only be answered by someone of a higher rank than either of us.'

Gilchrist smiled. 'Where are you staying?' she said.

'They're coming back for me,' he said.

'Do you know where you're staying?' Heap repeated.

The man shook his head.

'Are your clothes anywhere around?'

He shrugged. Gilchrist pointed up the road to the club under the arches. 'You were in there last?'

He nodded.

'Your friends still there?'

'Maybe.'

'What's their uniform?'

'What?'

'What did you choose for everyone to wear on your stag night?'

'Clockwork Orange.'

'Arty. OK. Don't wander off.'

Heap and Gilchrist got back in the car and drove the twenty yards down to the club. The din of the music cascaded out of the open doors. There was a strong smell of stale booze and piss around the entrance. They walked over to the doormen and flashed their warrant cards.

'You have a package for us?' Heap said. 'Your boss is supposed to give us a whole lot of documentation so we know you're not operating illegally and we don't need to close you down.'

The biggest bouncer reached behind a counter and produced a large envelope. Heap took it.

'Thanks,' Heap said. 'Listen – is there a gang of guys in there wearing bowler hats with black paint round one of their eyes? I mean each of them with one eye painted, not just one eye among them all.'

Gilchrist glanced at Heap as the biggest bouncer nodded.

Heap pointed back to the lamppost. 'Make sure they take care of their friend when they stagger out, will you?'

Whether his friends could even look after themselves after a night and half a day pub- and club-crawling was a moot point. They all looked back at the lamppost. The man had gone. Instead there was a small woman standing there. Something was dangling from her hand. She was swaying. She looked familiar.

Gilchrist and Heap walked back to the car and the woman moved towards them. She was smartly dressed. Cashmere coat. She was Asian. Her mouth hung open. She had a kitchen knife in her hand. It was bloody.

Gilchrist watched with horrified fascination as a fat globule of blood slowly separated from the knife's tip and dropped to the concrete. She imagined she heard the splat as it landed. And the next one.

Gilchrist gave Heap's arm a cautionary squeeze. He glanced at her other hand sticking out of her pocket where she was tapping in the code on her mobile asking for urgent back-up.

Gilchrist's attention never wavered from the knife. She wasn't scared but she didn't intend to tackle this woman unless it was absolutely necessary. She hoped Heap felt the same.

'You recognize her, don't you?' Heap said as they drew closer.

'The mother who lost her son – the one standing at the side of the road?'

'Her hands are covered in blood.' Gilchrist looked beyond her, trying to locate the drunken groom. 'Do you think she's stabbed that guy?'

'No. I think she's hurt herself. That's her blood.'

They stopped in front of the woman.

'Can we help?' Heap said.

Gilchrist scrutinized her face. She looked up at Gilchrist, her mouth open in a rictus of misery. There was something particularly distressing because the planes of her face were flat, the eyes expressionless. All emotion was in the silent scream of the open mouth.

The woman said nothing. Just stood there, blood dripping slowly from the knife and off the fingers of her other hand. Heap gestured towards the knife.

'Do you want to drop that?'

The woman didn't respond. Heap moved his hand, almost casually, to his belt. Gilchrist hoped he wasn't going to Taser her.

'Do you speak English?' Heap said.

The woman gave the smallest of nods.

'We want to help you,' Heap said. 'You're hurt.'

The woman ignored him, her eyes on Gilchrist. Gilchrist glanced

beyond the woman. Far off at the other end of the drive she could
see a police car slowly approaching. She guessed there was by
now another one hidden round the bend behind her.

'What is your name?' Gilchrist said.

The woman said nothing again.

The police car worked its way through the chicanes. It was now
about two hundred yards away.

The woman, her mouth still open, worked her jaw, as if she
was trying to devour something. Heap took his phone out and
ordered an ambulance.

'You haven't hurt anybody else, have you?' Gilchrist said.

If there was a reply Gilchrist missed it because of a sudden
explosion of chanting from the entrance to the club behind her. It
was the drunken repetition of a single line: 'Who's getting married
in the morning?'

Half-a-dozen raucous male voices. Jeering and laughter.

'Where's the bloody lamppost?' someone shouted.

Gilchrist didn't take her eyes off the woman but in her peripheral
vision a gang of drunken men in bowler hats staggered across the
road towards the lamppost with the vomit beside it.

'Where's the bloody groom?' someone else called as everyone
sniggered.

Gilchrist flicked a glance across. That's what she was wondering.

She hoped they'd find him wandering on the beach. She looked
back at the woman. The woman now seemed to be scrutinizing
Gilchrist's face as intently as Gilchrist had scrutinized hers. The
knife was still pointing towards the pavement.

The police car halted beside the woman. As a door opened, the
woman nodded at Gilchrist, let the knife clatter to the pavement
and said just two words: 'My son.'

She turned to the rear passenger door of the police car and stood
as if awaiting instruction.

There were shouts from across the road. One of the men was
down on his hands and knees being sick. The others were gathered
in a loose semi-circle looking down at something just out of sight
over the lip of the shingle incline.

'Wakey-wakey,' they chanted in rough unison as the woman
collapsed into the back seat of the car.

# EIGHT

You're looking at yourself in the mirror. Your ribs ache. *Your* ribs. You can't get over this disjunction between what you see and what you are and what you feel. They must be your ribs but the feeling is outside you. As so much is outside you.

Lately you have often been feeling as if you are looking down on yourself from the corner of the room. The feeling is so strong you fear you are fracturing down the middle.

Your mobile phone rings for the first time in weeks.

'Jimmy?' your friend Bob Watts says when you answer.

'Bob.'

'Bloody hell. I can't believe I've actually got through to the elusive Mr Tingley. I've been trying for an age.'

'Connections have been a bit iffy,' you say quietly. You slide open the glass door and step back out on to your veranda. 'I read about your new job, Bob. Looks like you outmanoeuvred the bastards. But tell me you're not going to reopen the Milldean Massacre case to go after your erstwhile friend William Simpson.'

'William Simpson will get his due retribution but I have no immediate plans to facilitate that,' Watts says. Then laughs. 'If only.'

You watch the water ripple in the pool, then say: 'You joke but I know it's not a joke for you.'

'That's as maybe.' You can tell Watts can hear something in your voice that he can't quite place. 'When are you coming home, Jimmy?'

You sit in the chair on your veranda and pick up the half-full glass of vodka on the floor beside it. 'Home being Brighton? In due course.'

'You OK, buddy mine?' There is concern in Watts' voice.

'In the pink,' you say.

'Yeah, right,' Watts says. 'What's going on, Jimmy?'

'I'm not myself,' you say, standing again and looking back into your room.

'Recuperation can take a long time,' Watts says. You are distracted for a moment. 'Jimmy?'

'I mean that statement very precisely, Bob,' you say. 'I'm a person I don't recognize or feel anything for. I feel as if I've been hijacked by somebody else.'

Watts clearly doesn't know how to respond to that. 'Are you still in Italy?' he finally says.

'Cambodia.'

'Cambodia? That's a bit sudden, isn't it? Holiday?'

You rub your eyes. 'Pilgrimage. Sort of. A kind of twelve step.'

'You've given up booze?'

'Far from it.'

Watts laughs. 'That's a relief. I can't imagine you without your rum and pep.'

'Can't get the peppermint over here so I've switched temporarily to vodka.' You swirl the vodka round in your glass as you say this.

'I hope it's Polish,' Watts says.

'It is.'

Another silence.

'What kind of twelve step?'

'People I need to apologise to. Ask their forgiveness. Things I need to apologise for.'

Watts says nothing.

'The problem is that pretty much all of them are dead.'

Watts knows better than to pry. You are probably his best friend but he knows scarcely anything about you. You and he are both to blame. Watts is useless at asking questions and you are brilliant at not answering them.

'You haven't got religious, have you?' Watts finally says with a chuckle that sounds forced.

'I've always been religious in my own way,' you say. Which is true.

'Buddhist over there, aren't they? Are you listening to the sound of the one hand clapping?'

There is a little patch of bamboo beside the veranda. It clacks in a sudden shiver of air.

'Not exactly.'

After a moment, Watts says, 'Revenge a factor in this?'

You say nothing.

He says again: 'Come home, Jimmy.'

'In due course,' you say. 'But first I could do with a favour.'

'You know you only have to name it,' Watts says.

'Can you find out about a shop for me – discreetly though. An antiques shop in the Lanes.'

'Sure. What do you want to know?'

'If the owners are around in Brighton. What their circumstances are. That kind of stuff.'

'Let me grab a pen,' Watts says. 'What's the name?'

'The shop is called Charles Windsor Antiques but I don't know if that's the actual owner. It's people who might be linked to it I'm interested in. But you've got to be discreet. I don't want anyone scaring off.'

'What have they done?' Watts asks.

You lean forward. You want to say but you find it difficult to get the words out. You don't think you have vocalised it before. Ever. You want to hang up the phone. But before you hang up, you exhale and say quietly: 'They killed my wife.'


Rafferty was holed up in a big house on the beach at East Preston, a posh village on the edge of Worthing. He looked little changed when he met them at the door in blazer and cravat. Gilchrist got a waft of alcohol as he ushered them into a large sitting room at the back of the house. It was ten a.m.

His lawyer was sitting in an armchair by the window. He stood and nodded to them.

The window looked out on a long stretch of lawn that ran to a short wall. Beyond the wall they could see high waves rushing up the beach.

Rafferty gestured for them to be seated on a long sofa. As they both sank into it, Gilchrist doubted she would be able to get up again with any dignity.

'Mr Rafferty,' Heap began. 'We want to talk to you about Hindu artefacts from Cambodia. Twelfth century.'

'Not my area of expertise. I'm more rural England. Graveyards. I thought you knew.'

'That wasn't always the case though, was it? You've had a long career at the Brighton museums. Worked your way up.'

'It's the British way. I'm sure you two have done the same.'

'You spent time as deputy director of the Royal Pavilion in the eighties.'

'Just after a bad time for the Pavilion. A load of fucking philistines ran the council in the seventies. Medieval banquets and horse races down the corridors. Those beautiful rooms used as council offices.'

'Your relationship with Cambodia?'

'I have no relationship. But knowing the wankers in power in the seventies in Brighton, we were probably twinned with Phnom Penh whilst Pol Pot was massacring everyone in sight with half a brain.'

'Did you buy some illicit treasures from Cambodia when the country was dying?'

'Excuse me,' the lawyer said. Rafferty waved him away.

'I wish,' Rafferty said. 'That's how you create a world-class collection. You think Lord Elgin paid actual price for the Marbles? You ever been to St Paul de Vence? No, don't even answer – no way you have. There's a restaurant there – La Colombe d'Or. The food is pretty good but not great. But people go there to see the artwork on the walls. Worth millions. You think the restaurant owner had millions to spend on it? Not at all. He gave Picasso free meals and in return Picasso gave him a couple of pictures. Same with the other artists. Braque, Miro, Fernand Leger.' He sniffed. 'All collections start with someone buying cheap.'

'But we're talking about artefacts that were known to be stolen.'

'You're a few years out – Pol Pot was long gone by the time I got the Pavilion. And I don't know what artefacts you're talking about. But I do know that nobody gave a fuck in the seventies about Angkor Wat.'

He turned to Heap.

'Big brain – when did UNESCO register Angkor Wat as a world heritage site?'

Heap shrugged. 'Years ago, I guess. Why do you ask?'

'Because I know that it wasn't until the early nineties. One of the greatest religious and archaeological sites in the world didn't have any kind of protection through war, civil war, the Khmer Rouge genocide and ten years of Vietnamese occupation.'

Heap tilted his head. 'You're well informed about its recent history for someone who has no interest in its cultural heritage.'

Rafferty grinned, almost wolfishly. 'You obviously never saw me polish off my General Knowledge round on *Mastermind* when Magnus was still in the chair.'

'Was I born then?' Gilchrist muttered to herself.

'What?' Rafferty said.

Gilchrist shifted, with difficulty, on the soft sofa. 'Just thinking aloud, sir,' she said.

'So you're saying that whoever looted these things was providing a public service?' Heap said.

Rafferty pressed his knees together. 'That's exactly what I'm saying. They left Cambodia through back-door channels? So what? They were taken out of harm's way. Elgin did the same – the Marbles would have been destroyed. The ones that remained in situ were pretty much destroyed, not least in the twentieth century by acid rain.'

'Elgin was a philanthropist?' Heap said.

'Are you two saying the world hasn't been enriched by having the Marbles on show in the British Museum for decades when they could have been destroyed entirely had they been left in situ?' Rafferty pretended to stifle a yawn. 'Indigenous populations don't usually care about their heritage until they discover there are people willing to buy it. They pull down temples to use the stones to build their own houses. We're no different in this country. Ever been to Avebury? Every house in the area is built from the stones that formed part of the original stone circle and processional route. The same around Stonehenge – a much inferior site in my view.'

'If we could get back to the question of these objects in the basement . . .' Gilchrist said.

Rafferty ignored her. 'Mainly, though, indigenous people flog the artefacts off or learn how to copy them and rip the West off with forgeries,' he continued.

'The objects in the Pavilion?' Heap repeated.

Rafferty steepled his fingers. 'Whoever bought these things has ensured they will be protected, celebrated and saved for the future.'

'They were hidden in a tunnel,' Gilchrist said. 'I think the only person who would have been celebrating these things was which-ever wealthy private collector bought them.'

Rafferty said nothing.

'You sure it wasn't you?'

Rafferty leaned forward. 'You know, I thought you were here to tell me what's happening with this other thing.'

'We're evaluating.'

'Evaluating?'

'Yes. Then we pass our papers on to the Crown Prosecution Service and they decide whether to take it further.'

'And the charges?' Rafferty said.

'Will be decided upon when the evaluation is complete,' Gilchrist said.

'As a matter of fact, sir,' Heap said, 'it would help us reach some decisions and speed up the evaluation process if you were willing to undergo evaluation yourself.'

'What kind of evaluation?' the lawyer said.

Rafferty pointed at him. 'Earning his money, you see,' he said.

The lawyer pursed his lips.

'A psychological one,' Gilchrist said.

Rafferty laughed an exaggerated, high-pitched laugh, rocking a little. He stopped abruptly. 'To see if I'm sane enough to testify, you mean?'

'Not precisely that, no,' Gilchrist said. 'And it will just be part of the mix.'

'Do you think I'm sane, Clarence Darrow?' Rafferty called to his lawyer.

'Of course,' the lawyer said shortly. 'You're as sane as the rest of us.'

Rafferty sneered. 'That leaves quite a lot of leeway,' he said.

'Are you willing to be assessed, Mr Rafferty?' Gilchrist said.

'What do you think, Clarence?' he said to his lawyer.

'It's your decision,' the lawyer said. 'You're not legally obliged to submit to any evaluation until and unless you've been convicted. Reports are usually asked for at that stage to assist sentencing.'

'This evaluation will help us decide whether we proceed at all,' Gilchrist said.

'There's some doubt?' the lawyer said quickly.

'We're trying to establish the facts,' Gilchrist said. 'Until we do so there is neither doubt nor certainty.'

'I'll do it,' Rafferty said. 'If I can do it here. I don't particularly want to leave my little bolthole. The public and the press have shown a surprising amount of interest in this matter.'

'We can arrange for the psychologist to come here,' Gilchrist said. 'But let me just go back to these artefacts discovered in the storeroom underneath the Royal Pavilion. Are you denying you put them there?'

'I am.'

'Do you know who did put them there?'

'Since I didn't know they were there I can hardly be expected to know the answer to that, can I?'

'Can you think who might have put them there?'

'Aside from God, Santa Claus and the Tooth Fairy, you mean?'

When you were younger you were scared of no man. You would steam in against anyone. But now you have to be more careful. More cunning. Especially with the drink you've been consuming lately. You haven't counted today – when did you? – but you know you are teetering on the edge of recklessness.

You take a deep breath. You are pretty sure the breeze that is shivering the bamboo is a through draught from somebody opening a door or a window in your room. Maybe more than one person. Maybe in your bathroom. You're pretty sure Sal Paradise has sent him or them back to finish the job.

You are wrong. Your bathroom is empty. You set the chain on the door. Your phone is ringing again.

'You dropped two bombshells on me,' Bob Watts says. 'First, that someone killed your wife. Second, that you have a bloody wife.' He laughs. 'I didn't know you'd even been married. Hell, I didn't even know you were straight.'

You rub your face and work your jaw for a moment. 'It was a long time ago. And it wasn't for long.'

'Jimmy, I don't know what is going on with you here.'

'What is going on with me is I find the men who killed my wife are still alive when I thought them dead. I find that one or more have been living in the same town as me. In Brighton.'

'They run this antiques shop?'

'Certainly one of them is linked. Will Rogers. But I don't know if he's there or here. Some investigator I am if he's there. How many times do I go down the Lanes, for Christ's sake?'

'Hardly ever, I would think,' Watts said consolingly. 'You never get beyond the Cricketers, do you?'

Your laugh turns into a sigh.

'You thought these men were dead?' Watts says.

You grunt.

'And you want revenge. I understand that. But there's more to this than your desire for retribution. We can use legal means.'

'Just find out about them, would you?'

'Sure – but do you hear what I'm saying about legal means of bringing them to justice?'

'I've been hearing about exploring legal means all my life, Bob. For me it's just an excuse for inaction.'

'Not on this occasion.'

'Says who?'

'Me, James.'

A beat.

'Just make discreet inquiries, old friend,' you say. 'Please.'

Watts breaks the connection but you keep your phone to your ear and make little grunts as if you are still listening to him. You are standing by your bed. You are pretty certain there is someone standing behind you. A creak on the floorboards, a quiet exhalation of air, a change in pressure in the room – you don't know what has alerted you, but you know you are right.

You take a chance.

'The vodka is in the fridge, Will,' you say half over your shoulder. 'Help yourself.'


'What is she saying?'

Gilchrist was standing by the window in her office looking down at the blustery promenade when Heap approached. It had been a very long day and her brain was turning into spaghetti.

She turned to Heap. 'The Asian woman – what is she saying?'

Heap shook his head. 'She isn't making too much sense, ma'am. Her son disappeared. We have him down as a missing person. As I mentioned to you before, a fortune teller told her he had died but he would return on Madeira Drive or in one of several pubs in town. She's been going into pubs and buying a pint for him for when he comes back.'

'How did she move from that to cutting her wrists?'

Heap spread his hands. 'That's the part she's a bit confused about.'

Gilchrist nodded.

'She did a bad job of it,' Heap said. 'But most people get it wrong.'

Gilchrist raised an eyebrow. 'There's a right and a wrong way?'

'You cut along the vein, not across it, to be most effective.'

'I'll remember that,' Gilchrist said.

'I can't imagine why you would need to,' Heap said.

'Why not?' Gilchrist said, vaguely flattered. 'You don't think I'd ever be tempted to kill myself?'

Heap shook his head decisively.

'Why?'

'You wouldn't let the rest of us off so easily, ma'am.'

Gilchrist watched Heap flush, then said: 'Let me come and have a word with her.'

'Her name is Prak Chang. Her missing son is called Youk.'

Prak Chang's wrists were bandaged. There were spots of blood on her smart jacket.

'I come here twenty-five years ago,' Prak said in halting English. 'I carried Youk.'

'Did you come here with his father?'

She shook her head. 'No father.'

'He was dead?'

'No father,' she repeated. She picked at a red mark on the back of her hand with a long purple nail. Not blood; it looked like some sort of eczema.

'Did you enter the country illegally?' Heap said.

'I have passport,' she said indignantly. 'I nurse.'

'You've been working as a nurse in this country?' Heap said.

Prak nodded. 'Private nursing home.'

'We'll need the name of it,' Heap said. 'For our records.'

'You still work in a private nursing home?' Gilchrist said.

Prak shook her head. 'Now I run it.'

'You had family here when you arrived?'

'No family.' Prak leaned forward. 'In my country many people have no family since the Khmer Rouge. It split up families. And killing. Lot of killing.'

'You lost your family in the seventies?'

'Everyone. Brothers, sisters, parents, uncles and aunts.' She scratched at her hand. 'My father was a doctor.'

'How did you survive?' Gilchrist asked gently. 'You must only have been a child.'

Prak looked down, the purple nail never stopping its scratching. 'If people really want to survive they find ways.' She dropped her voice. 'I find a way.'

'That was many years before you came here.'

Prak looked up, her face hard. 'People never stop looking. They don't know whether families are alive or dead. So many years after they still don't know. They still hope. Old people like me trudging through malaria jungles searching for their missing families. Disappointed in refugee camps that have turned into towns after so many years. We have a TV programme now. Reality TV. Long-separated families reunited. Very popular among older viewers.'

'Where is Youk's father?'

'No father,' she repeated.

'There must have been,' Gilchrist said. 'Do you mean he's dead?'

The woman looked at her with the same intent expression on her face. 'I do not know who the father is.'

Heap interrupted. 'What prompted you to leave Cambodia and come here?' he said.

'A fortune teller in Battambang.'

'Told you to leave Cambodia?'

'I cut the cards seven times and she told me the child I carry is a boy. Youk. She told me to take him to a place of greater safety.'

'She warned you about giving birth in Cambodia?'

She looked down at her hand, bright red now from where she had been scratching it. 'She said he would die in Cambodia.'

The irony hung heavy for a moment.

'The fortune teller here tells me a man often meets his destiny on the road he takes to avoid it.'

'The appointment in Samarra,' Heap murmured.

'What?' Gilchrist said.

'A man in Baghdad sees Death staring at him in the marketplace and thinks it means his time has come. He borrows a horse to escape his appointment with Death. That night he arrives in Samarra and the first person he meets is Death. He complains to Death: "I saw you staring at me in Baghdad. I thought my appointment with you was there. Why am I meeting you here?" Death says: "I was staring because I was surprised to see you in Baghdad. My appointment with you was always in Samarra."

'You think Youk couldn't evade his destiny?' Gilchrist said to Prak. 'Is that because the same people you tried to get away from in Cambodia found him here?'

Prak looked immediately suspicious. 'Who said there were people I tried to get away from?'

'Sorry,' Gilchrist said, showing her palms. 'I thought that's what you meant about the fortune teller advising you to leave Cambodia for somewhere safer.'

Prak looked down. She remained silent until Heap said: 'Tell us about the last time you saw Youk.'

'He lived with me. He came home after work and he went out and he never came back.'

'Do you know where he went?'

Prak nodded. 'A house in the Lanes.'

'The north Lanes?' Gilchrist said, puzzled. She didn't think there were any houses in the main Lanes. 'Whose house?'

Prak looked equally puzzled by Gilchrist's question. 'A beer house.'

Heap twigged first. 'A public house,' he said.

Prak nodded again. 'Bath Arms,' she said.

'Was he meeting someone there?' Heap said.

Prak shrugged. 'He drank beer there often.'

'He was a regular?' Heap again.

'I think so. I leave a drink for him there but he never drink it.'

Gilchrist frowned. 'Now, you mean?' she said after a moment.

'Fortune teller thinks he return either to pub or beach.'

'The pub I understand, but why the beach?' Gilchrist said. 'Did he go to that part of the beach a lot?'

'There was a nightclub there.'

'Who was this fortune teller?' Heap said. 'Do you have his or her contact details?'

'He has a place on the seafront in one of the arches.'

'Cambodian?'

'Yes. He advised Tallulah Bankhead.'

Gilchrist frowned at Heap.

'That's the Romany place,' he said. 'Xavier Petulengro – but I think it's a brand name. His grandparents probably advised Tallulah.'

'Tallulah is a film star, yes?' Prak said.

'And a very naughty girl,' Heap murmured.

'Petulengro doesn't sound Cambodian to me,' Gilchrist muttered

'I think different fortune tellers hire it by the half day or day,' Heap said.

'What kind of work did Youk do?' Gilchrist asked Prak.

'Labour. He loaded and unloaded things at Shoreham.'

'And he worked for the port authority or for a company using the port?'

Prak's eyes never left Gilchrist's face as she thought about the question.

'All I know is that he worked there.'

Gilchrist nodded. 'All right, Prak. Now, have you anything more to say about your suicide attempt?'

'My life for his,' she said simply.

'You don't know what has happened to him,' Gilchrist said. 'If he is alive he would not want to return and find you dead. And if, by some sad chance, he is dead then your death would achieve nothing.'

'If he is dead it would bring me to him,' Prak said. 'I have nothing but my son. I am nothing without my son. My one good thing.'

Gilchrist gave her a rueful smile. 'We'll have someone take you home. And we'll do our best to find out what happened to your son.'

'Youk,' she said.

'Yes. We'll find out what happened to Youk.'

Prak put her purple-nailed finger below her eye. 'This programme on Cambodian television. I could never do that. Families are reunited with much emotion. A lot of tears. It is moving but it is show business. Reconciliation is a personal thing.' She touched the side of her eye. 'Beside, I have no more tears to cry.'

Gilchrist and Heap were just leaving the station when Karen Hewitt called them over to the front desk. A tall, tanned, broad-shouldered man in a dark suit was standing beside her, dwarfing her.

'Sarah, I was just about to phone you. This gentleman is asking for you.'

Gilchrist looked the man up and down. And up again.

'I'm asking for you if you're the officer in charge of the investigation into stolen artefacts,' he said. He had an American accent. He smiled and held out his hand. 'George Merivale, FBI.'

She shook his hand, then introduced Heap. 'We're not exactly investigating the stolen artefacts,' Gilchrist said. She frowned. 'But how do you know about them?'

'They showed up on one of our lists and that set off a signal in our system.' He smiled again. 'Didn't you put them up there?'

She shook her head. 'I might have looked at the Ten Most Wanted database once on a slow day.'

He smiled again. Flawless American choppers.

Gilchrist looked at Heap. 'Did you?'

Heap shook his head. 'Probably the curator at the Pavilion,' he said. 'Ms Rutherford.'

'Bit out of your jurisdiction, aren't you, Agent Merivale?' Gilchrist said.

'George, please. Actually, I'm not. I work with UNESCO. Pretty much a worldwide remit.' He looked at his watch. 'Listen, I don't suppose I could explain my business over a drink if you're nearly done for the day? I'm staying at some feng shui hotel opposite your library in Jubilee Square.'

'Very nice,' Gilchrist said. She knew the rooms in the exceedingly modern four-star hotel only from hearsay but she had drunk in its bar, with its banks of giant screens showing eccentric images and its fish tanks in each corner.

Gilchrist glanced at Hewitt. Hewitt inclined her head.

'Perhaps a coffee,' Gilchrist said.

Hewitt's restricted smile almost managed to be sardonic.

In the hotel bar Agent Merivale ordered a pint of beer, Gilchrist ordered wine. Heap was havering but saw Gilchrist's look. He also ordered a pint.

'Not from California then?' Gilchrist said as they got settled.

Merivale frowned whilst they chinked glasses. 'Actually, I am. What prompted that comment?'

'I thought people only drank water over there – the health thing, you know.'

He chuckled. 'There are a few desperadoes around. We take our lead from *Mad Men*.'

The actor Jon Hamm. *That's* who he reminded her of. She could almost smell the pheromones.

'What exactly is your remit?' Gilchrist said.

'Tracking down stolen artwork. Artwork in the widest sense.'

'Stolen from museums and so on?' Gilchrist said.

'And archaeological sites – open-air museums if you will. Ancient sites are being looted on an epic scale. Some are now little more than rubble as looters hunt for treasure.'

'You think what we have here is some of that?'

'I do. Cambodia is in the worst position. For centuries the ancient Khmer built stone temples for their different gods. Many of these temples are lost to the jungle. Profiteers who know where they are can rip statues and reliefs from the walls with impunity, destroying other remains in the process.'

'Is this big business?' Gilchrist said.

'Medium size. Montague Pyke, one of the world's biggest auction houses, has offices in South East Asia. It has been selling pieces of Khmer art as part of its annual auctions for years. It rarely provides the provenance. And where there is no provenance, more often than not there is theft.'

'How many objects are we talking about?'

'Around four hundred Khmer artefacts have been auctioned in New York in the last fifteen years. Pretty much all were sculpture – statues or reliefs. Only a fifth had provenance. Over half were from the twelfth century – the Angkorian or Angkor Thom period.'

'And each one worth a fortune?'

Merivale shook his head. 'Not a fortune, no. Just over half were big sandstone objects. They went for somewhere between eighteen and twenty-eight thousand dollars apiece. You'd think bronze pieces would be worth more but they're usually smaller – average price is eight thousand dollars. But it adds up.'

Merivale took a longer drink of his beer.

'You probably know Vietnam occupied Cambodia for about ten years from 1979 to 1989? When the Vietnamese withdrew it left a power vacuum which competing political factions, each with their own armies, tried to fill. The Khmer Rouge was still around, in the jungle near the Thai border. Arms dealing, drug trafficking, antiquities smuggling all skyrocketed, but the Khmer Rouge controlled the best routes to Bangkok – which is Smuggler Central in Asia.

'In 1993, UN-sponsored elections allowed the securing of the Angkor Wat site but that still left the ones deeper in the jungle vulnerable. In 1998 the Khmer Rouge surrendered and you'd think that would be an end to the looting, but in 1999 sales of looted stuff increased by well over two hundred per cent.'

'That doesn't make sense,' Heap said.

'On the face of it, I agree,' Merivale said. 'But the removal of the Khmer Rouge opened up those smuggling routes to Bangkok to every other smuggler around. They didn't have to worry any longer about getting their stuff ripped off by the Khmer Rouge or paying an extortionate tithe. In addition, the newly opened territory included some incredible temple complexes that the Khmer Rouge had been monopolizing.

'Koh Ker, the tenth-century capital, is one of the most heavily looted sites because it's so isolated. Poor roads and a harvest of landmines make for a solitary existence. And every apsara at the temple of Phnom Banan in the north-west has been decapitated so that the heads could be sold off.'

Heap looked at Gilchrist. 'There were heads in some of those boxes.'

'What's an apsara?' Gilchrist said.

'A representation of a female deity.' Merivale took another long pull on his beer, almost finishing it. Heap had scarcely got started on his. 'So in 1999 the US agreed to ban the import of Khmer sculptures and architecture elements unless accompanied by an export permit. Montague Pyke's sale of Cambodian artefacts dropped by eighty per cent. Guess they just couldn't take stuff with no questions asked any more so the supply dried up.'

'Where do you come in?'

'All the US government intelligence bodies are concerned about this stuff. But the FBI Art Crime team has been busy since 2004. Back in 2008, hundreds of federal agents from different agencies conducted a massive raid on owners, curators, registrars and collection managers from sixteen museums and galleries in California and Illinois. Mostly this was about pre-Colombian art but there was some South East Asian art involved too.'

Heap finally took a proper swallow of his beer. 'What was the result?' he said, a foam moustache on his top lip.

Gilchrist, mother-like, wanted to brush it off for him but Merivale made a little gesture with his index finger and Heap wiped his own hand across his mouth.

'Frankly, disappointing,' Merivale said. 'We seized loads of objects, interviewed a bunch of people. We indicted some but prosecuted only one person a couple of years later.'

'Successfully?'

'Oh, yeah. In 2010 Homeland Security went after him specifically. They called it Operation Antiquity. We'd had him in our sights for a long time. He'd been importing South East Asian items through brokers in Thailand and Cambodia for twenty-five years.'

'Did he own up?' Gilchrist said.

Merivale nodded. 'He spilled on the entire operation. Turned out his Thai and Cambodian brokers used private diggers to loot ancient sites. For twenty-five years this guy had been falsifying documents to get stuff into the US. We reckon that because of him Thailand lost a third of what remained of its ancient Ban Chiang culture.'

Gilchrist couldn't get excited about all these lumps of stone.

Merivale, though, that was something else. 'But that was just one end of it.'

Gilchrist focused on the subject, not the man. 'What was the other end?'

'The artefacts came in on container ships with a load of cheap tourist "handicrafts". They declared the whole shipment low value. They sold the artefacts to some private buyer for a much higher sum. The buyer then donated the artefacts to a museum, claiming for them an even higher value. That higher amount would then be written off his tax bill as a charitable donation.'

'Clever.'

'Very. One intercepted shipment had a second-century Dong Son bronze container and a seventh-century Khmer sandstone head – let's not even get into whether the head had originally been attached to something. Altogether these were worth some $35,000. Coming into the country they were declared at Customs as having a value of $250.'

'We're still talking pretty low value items here.'

'Well, the value to the country they have come from is much higher – plus the money is cumulative.'

'So I'm gathering,' Gilchrist said. 'These countries leave these things rotting in the jungle though, don't they?'

Merivale shrugged. 'Not my business. I just want to be sure US museums are finally looking properly at their acquisition policies.'

'Doesn't that just mean the crooked dealers will turn to private collectors without scruples to make their sales?' Heap said. 'If it looks good they won't ask too many questions.'

'They already do but we're on their trail too. We've wised up to the tricks of their trade. It's tough, though. Looted stuff is often auctioned on the Internet. It can change hands pretty quickly. But anyone buying cultural or historical stolen property is breaking both US and international laws.' Merivale prodded the table-top. 'And we will track them down.'

Heap gestured vaguely around. 'Which is how you ended up here?'

Merivale looked into his empty glass. 'I was on a stopover in London en route to a conference in Budapest and I saw the Looted Artefacts database had been alerted to some stuff discovered here.' He smiled. 'I read in one of your newspapers that the Director of the Pavilion has been arrested for body-snatching or whatever the hell he's been doing. I'm not interested in that, but if he's in the looted artefacts business . . .'

Heap's phone buzzed. He excused himself and walked out to the foyer.

'How can we help?' Gilchrist said to Merivale.

'First off, let me see the objects in question. I'm then going to have to requisition them for further examination. I hope you don't see a problem with that. Second, I don't suppose you'd consider having dinner with me tonight?'

Gilchrist flushed, caught off guard.

Merivale put his hands up. 'I don't know anybody in town and I figured we could exchange some notes about the case over a good meal.'

Gilchrist nodded slowly, looking at Jon Hamm. 'OK. Sure. Is Heap invited too?'

Merivale gave her the full wattage smile. 'Preferably not.'

They arranged to meet in an hour in Carluccio's across the road from the hotel. She left him in the bar and joined Heap in the foyer. He was still on the phone. She stepped out into the sunshine and waited for him.

When he came out, he said: 'That was legal, ma'am. Rafferty isn't the only one up to this bizarre stuff. There's this woman they were going to charge with necrophilia in Sweden. Thirty-seven years old. She admits she's a bit odd. In her flat police found six skulls, a spine and a large number of other bones along with body bags and morgue pictures. There were photos of the woman performing sex acts on a skeleton. There were two CDs entitled "My necrophilia" and "My first experience". They couldn't make a charge of necrophilia stick since it was a skeleton, not a cadaver, so she was charged with violating the peace of the dead.'

Gilchrist shook her head.

'She admits she's a bit odd,' Gilchrist repeated slowly.

'Ma'am. Meanwhile, in Austria, a forty-seven-year-old man is being charged with disturbing the peace of the dead after police found fifty-six human skulls and fifty-five other bones at his home. He'd done a Rafferty except he'd taken them all from the same graveyard. The only reason he was caught was because he tried to sell three skulls and two thighbones at a flea market.'

'Is that charge on our statute books?' Gilchrist said.

'Legal are checking,' Heap said.

Gilchrist nodded. 'Let's get rid of this as quickly as we can. It's sick but it's a side issue in relation to our regular policing.'

'Ma'am.'

'I'm going to pop back to my flat,' Gilchrist said. She knew she was flushing. 'Agent Merivale wants to continue briefing me this evening.'

'He wants to continue briefing you?' Heap repeated.

'That's right.'

Heap looked at his feet for a moment then muttered: 'Overpaid, oversexed and over here.'

'What's that?' Gilchrist said sharply.

'Nothing, ma'am.' Now Heap was blushing, but with an impish smile on his face. 'Nothing at all.'

# NINE

A bell above the door jangled as Bob Watts entered the antique shop. A woman behind a desk at the far end of the shop looked up and smiled at him. Her hair was drawn back tightly to accentuate the perfect oval of her face. Incense drifted around her from burners at either edge of the desk.

Watts smiled back and looked around him. Buddha heads and torsos carved from stone or cast in brass. Big pieces of French colonial furniture: chests, cupboards and bedheads made from teak or some other hardwood. He'd seen similar modern versions in the Lombok shop, imported from Thailand.

The woman let him browse but when he approached her desk she looked up and gave him the same neutral smile, one eyebrow slightly raised.

'How old are these pieces?' Watts said.

'Their ages vary,' she said, with the hint of an accent. 'Did you have a particular piece in mind?'

Watts pointed behind her. 'That Buddha there, for instance. It looks really old.'

The woman glanced behind her. 'It's not. Late nineteenth century. Burmese.' She gestured back into the shop. 'That one down there is much older. The brass one? Sixteenth century from Thailand.'

Watts nodded. He pointed at the furniture.

'Suppose you can't get stuff like this any more, given it's made from hardwood.'

'They farm teak so you can still get it, but modern furniture doesn't have that patina of age.'

'Age can be imitated though, can't it?' Watts said.

'Faked, you mean?' the woman said. 'Of course. There are unscrupulous people in this business as in any other.'

'I'm trying to place your accent. I'm guessing French.'

'You guess correctly.'

'Have you been in Brighton long?'

She gave him an appraising look. 'Why would you want to know?'

Watts recognized that he was hopeless with women. He grinned, feeling foolish. 'Sorry. I wasn't prying. It's just that if I lived in France I can't imagine I would want to move to England.'

'I have never lived in France,' she said, a small smile playing on her lips.

'Ah,' he said. 'That makes two of us. You're French-Canadian?'

She gave him that appraising look again. 'I was born and raised in *Indochine*.'

'Vietnam?'

She nodded. 'My parents were plantation owners too stubborn to leave during the Vietnam War.'

'They lost everything?'

'Let us say their circumstances became rather straitened.'

'Straitened.'

She smiled. 'Indeed. And not long before Saigon fell they decided it would be politic to take what money they had left and move to Cambodia.'

'Probably wise.'

'It was wise until Pol Pot's Khmer Rouge took over the country four years later.'

'They lost what little they had retained?' Watts said.

'The French embassy arranged transport out of the country for all non-Cambodians just before Phnom Penh fell to the Khmer Rouge. They took what they could carry, including me.'

'Where did you go?'

'Laos.'

Watts frowned as he thought for a moment. 'A safe choice – at least, I can't think of anything horrible happening there.'

She smiled, a broader smile than before. 'You're right.'

'So that's where you were brought up.'

'Well, we moved back to Cambodia a decade later, in the late eighties, once the Vietnamese had gone – you know they invaded in 1979 and toppled Pol Pot?'

Watts was relieved he'd finally arrived at where he wanted to be. He gestured round the shop. 'Is that how this all got started – importing stuff from Cambodia?'

'In fact not. This business is nothing to do with my family. It is run by Englishmen. But the objects are from all over *Indochine.*'

Watts reached out and picked up a card from a pile on the edge of the table. He read the front and turned it over. 'An office in Siem Reap,' he read aloud. 'That's Angkor Wat, isn't it?'

She nodded, frowning slightly.

'Do you have things from there?'

Her frown deepened. 'Of course not,' she said. 'Angkor Wat is a protected site. Nothing can be taken from there.'

'I know that, but I assumed things were taken in the past before it became protected. Presumably those objects turn up from time to time quite legitimately?'

She was appraising him again. 'Do you know how many Cambodian artefacts are in the British Museum?'

Watts had bad memories of a woman from the British Museum he'd been involved with so he was thrown for a moment. Recovering, he said: 'I've a feeling you know the answer to that.'

'Three. Three objects out of however many thousands of artefacts the museum possesses. The Vietnamese collection is scarcely bigger. They have a few pieces from Burma and Thailand but that part of their Asian collection is really poor.'

'What conclusion do you draw from that?'

She laughed. 'The conclusion I draw,' she said, lingering on the phrase to let him know it was the formality of the question that had amused her, 'is that nobody originally recognized the value of objects that seemed to be mimicking Chinese originals – and that now nobody is allowed to export any artefacts from these countries.'

'But that confirms my original point. If nobody valued them the colonists would have chipped nice bits of the temple decorations off and brought them back with them over the past couple of hundred years just as souvenirs.'

She nodded. 'Undoubtedly. And over the past thirty years a number of pieces from the Angkorian period have come on the market.' She gave a little shrug of her shoulders and looked him in the eye. 'Not through this shop, however.'

He nodded, thinking: with your denial you've put a notion in my head that wasn't there before.

'So – the owner or owners.' Watts looked at the card again. 'Is anyone around?'

It isn't Will Rogers.

'You haven't changed much,' Frank Howe says when you turn to face him. 'Still skinny as piss.'

'Nor you,' you say evenly, though in truth you're surprised at how bloated he's become: heavy jowls and big belly, all his muscle turned to fat. He still has a moustache, though smaller now, carefully trimmed. Grey.

'Good to see you, Jimmy,' he says.

You half expect him to offer his hand but both arms remain loosely hanging by his sides. He is showing no weapon but that doesn't mean he isn't armed. And his eyes haven't lost their watchfulness.

'You were expecting me to come and find you?' you say.

Howe turns to the fridge and bends to open it and take out the vodka. He gestures to you with the bottle. You nod and he pours two big shots, almost emptying the bottle. He stretches his arm out to offer you your glass.

You take it and he tilts his glass at you. You both drink.

'One day, of course, I knew you'd come,' he says. 'I haven't exactly been hiding.'

'But then I did think you were dead.'

'We've all been in plain sight. Maybe you just needed better spectacles.'

'I thought you were dead so I wasn't looking.'

Howe shrugs. Although he's overweight there was something almost balletic about the way he'd taken the vodka from the fridge. Economy of movement and effort. When you decide to move, he's not going to be easy.

'I need to know where the others are,' you say.

'How do you know they're still alive?'

'Because those kind of bastards never die, however much they deserve their comeuppance.'

'So are they going to get their comeuppance? Am I?'

You don't reply. Keep the bastard hanging.

'We didn't do so much to you.'

You keep your voice level. 'You took my wife. You killed my wife. You lied to me about that and everything else.'

Howe shrugged. 'How were we supposed to know she was your wife? You said bugger all about that.'

'Would it have made any difference if I had?' You take a step towards him. 'And don't fucking shrug about this.'

Howe puts a pacifying hand up.

'Sorry. But we didn't kill her. The Khmer Rouge did.'

'You say.'

'It's true.'

'In the same ambush you were all killed in and you died trying to save her. Yes, I heard.'

'We got lucky.'

'Did Paradise believe your story or was he just stringing me along when he told it me?'

Howe walks to the window and looks out. 'You survived, didn't you? You're still around.'

'It's not about me. And surviving isn't the same as living.'

Howe turned. 'For Christ's sake, Jimmy. Save me the fucking violins. If you couldn't get over that you're not the kind of man I took you for.'

You think back. How had you dealt with it? By hardening your heart? Throwing yourself into your work? Both those things.

You take another sip of your drink. You know you can't blame Howe and the others for what you've done with your life.

As if reading your thoughts, Howe says: 'Rogers says freedom is what you make of the hand you've been dealt.'

You snort. 'Thanks for the bumper sticker.'

'Sartre actually.' Howe grins. 'Or maybe Camus. One of those existential fuckers anyway.'

'What actually happened to Michelle?'

'What did Sal Paradise tell you happened?'

'A pack of lies, presumably.'

'A mix of lies and truth, actually. The truth is she did die pretty much as he said. She'd tried to get away from us but we caught up with her and she was with us when we were ambushed. The lie was that not all of the rest of us died with her and her father in that ambush.'

You look at the glass in your hand. 'Somebody has to pay. She was innocent.'

'Jesus, Jimmy – nobody is innocent. Her father was helping us do the looting. She was helping him.'

You think for a moment. 'That's why they were back in Cambodia in the first place? She wasn't in any condition to help anyone.'

'Before. That's how they were caught. Trying to take stuff out by sea. They were working for Paradise too.'

You mull over this for a moment. 'I can't believe that of her.'

'Hey, listen, I'm sure her father and Paradise played her – told her this stuff was going to be destroyed otherwise, blah, blah, blah. But it came down to the same thing. It isn't too difficult to persuade someone to do something if you apply the right pressure.'

'Michelle wasn't like that. She wasn't corrupt and she couldn't be coerced.'

You are surprised how heated you sound.

Howe made a noise that was half grunt, half laugh.

'Everyone can be coerced, Jimmy boy.'

'You would say that, wouldn't you?' you finally say.

Howe shakes his head. 'You don't have a fucking clue what's going on now and you didn't have a fucking clue then. You are *so* naïve.'

You're a bit old to do a drop kick but you're picturing the heel of your foot connecting with the underside of your former friend's chin just the same. It's satisfying. Very.

'Do tell me what I'm missing,' you say, controlling yourself and taking another sip of your drink.

'Look, we were all working for Sal. The mission wasn't to get three sailors or three spies; it was to get out the valuable stuff from Cambodia. And Westbrook told Paradise there was some juicy stuff in the National Museum that nobody knew about.'

'Which you and the others went to get, leaving Rogers and me behind.'

You frown. That doesn't sound right now. Howe sees your look.

'We needed to take the truck to start loading. Rogers knew where we were headed. We were waiting there.'

You take another sip of your vodka. 'I'm working for Sal too.'

That throws Howe, you can see, but he tries for nonchalance and a mirthless grin.

'I know,' he says. 'That's why you're not dead already.'

'You think you could take me?'

'Don't be a spaz.' He pats his belly. 'I haven't done my own dirty work for years. There's a man with a rifle in the room opposite just waiting for my signal.'

It's your turn to smile. 'Long lens on the rifle?'

'Of course,' he says, frowning at your smile.

'Well, that's not going to work, is it?'

Howe looks suddenly uneasy but tries not to show it. 'Because?'

'Because he can't be aiming at me if he's looking at you for your signal.'

'You're working for Sal,' Howe says.

'I said I'd deal with someone for him.'

Howe tries to keep the bonhomie going but his eyes are fearful. 'Not me. He needs me.'

'Does he? Do you think he has ever actually forgiven you – any of you – for what you did?'

'We made restitution. Gave him the stuff.'

'All of it?'

'All he wanted.'

'And he was happy with that?'

''Course he was. We've been working for him ever since, haven't we?' Howe finished his drink in one gulp. 'You're winding me up.'

You keep your smile. 'A bit. His name is Harry Nesbo. The man I'm looking for.'

'Don't recognize it.'

'That won't be his only name.'

'Then how am I supposed to know him?'

'He's . . . distinctive. Weird.'

Howe laughs. You join in, watching him.

'He's weird,' he finally says. 'You shitting me? This is Cambodia. Weird westerners is the fucking norm.'

You're still laughing as you reach to put your phone and your glass on the bedside table beside the lamp.

'Anyway,' he says, chortling then suddenly suspicious. 'Why would you do anything for Sal Paradise?'

You tug the light flex out of the wall socket and in the plunging darkness whisper: 'So he'll let me kill you.'

\*  \*  \*

Gilchrist was nervous about dinner with Merivale. She couldn't decide what to wear and ended up with her summer uniform of T-shirt, jeans and plimsolls. It was her winter uniform too, actually. She wished Kate had still been living with her to advise on applying make-up for the no-make-up look. There was a dab of perfume and, OK, a bit of lippy.

They met in the Coachhouse. Merivale too was in jeans and a T-shirt and some chunky American boots. She couldn't help noticing that he was, as they say, ripped.

'I remember this as an antiques shop,' she said when they were settled at a table by the open windows looking into the narrow courtyard.

'Seems to me Brighton is one big antiques emporium,' Merivale said. 'You a local girl?'

'Born and bred.'

'From one of those estates I saw on the way in?'

Gilchrist gave a little grimace. 'Let's talk about my past another time.' She smiled. 'Or at least when I've had a few more drinks.'

He smiled. 'The time could be now.'

She shook her head. 'Now there are crimes to combat.' She gestured at his hands, clasped on the table. They were rough and scarred. 'Those aren't office worker's hands.'

'I like to get out of the office whenever I can.'

'And that tan isn't from a sunbed.'

'To be honest it's more windburn than sunburn. I spend a lot of time out in the elements.' He looked down, clenched and unclenched his fists. 'I've never been a workout down the gym man,' he said. 'I like doing more natural physical stuff.'

Gilchrist was alert to a double entendre but Merivale didn't leer or tip it in any way. One up to him.

They ordered two steak salads and a bottle of red wine. She was aware he was watching her but she was doing the same. She guessed it was two coppers who were so used to trying to figure out people that neither could turn it off. Usually, of course, she was looking for something that was a bit off. There didn't seem to be anything off about Merivale. Far from it.

'Had you heard of the temple complex at Koh Ker before I mentioned it?' he said when they'd taken their first drink of wine.

'I thought I was good knowing about Angkor Wat.'

Merivale smiled. 'It was the tenth-century capital of Cambodia. It's remote so not as well known as Angkor Wat. Wonderful statues were chiselled there. Wonderful.'

'You've been there?'

Merivale nodded. 'Several times. It's magnificent and tragic. Its remoteness makes it one of the most heavily looted sites in Cambodia. A combination of poor roads and unexploded landmines has kept it isolated. Which means looters can really go to town without fear of interruption.'

'You think some of the stuff we've found . . .?'

'Too early to say. The National Museum managed to remove quite a number of the most important pieces but, for the rest, well, museums around the world are exhibiting them and many are in private collections. All looted.'

If Gilchrist was honest she couldn't get excited about this artefact stuff. She didn't really value art, probably because she was not interested in it.

'That's terrible,' she said, doubting how convincing she sounded. He didn't seem to notice.

The food arrived.

'We've been on this stuff for over ten years,' Merivale said, between mouthfuls. 'Trying to get back up the pipeline for stolen Thai antiquities. We've uncovered a couple of scams. The first was the one I told you about earlier, with objects being appraised at inflated values and then being donated to museums for fraudulent tax write-offs. What I find interesting is the close link between the experts and the exploiters, the crooks and the collectors.'

'Meaning?'

'A woman called Hilary Black helped us. She's an expert on South East Asian ceramics. She'd lived in Thailand for years, just outside Bangkok. She'd tipped us to a suspect dealer. She said that in his warehouse she'd seen human arm bones strung with antique bronze bracelets.'

Arm bones? Was this some link to Rafferty? Gilchrist put her fork down.

'What she didn't say was that she was the one who'd sold those bracelets to him, plus Thai ceramics from burial sites on the Burmese border and a bunch of other antiquities – Neolithic stone tools and so on.' Merivale tapped the table with the end of his fork. 'They were all stolen objects that her signature had made legitimate. Turned out she was also making inflated appraisals for a couple of LA-based Asian art dealers. God, we were pissed. The next time she touched down in the US we arrested her.'

'What happened when it came to trial?'

He shook his head. 'Maybe later – wouldn't want to spoil your dinner.'

They ate in silence for a moment.

'Criminals don't specialize any more,' Merivale said abruptly. 'They're portfolio workers. They know all about diversifying. If you're smuggling drugs you may as well smuggle people and antiquities whilst you're about it. And antiquities serve other purposes.'

'Such as?'

'Money-laundering and tax evasion.'

'But the stuff you mentioned wasn't worth very much.'

'Well, the standard stuff, worth a few thousand dollars, is just part of it. There's also the rare stuff. And the irreplaceable, priceless stuff. The museums can't touch such objects easily or they'll be in serious doo-doo. So these pieces are going to the private buyers. It disappears from public view and appreciation for decades, sometimes forever.'

'So what do you think happened here at the Pavilion?'

Merivale spent a few moments chewing his food. 'Maybe Rafferty was using the American model. He got this stuff donated to the Pavilion as a tax write-off.'

'And then never displayed it?'

Merivale shook his head. 'That doesn't make sense, I agree. I'll understand more when I know what we have. Are you OK with us getting our own experts in to take a look?'

'Of course,' Gilchrist said.

When the plates were cleared away and they were deep into the second bottle of wine, Gilchrist said: 'This woman? This Asian art expert.'

Merivale looked out into the courtyard. 'It never came to trial. Over the weekend in prison Black complained of stomach problems. She had uncontrolled diarrhoea. She began vomiting what appeared to be excrement. She asked for urgent medical attention and was told she'd need to wait until the morning.'

He stopped.

'And?' Gilchrist said.

'And she died in the night. In her own filth. Death certificate said she had peritonitis brought on by a perforated ulcer.'

'No foul play then?'

Merivale just looked at her.

The conversation got brighter after that. Unusually for a man, he asked most of the questions. Perhaps unusually for a woman, she felt uneasy answering them so fobbed him off. But something was definitely happening.

The heat was palpable when they walked out on to Middle Street. They looked at each other. Neither could stop looking.

'Shall we go back to your hotel?' Gilchrist asked. Damned pheromones.


You rise at four, a little groggy. The hotel has bicycles. It seems apt that you use one of them to cycle out to Angkor Wat to see the dawn before you leave the country. The bike has no lights. That too seems apt.

Actually, hardly anything else on the road has lights either. It takes thirty minutes to reach the site, riding in the gutter as lorries and cars swish by you. Motorized tuk-tuks pass you with couples swathed in blankets huddled inside them. It is cold but you like it.

Somehow nobody side-swipes you as they pass. You come off the road, the bike rattling on the rough path, and head into the jungle. Trees push at you, the bike tries to dump you in potholes. It's humid now and you are drenched in sweat.

There are insect noises, the *cucurrus* of a creature that is loud way beyond its size. But then the ruins of some temple or palace loom before you and suddenly you are surrounded by hundreds of shadowy people, all here to see the sun rise behind the towers of the temple.

You sit at the edge of the lake with everybody else. There are purple lilies on the lake, closed now. Over the next hour, as the sun rises over the parapets, the lilies slowly wake. You witness the dawning, in all its shades, mediated by the zip of hundreds of camera flashes. It's a kind of lightshow. Then the swollen yellow sun rises between the two towers, wreathed in morning mist. You watch its reflection in the dark water among the blossoming lily pads.

You met Michelle when you were fifteen. You were interested in archaeology and soldiering. You had romantic notions of being a scholar-soldier like Paddy Fermor or T.E. Lawrence. You met her in the Ashmolean in Oxford. You were standing either side of an Egyptian mummy. You clicked. Aside from being beautiful – part French, part English, half Cambodian – she was sharp as a tack and warm and friendly and took the piss out of you something terrible.

Her father was an archaeologist for the Louvre. He disapproved of you in your one brief meeting – so brief he didn't recognize you the next time you met. You were an oik with a brain, with too many street fights showing on your knuckles, too much interest in soldiering. But then he would have disapproved of anybody. He wanted Michelle to pursue her interests to the utmost. But if she must get involved with somebody, the last person he wanted was you.

He told her all this and she told you. It made no difference. You continued.

But she was a wraith. You don't mean skinny like these sad girls now. You mean more . . . elusive. Jesus, you wish you knew words. There was something about her that was insubstantial, dream-like – even non-existent.

You married in secret. She was pregnant. You were both young. She had an abortion. Woman's right to choose and all that. Except it wasn't her choice. It was at her father's insistence and she acquiesced.

You know it was hard for her. The culture she'd been brought up in . . .

'You don't understand,' Michelle had shouted at you, pulling away from your embrace and stepping out from the shelter of the parapet into the rain. 'It isn't easy for me.'

She'd told you in the kitchen garden of Fulham Palace by the Thames on a blowsy day, thunderclouds broiling in the sky, the rain suddenly pelting down, trapping you in this shallow stone porch.

'I thought your father brought you up to be free?' you said, reaching out to draw her back in.

She pulled away from your arm. She was already drenched. Now the rain was like a curtain between you. You felt you were parting it as you stepped down to join her.

Michelle jabbed at her own face with a long finger. 'My father is white but everyone sees an Oriental. A slanty-eye. They don't know if I'm Japanese, Chinese, Korean, Vietnamese or Thai. Most people don't even know Cambodia exists.'

'So?'

'So they make assumptions about how I'm supposed to behave. They think we *Orientals* are all tea ceremonies and geishas, or mail-order brides, submissive and pliant.'

'Nobody who has known you for half a second would think that,' you said, reaching out to her again. She stepped away from you, into a puddle. Your eyes were stinging, the rain flooding you. Her dress was clinging to her. You were trying to push down the thoughts the sight of her in the rain inevitably produced.

'Your father gave you a liberal education,' you said. 'He encouraged you to be yourself. How do you get from that to obeying him about an abortion?'

'My father is liberal, yes he is. But he is also half French and I am his daughter. That makes him the most illiberal liberal in existence.' She bared her small, pointed teeth in a cold laugh. 'The French demonstrated with the guillotine during their glorious revolution that there is nothing more fascist than a liberal fervent about freedom.'

'Can we focus on the abortion?' you said. You reached out your hand. 'And can we get out of the ruddy rain?'

Michelle stepped past you back beneath the portico. You sloshed in after her.

'I had an enlightened education, it is true, but I am also a Cambodian woman. Do you think my mother was equal to my father? I love him but he is a colonizer, like all men. Paternalistic. He claimed to know what was best for her, he claims to know what is best for me.'

She took your hand. 'I'm sorry, Jimmy.'

You squeezed her hand. 'I'm not a colonizer. You're my wife.' You smiled. 'There's always our next one.'

She looked at you for what seemed a long time. You held her look though you wanted to blink the stinging water from your eyes. You couldn't read her expression. You'd never been able to but had never dared say it in case it fed into the old stereotypes about Oriental inscrutability.

You sat on a stone bench, side by side, holding hands but unspeaking, until it was time for you to go. You had a train to catch back to your barracks. The rain had stopped but plump beads of water plopped from the arch masking the garden beyond.

'Leave me here,' she said when you stood. 'I want to walk in the gardens after the rain. Smell the air.'

'And see if the rain has brought anything up from beneath the soil?' you said with a smile. Six months earlier you'd both volunteered for a dig in Tuscany, in the fields around the hill town of Chiusi. There the number of Etruscan finds you made on a daily basis during the wet months had almost become a joke. Things buried years ago would slowly rise to the surface after heavy rain.

A kiss then you left her there, sitting in the garden of Fulham Palace. You left her reluctantly. You consciously didn't look back, though you ached to do so. A superstitious dread was rising in you that if you looked back you would somehow trigger some ur-myth: that she would turn into a pillar of salt or be lost to Hades.

Hades worried you most. You'd gone on from Tuscany to Turkey and during that dig had once stood at the mouth of Hades – or what archaeologists had identified as the cave the ancients believed to be the entrance to Hell. You didn't know if there was a Cambodian equivalent of such myths or of such a cave. Of course, Pol Pot was turning the entire country into a living hell.

But that was not to be your fate. Or hers. Instead, she simply disappeared from your life. Vanished. Unreachable. Over the next two years there were times you wondered if you had entirely imagined her. Even when she contacted you to say that she was back in Cambodia with her father you didn't know that you believed it was her. Not until you saw her nailed like a bat to a barn door in the playground of Security Prison-21.

Gilchrist didn't know where she was when her phone woke her. She had dragged herself unwillingly from Merivale's bed in the middle of the night and come home but it took her a moment to figure out she was actually back in her own bed.

'Bellamy?' she said, her voice croaky.

'I hesitated to call, ma'am, as I didn't want to disturb you . . .'

'Enough with the innuendo, Detective Sergeant. What is it?'

'Don-Don has just phoned to say he's opened that metal door at the back of the store. It leads into a tunnel. And in the tunnel he's found a body.'

'I thought that was the point of the exercise: to find all the bodies Rafferty had dug up.'

'This is no bag of bones, ma'am. This is a murder victim.'

Gilchrist got out of bed and walked towards the bathroom, still holding the phone to her ear. She was aching in odd places but now wasn't the time to remember why.

'Youk?'

'Hard to say, ma'am – face bashed in, I believe. But it has to be a possibility.'

'No identification on him?'

'None.'

She reached in and turned the shower on. 'I'm on my way,' she said. 'I'll meet you at the Pavilion.'

'Shouldn't I stay out of it as Donaldson made the discovery?'

'OK then, check out Youk's old address. I'll phone you in a while.'

'Righty-ho, ma'am. Might we expect to see Agent Merivale today?'

Did she hear the cheeky sod chuckle?

'Fuck right off, Detective Sergeant.'

'Certainly, ma'am,' he said, ending the call.

# TEN

I t actually takes you forty-five hours to fly from Siem Reap to Budapest. And that's the quick way, via Singapore and Frankfurt. A long time for your quarry to remain unaware. A long time for you to think about what you are doing.

You check into a five-star hotel beside the Danube. You've read about the importance of this broad river over the centuries. A conduit and a barrier.

There is a Chinese restaurant directly opposite that you mean to try later. For now you hit the bar and gaze blankly out at the broad, brightly illuminated Danube. The river traffic is mostly restaurant boats plying between the bridges.

You were in Budapest because Howe had told you where to find the other two. He'd also told you what Sal Paradise was up to, then and now.

'The older, pre-Khmer Rouge guys – the tunnel rats and Viet Vets – still dominate in Vietnam, hunkered down in Hanoi and Saigon. Excuse me – Ho Chi Minh City. They're handling the heroin and the antiquities and the people trafficking. A nice little combination – the three get sent together.'

'And here it's Sal Paradise?'

'Not just him. There's another guy behind him. We never see him.'

'You do the people trafficking and the heroin?'

'Fuck off – I'm strictly antiquities. Paradise handles all the rest.'

People traffickers. There are such people. People without feelings. More than you would like to believe. For a while you worried you were such a person until you figured out the difference.

'If there's a reception party waiting for me in Budapest I'll come back for you,' you said to Howe.

Howe nodded. 'I know.'

You killed him even so. You can't seem to process that.

You're supposed to meet somebody in the Liszt Museum. Cloak and dagger but you don't need to argue unnecessarily with Sal

Paradise. The museum is in an apartment where the composer and pianist used to live. You climb a couple of flights of stairs and go into a small foyer. Your shoes squeak on the waxed wooden floor. You are the museum's only visitor.

The rooms are deserted. Your contact is not here unless it is the elderly woman who took your entrance money at the makeshift counter in the foyer.

You read on a notice on the wall that Liszt, like all great pianists, had an unusually large hand span, which made his compositions almost impossible to play by anyone with smaller hands. There is a plaster cast, and a bronze cast, of one of his hands. They are different sizes, which confuses you.

You are looking at his death mask, covered in warts, when your contact finally arrives. She doesn't speak, simply places an A4 envelope on the glass cabinet you're looking into and walks away. You examine Liszt's warts for five more minutes then leave the museum.


'What have we got, Detective Sergeant?' Gilchrist said as she joined Donald Donaldson in the store halfway down the Pavilion tunnel.

The hard hat he was wearing looked like a joke one from the seafront because of his enormous head. Coupled with his white forensics onesie it made him look like a gay polar bear circa Village People.

He indicated the half-closed metal doorway at the back of the store. Bright lights spilled out from arc lamps. 'When we forced the door open first thing this morning, we found a body. We're assuming male.'

'Is it still there?'

'Forensics will take all day, ma'am.'

Donaldson was avoiding her eyes as they talked, still clearly pissed off with her. She couldn't blame him but she couldn't let his moodiness get in the way.

'Any indication of ethnicity?'

'Best talk to Mr Bilson about that, ma'am.'

'I will do. And the tunnel?'

'Doesn't lead anywhere – it's blocked up a few yards in.'

'Do you think it's been blocked for a long time?'

Donaldson stared at her. 'I had assumed so.'

'OK. I'd like the blockage clearing – but with the understanding the tunnel is a crime scene. Could you ask Bilson if he has a moment for me?'

She looked round the storeroom, which was now totally empty of boxes and black bags.

'Do I have a moment for the delectable Detective Inspector Sarah Gilchrist?' a tall man with a sharp face said, bending as he came through the small doorway. 'My dear Sarah, I have much more than that for you.'

'I'm sure, Mr Bilson – it's perhaps as well you're in your onesie so you can't demonstrate exactly what.'

'True, true – and these are such a pain to get on and off. I don't want to come any closer because then I'll have to put another one on.' He tilted his head and looked at her speculatively. 'Might be worth it though.'

'It wouldn't be,' Gilchrist said. 'Trust me on that. So what have we got?'

'Give me a chance, Detective Inspector, I've only been here five minutes. I usually take at least seven to solve your case for you.'

She pretended to look at her watch. 'I can wait.'

'I can tell you the person who left the body here or committed the murder here – I don't know which yet – either wanted to prevent the smell of decomposition or he read a lot of old crime fiction.'

'Because?'

'He covered it in quicklime.'

Gilchrist nodded. 'Which do you think it was? He thought it would speed up decomposition or he wanted to slow it to avoid the smell?'

One of the few things she remembered of all the many things Bilson had told her over the years was that, contrary to popular misconception from fiction films and books, quicklime did not destroy bone and tissue. It leached the water from a body and that set off a chemical reaction in the quicklime which produced slaked lime. This preserved the body, mummifying it. It also prevented the microorganisms breeding that broke down the body and in doing so produced the foul smells.

'So what can you tell me?'

'His face has been bashed in, so not much there. His teeth have been looked after by a British dentist – the fillings are distinctive. Judging from the hair and what I can make out of skin colour from patches as yet unmummified I'd say he was of South-East Asian ethnicity. Possibly Chinese.'

'Possibly Cambodian?'

He gave her a sharp look. 'Perhaps. You have a supposition you want me to confirm, I take it?'

'If I knew what a *supposition* was I'd say "possibly". Can you take a DNA sample? I'll have one for you to try to match later in the day.'

Bilson gave a little mock salute. 'Until then, Sarah.'

She half-bowed. 'Until then, Mr Bilson.'


'So you're offering your services,' Sal Paradise had said to you as you sat beside your pool coughing up vodka. 'In return for what?'

'I told you – I want to know what happened to this woman Michelle in Cambodia in late 1978.'

'I seem to recall I told you at the time. She was killed in an ambush along with her father.'

'So you do remember her?' you said.

'Vaguely.'

'Well, you'll remember that you told me she had been killed along with my former colleagues. But my former colleagues are still alive.'

'Not all of them,' Paradise said. 'Only Mr Rogers and Mr Howe survived.'

'They work for you now?'

'In a loose sort of way – although actually they are answerable to someone else.' Paradise leaned forward. 'But you're saying you're good enough at whatever you do for me to consider using you?'

You'd got your breath back by then. You put your hands behind your head and grabbed the ankles of the man standing there. At the same time, you rolled back, using your momentum to kick him with both feet in the face.

As he fell back against one of the other men you did a kind of breakdance spin to the side, taking your weight on your hands and arms to scythe your legs low into the legs of a third man. Neal you dealt with by jumping to your feet, grabbing his wrists and turning them out, breaking both his arms. It was easy but horribly noisy. The crack of bone seemed to reverberate in the yard until his screams took its place.

You glanced at Paradise, still in his seat.

He shook his head. 'Shut him the fuck up, will you,' he said in a bored voice. 'He's giving me a headache.'

You obliged Paradise with a short jab to Neal's chin. His head snapped back and you caught him round the waist and lowered him to the floor. When you've broken a man's arms you don't need him to fall on them as well.

You turned to Paradise.

'OK,' he said. 'There's this man I need dealing with. Guy called Harry Nesbo.'


Gilchrist invited Donaldson to join her and Heap upstairs to examine the artefacts. In the Pavilion entrance, Heap and Donaldson studiously avoided each other until a beaming Merivale loped across the gardens, raising his hand in a little wave. Gilchrist was aware of Heap watching her so merely nodded her head at the FBI agent. Plus she was peeved. She was feeling exhausted and was sure she looked it. Merivale looked fresh as a daisy. Bastard.

She introduced Donaldson and told Merivale about the corpse. Rutherford joined them. She gave Merivale the once-over as they walked towards her. Introductions made, she hung back with Gilchrist for a moment, raised an eyebrow and wafted her hand in front of her face as if cooling herself down. Gilchrist looked down to hide her grin. He was a hunk all right.

'What are you looking for in particular?' Rutherford asked Merivale as she led them down the long corridor towards the banqueting hall.

'Whatever we can find,' Merivale said, looking to left and right at the nodding Chinese statuettes on either side of them.

'I've been checking with the Museum Association,' Rutherford said. 'Apparently the Holy Grail in missing Cambodian artefacts is a bronze figure of Ganesh from the thirteenth century.'

Merivale gave her an assessing look. 'That's true,' he murmured. 'You have it here?'

Rutherford shook her head. 'I don't think so – but wouldn't that be something?'

'You haven't finished unpacking the boxes?'

'In fact, we stopped when we realized what we had. We need more expert hands. A British Museum expert is joining us.'

'You know I'm going to have to take over these artefacts?' he said politely.

'I guessed,' Rutherford said.

'I'm intending to get them moved to a secure place as soon as possible,' he said, addressing both Gilchrist and Rutherford.

Gilchrist nodded. 'Ganesh is who, exactly?' she said.

'The elephant-headed god in the Hindu pantheon,' Rutherford said. 'There's one of him in the British Museum from Cambodia where he is represented with breasts and four arms.'

'Breasts?' Heap said.

Rutherford stopped in the corridor and looked over her glasses at him. 'What – you accept the idea of him having the head of an elephant but you worry about the fact he has breasts?'

Gilchrist and Heap laughed. Gilchrist thought about the hermaphrodite they'd encountered a few months earlier who'd had both breasts and penis.

'I wasn't worrying,' Heap said, red-faced. 'I was clarifying.'

'He's the god of success and a remover of obstacles,' Rutherford continued. 'You can see why he was popular with traders and merchants heading out from India in the twelfth century. They took him with them as they spread out over South-East Asia. In Indochina Hinduism and Buddhism were practised side by side, so they influenced each other. Buddhists like Ganesh too.'

'What makes this one so special?' Gilchrist said.

Rutherford glanced at Merivale to see if he wanted to answer but he said nothing. 'It's size,' she said. 'It's massive.'

'How massive?' Gilchrist said.

'Some twelve feet high. That's how I'm pretty sure we haven't got it – we don't have a box that big.'

Gilchrist frowned. 'Is that so big?'

Merivale did come in now. 'Well, he was often depicted in bronze in ancient Cambodia but on a small scale,' he said. 'The ancient Khmer preferred to work in stone but you can't carve stone easily in miniature. Particularly a small figure with multiple arms and a trunk.'

'And breasts,' Heap murmured.

'But this is the only known example of one cast in bronze of such a size.'

'Is bronze valuable?' Heap said.

Merivale glanced at Rutherford.

'It partly depends on the value of the metals used to make the bronze,' Rutherford said. 'Different metals were used to achieve different colours: gold, silver, copper, pewter, bismuth and so on.'

'It's the art in the piece that has the value, not the materials,' Merivale said. 'Didn't some London park have a Barbara Hepworth bronze stolen from it for its scrap value? That would have been nothing compared to its worth on the art market.'

'How rare is this piece?' Gilchrist said.

'It's unique – until another one turns up, of course.'

'Where was it stolen from?'

Merivale looked at Rutherford, who shook her head.

'I don't have that information.'

Merivale shrugged. 'Me neither.'

She led them into the banqueting room. She pointed at the boxes in the centre of the room. 'There it all is.'

Bob Watts went back to the Bath Arms for a pint. It was crowded and he ended up sitting near a guy who was talking to himself. Never a good sign but made worse by the fact that actually the guy would clearly much rather be talking to someone other than himself. Watts realized it was the security guard from the museum again.

Watts focused on his drink and tried not to think about what wild conspiracy theory the man might wish to share. Watts was feeling foolish that he had been so open in his inquiries at the shop. He thought he'd been doing OK with the Frenchwoman until it was time to leave, just after he'd asked whether the owners were around.

'They're rarely around,' she said. 'They spend most of their time away. As you see, we have an office in Siem Reap. We also have connections in Budapest.'

'Siem Reap is where Angkor Wat is?' Watts said.

'It's the nearest town, yes.'

'You import Hungarian objects too?'

'Not so much. It's more of a distribution point for the Asian things we sell around Europe.'

Watts frowned. 'I assumed you would ship these big pieces in by sea.'

She looked perplexed. 'We do.'

'Hungary is land-locked.'

She laughed. It was a nice laugh. 'I guess you've never heard of the Danube.'

'I know it empties into the Black Sea. That doesn't seem too direct a route from China.'

He couldn't figure out her smile. 'I'm not an expert on maritime export routes,' she said, still smiling. 'I leave that to my bosses. All I know is that our goods come into this country via Newhaven. Legitimately.'

'I wasn't supposing anything other than legitimately.'

'You seem to be taking an inordinate interest in our business,' she said with a tilt of her head.

'Curiosity about things is my strength and my weakness,' he said, an apologetic smile on his face. 'I like to figure out how things work.'

She seemed to accept that. She looked at him but didn't say anything.

'OK, well, I'd better let you get on,' he said.

'You were just looking,' she said, her eyes not leaving his.

'Wandered in on a whim, I admit.'

She smiled at him again. She was a very good-looking woman.

'So you're not going to ask me out on a date?'

He was actually quite surprised but then he was useless with women. He was out of his depth. Again.

'Is that what you think I was building up to?'

'Lot of wasted effort otherwise, surely?'

'Whatever happened to the simple art of conversation?' he said, almost plaintively.

She smiled back at him. 'You really think any conversation is simple?'

He shook his head. After a moment he said: 'Do you mind if I ask your name?'

She held out her hand. 'My name is Monique.'
He gave her hand a gentle shake. 'I'm—'
'You're Bob Watts, our new police commissioner.'
So much for being discreet.


You are at the flea market on the outskirts of Budapest. It is bitterly cold and everyone is in warm hats and thick coats. Everyone except you. You are wearing warmer clothing than in Cambodia but it is still not right for this harsh weather.

A sprawling, haphazard place, part shanty town, part junk yard. Boardwalks of splintered and rotting wood sinking into mud, odd slabs of concrete and uneven paving stones.

It stinks of desperation.

A man with raw hands stands in the open beside what looks like a small trash heap. You look closer and see it is made up of old tools and spare parts all tangled together: nuts and bolts, spanners and hammers, spools of wire, cogs and chisels. Beyond him an old lady huddles in a fur coat and Cossack hat beside a table on which she has a few vases and wine glasses. She has a look on her face that suggests her cupboard is now bare.

You walk down a narrow alley between tiny wooden stalls. As you near the end of the alley, the stalls have crude wooden rooms behind them containing paintings in heavy frames hung above old desks and chests of drawers.

Your quarry, Harry Nesbo, is fifteen yards ahead of you. At this end of the alley he has slowed down. He asks a bleached blonde woman the price of an old mirror and shakes his head. He offers another price and the seller shakes her head. He nods and moves on.

You can't hear whether the man speaks Hungarian or Russian. Hungarian, you know, is a unique language, unrelated to any other European language. Is this man Hungarian? You don't know anything about him except for a memorised photograph.

He's a job.

You look at the mirror as you pass. It is badly silvered and the frame is chipping at top and bottom. You look into it. You do not recognize the man it reflects.

Your quarry is now in the open, walking between lines of tables selling old metalwork, locks and glassware. As he holds a big lock in his hand he casually looks back down the alley. It is too late for you to hide.

'How much?' you say in your passable Russian to the bleached blonde, pointing at the silvered mirror. You can speak Hungarian too, though mostly it's obscene slang. She quotes a price in Euros. It's high.

'It is damaged,' you say, indicating the frame.

She looks at you contemptuously. 'It was made in 1850,' she says, as if talking to a child or an idiot. You feel like the latter.

You shake your head and turn to move on. You are aware the man was watching the exchange. You see him catch her eye and shake his head wearily.

You pretend not to notice and move off to look at a table of medals. You feel exposed in this outdoor section and unsure whether you have been spotted. You are also freezing, your fingers and ears pinching.

You duck into a big room. It has electricity – a television is playing – but there is no heating.

This is a furniture room but with a lot of books and paintings. You are examining a scratched art deco bureau when your man enters the room from the opposite end. He pays you no attention but drifts towards a bookshelf. You are watching in a mirror, aware that the reflection of your own pinched face is blue with cold.

The man riffles casually through a pile of magazines. He starts to look in your direction so you turn away from the mirror and focus on a horrible vase. When you casually glance back your quarry is gone.


'It's huge,' Gilchrist said, looking around the banqueting room and up at the enormous crystal chandelier, hanging from the claws of a dragon at the apex of a dome decorated with the moon and stars and images of curious beasts.

'It looks extra big because we've taken out the centre table,' Rutherford replied. 'We're starting a refurbishment here in a couple of weeks. It took us a week to move the table.' She saw Gilchrist's puzzled look. 'The main table is laid as if for a nineteenth-century dinner party. It's for display only – we never use it for real.'

'Of course,' Gilchrist said, wondering if she had ever been in here since a school visit when she was ten that she only vaguely remembered.

'Takes almost a week to clear the table because there are so many items on it and each one has to be carefully handled,' Rutherford concluded.

Rutherford saw Merivale hovering by the half-dozen open crates and walked over to join him.

Gilchrist gestured at the ceiling and said to Donaldson: 'You'll feel right at home here, Don-Don.'

Donaldson looked up and frowned 'Don't get you,' he grunted.

'I think the detective inspector is referring to the all-seeing eye,' Heap said, pointing to the eye within a triangle and circle high on the canopy among stars and planets.

'There are lots of Masonic symbols scattered among the fantastical beasts,' Rutherford called back. 'The Prince of Wales was a keen Mason – he had his own lodge for almost fifty years and was Grand Master of the whole shebang for nearly twenty-five years. The other members of his lodge would have been tickled to see these symbols.'

'You have no reason to believe I'm a Mason,' Don-Don said quietly to Gilchrist, throwing a glance at Rutherford. Donaldson leaned in to Gilchrist and hissed: 'And it's not illegal if I were to be one. I believe the Labour government some fifteen years ago decided against a public register of Freemasons in the police.'

'That's right,' Gilchrist said, regretting her remark. 'But officers could voluntarily disclose their membership.'

'Nobody in Brighton did,' Donaldson said. He smirked. 'But then keeping your membership secret is rather the point of a secret society, isn't it, ma'am?'

A female voice from the door:

'Anjelica – sorry I'm late.'

They all turned. A strikingly attractive woman walked in, smiling at Rutherford whilst acknowledging the others. She was in high heels and knew she had good legs since she wore a short, canary yellow dress that showed them off.

'Charlotte,' Rutherford declared, hugging her and exchanging air kisses. She turned. 'This is Charlotte Byng.'

As everyone was introduced, Gilchrist felt a twinge of something she didn't want to recognize as jealousy because Merivale was looking at Byng appreciatively. Wolfishly, in fact. She looked at Byng's slender shape and felt like a heifer.

'Charlotte is one of the experts in the South-East Asia section of the British Museum,' Rutherford explained.

'Sorry I'm late,' Byng said. 'A day late, actually – sorry about yesterday too.'

Rutherford murmured something and gave her arm a squeeze.

'So what have you uncovered so far?' Byng said as she joined Merivale at a trestle table on which a handful of items had been laid out.

'Well, there's a male head and upper torso – obviously sheared off from a full statue.' Merivale indicated a sandstone carving some three feet high. The right hand was raised palm out. There was a symbol carved on it.

'Thirteenth century, I'd say,' Byng said.

'What does that gesture mean?' Gilchrist said.

'The gesture is called *abhayo mudra*,' Byng said. 'It offers peace.'

'Who do you think it is?' Merivale said.

Byng shrugged. 'Hard to say. We'd need to know where it has come from to know that. He's wearing a kind of crown so it may be a Buddhist bodhisattva or a form of Vishnu, the Hindu god.'

Gilchrist pointed at a tiny bronze statue some six inches high and about the same length. 'What is that?'

'That's Ganesh riding on a rat,' Byng said. 'His favourite form of transport.' She indicated another bronze statue, this one about four feet high. 'There he is again.'

This time Ganesh was sitting cross-legged with one pair of hands placed on his knees. His second set of arms pointed upwards but were broken off at the wrist.

'So has the British Museum got the Cambodian equivalent of the Elgin Marbles?' Heap said to Byng.

'Actually not,' she said. 'Have you ever read *Gods, Graves and Scholars*?'

'Not for a long time,' Merivale said.

I've never heard of *Gods, Graves and Scholars*, Gilchrist thought but didn't say.

Donaldson just grunted.

'It was the book that started a whole generation of archaeologists off. It romanticised the early archaeologists, who were as much explorers as academics. Hacking through jungles, digging up deserts, working from myths and legends.'

'It's what got you started?' Merivale said.

Byng laughed. 'Should I be offended? Surely I don't look that old? It was published just after the Second World War.'

'Why do you mention it then?' Gilchrist said. She wasn't sure of her tone but Heap glanced at her so she knew it wasn't good.

'The book typifies the attitude then to what were regarded as the great civilisations, the ones worth studying. And the British Museum original collection reflects that approach. We have Greek and Roman and Egyptian and Assyrian at the core. Then we have some Mesopotamian and a little Phoenician. A hint of Mayan and Aztec. Some Indian. But Cambodia and Vietnam? Only a couple of glass cases. Angkor Wat – not a thing.'

'But now – you acquire things all the time, don't you?' Gilchrist said.

'It's not possible to build a big collection from abroad any more. Attitudes to important objects leaving their home countries have changed dramatically. There is very little from Cambodia in the whole of the United Kingdom.'

'So you were surprised when you heard about a hoard of stuff from Angkor Wat in Brighton,' Gilchrist said.

'I was astounded . . . and unbelievably excited.' She looked at them. 'If it reached here legitimately.'

'Well, there's the thing,' Gilchrist said. 'That's what we're trying to figure out. You've heard about Bernard Rafferty?'

Byng glanced at Rutherford. 'I hope you're not expecting a comment.'

'I'm just saying that he is linked to the hoard in a way we're still trying to ascertain.'

Byng frowned as she thought for a moment. 'I don't quite get the link. Although he probably knows Charles Windsor.'

'Charles Windsor?' Gilchrist said.

'Yes. One of the world's few great authorities on Khmer art, particularly from the Angkor period.'

'Why would he know him?' Gilchrist said.

Byng looked at her, then at the blank faces of Heap and Donaldson. 'Well, because he has a shop in Brighton.'

You hurry back into the open and down the narrow lane towards the woman with her vases and the man with his scrapheap. Two men appear in front of you. Big men. They block your way. You're aware of someone looming just behind you.

You're standing near the scrapheap. The man with the raw hands has made himself scarce. You reach down and pull out a wrench and swing it at the nearest man's head. He falls against the second man and you turn and the third man is right behind you – near enough to take the wrench full in his face.

You turn back and swing at the man who is unbalanced but as yet unhurt. He puts his arm up to block the blow so you jab at his face and then again. You drop the wrench and head for the road.

You see your quarry beneath the flyover getting into a black Mercedes. He has a parcel in his hand but where it came from you have no idea. A beaten-up taxi is idling near you. You get in. You can't exactly ask the driver to follow that car but there is only one road back into town so you give the name of your hotel. You ask the driver in Russian to turn the heating up. He shrugs. No heating. He points to his own hat with ear flaps.

'Get a hat and coat like everyone else,' he says in Russian. Muttering, in Hungarian: 'Fucking Russki idiot.'

You're cold, you're cross with yourself for cocking up your job at the flea market and you have no idea how to follow your quarry without tipping your hand. However, the driver has pissed you off and you have a gun so you seriously contemplate shooting him and taking his cab.

'I need to stop here,' you say, indicating the verge along the side of the road.

'You said hotel.'

'I'm going to be sick,' you say in Russian. 'Don't want to mess up your car.'

'Shit, piss, wank,' the driver mutters in Hungarian. 'Fucking *kulak*.'

He veers over to the verge and slams on the brakes.

You roll out of the back seat and fall on your knees in freezing mud. You're pretty sure he isn't going to drive off without you. Taxis don't queue at the flea market unless the driver is desperate for money.

The mud has immediately soaked into your trousers. That irritates you even more. You do the gagging noises and dry heaving and wave behind you with your left hand to get the driver to come over. Nothing happens.

You put your forehead in the mud and keep waving your hand. You hear cursing and footsteps and the driver, somewhere to your left, says, in Hungarian: 'What do you want, fuck face?'

You sit up straight and from the kneeling position stand, with a sucking noise as your knees come out of the mud. The driver is looking down at the verge and there's a perplexed look on his face because there's no vomit to be seen. You note his coat is open.

You hit him in the throat and knee him between the legs and drive a punch into his solar plexus, deep beneath his diaphragm. Now there is vomit. His, projected over your shoulder. You turn and let him slide down to the mud, snatching his hat off his head as he falls.

You look inside the hat, turn it round and round. Looks pretty new and not too greasy. You jam it on your head and jump into the taxi. You force your way back into the traffic and go hunting for your quarry.

The driver isn't going to be feeling too good anytime soon. But at least you didn't kill him.

# ELEVEN

S oon after Byng dropped the bombshell about a Cambodian art expert with a shop in Brighton, Merivale left for another appointment. He suggested to Byng that they meet again at the safe UNESCO storage space to which he was going to move the artefacts. Gilchrist tried not to be jealous, although actually he left almost brusquely before Byng had quite agreed. Gilchrist was still staring after him when Donaldson too got up.

'Well, this has all been very interesting but I've got a murder to investigate. If you'll excuse me, ma'am. Ladies.' He glanced at Heap. 'Detective *Sergeant*.'

'I should go too,' Heap said. 'Go and check out Youk's digs.'

'Stay a bit longer, Bellamy,' Gilchrist said. 'I'll go with you. I want to hear more about this Windsor man. Tell me, Charlotte – do you think he should be called in to examine what we've found here?'

Byng glanced at Rutherford.'Probably not. But I think it would be worth talking to him, if he's around.' She indicated the sofas. 'Shall we?'

Once settled, Byng said: 'Charles Windsor has got a "special arrangement" with several museums in Europe and America.'

Gilchrist hoped she didn't sound impatient. 'For now, tell me about him and Brighton.'

Byng looked at her. OK, she obviously did sound impatient.

'As I said, he's a world expert on Khmer art,' Byng continued. 'He has written the definitive book on it. But he's under investigation in the US at the moment. A federal seizure lawsuit has been issued there on behalf of Cambodia for the return of two statues illegally removed from the country in 1975.'

'Are either one of these statues the Ganesh you talked about?' Gilchrist said to Rutherford.

'The big brass one?' Byng said to her friend.

Rutherford nodded.

'No. These are something else.'

'What does Windsor say?'

'He denies the accusations, of course. But he's got form. He's been implicated in the sale of looted artefacts to the New York, Chicago and Philadelphia museums.'

'Quite an entrepreneur,' Gilchrist said.

'Quite so,' Byng said. 'In the main one, the federal lawyers say Mr Windsor – who is identified in court papers only as "the Collector" – bought a twelfth-century sandstone statue of a Khmer warrior sometime in the early seventies knowing that it had been looted from Koh Ker during the Cambodian civil war.'

'They're only bringing this up now?' Heap said.

'Well, it was only in 2007 that at Koh Ker a pedestal and a pair of feet, without the rest of the statue, were uncovered. A couple of years later a French widow approached Montague Pyke about selling this sandstone statue of a Khmer warrior her husband had owned since 1975.'

'Somebody saw that the statue and the feet on the pedestal matched when Montague Pyke posted a photo of it in its catalogue?' Heap said.

Byng nodded.

'Exactly. The Frenchman had bought it at auction in Paris. The court papers say Windsor assisted with export licences that concealed what the statue actually was when it was shipped to Paris for that 1975 auction. The papers also say that Windsor had bought it from a Thai dealer in Bangkok in the early seventies who ran an organized gang of looters.

'So the sale was suspended. But the auction house is fighting the United States government's effort to seize the statue, arguing there is no evidence that the statue was looted or is even the property of the Cambodian government.'

'And Windsor?'

'He's annoyed because he says he is being smeared. He's not a defendant in the case. The court papers don't provide the evidence to support the US's depiction of him. He says he has never owned the statue although he wanted to. He simply recommended to the London auction house that they bought it from the Thai dealer.'

'What does the auction house say?' Gilchrist said.

'That Cambodia can't lay claim to a statue that was abandoned in the jungle fifty generations ago.'

'What do you think about that argument?' Heap said.

Byng crossed her legs and Heap flushed, bless him.

'The US government's view is that the statue is still Cambodian property because the state has never transferred it to anyone else. It's stolen property.'

'And your view?' Heap said.

'Officially we all work to a 1970 UNESCO convention preventing the illegal transfer of cultural property – but it is no longer fit for purpose.'

Byng clasped her hands on her knee. Heap was riveted. Gilchrist smiled to herself. This woman did have great legs. When she'd crossed them earlier it had almost been a *Basic Instinct* moment. Almost. And, dammit, the woman was bright. Gilchrist was trying hard not to hate her.

'The looting is one thing but all a government has to do is issue export licences and it can flog off its entire cultural heritage quite legally. If in Syria Assad had decided to empty the museums to buy more chemical weapons to attack his own people, he could have done so quite legally.'

Heap frowned. 'What's the deal when iconoclasts take over a country? I remember the Taleban blowing up those Buddhist statues at Bamiyan when they took over Afghanistan.'

Gilchrist nodded warily as she had no idea what he was talking about.

'You know those statues dated back to the second and fifth centuries?' Byng said. 'And in the Balkans in the civil war, ancient monuments of special cultural significance were targeted by all sides: churches, mosques – even bridges. The Sarajevo National Library was burned to the ground.'

'Nothing new there,' Heap observed. 'We had our own dissolution of the monasteries in Henry VIII's time and Oliver Cromwell was pretty iconoclastic during our own Civil War.'

Byng was taking more time to deal with Heap, Gilchrist noticed. Big Brain had that effect.

'True,' Byng said, leaning towards him. 'But you kind of hope everyone but ignorant fundamentalists of whatever religion have learned about the importance of cultural heritage by now. And certainly some countries are getting more gung-ho about getting stuff back.'

'You mean Greece and the Elgin Marbles?' Heap said.

'I was thinking of Egypt. The latest government is suing English and Belgian museums for the return of tomb carvings. It says that if the museums don't return the artefacts archaeologists from these museums won't be allowed to dig in Egypt. Not that it'll be safe to dig there any time soon in any case. They've been asking for the Rosetta Stone back from the British Museum since 2004 but that's not going to happen.'

'But if something ancient is in a country then I guess it belongs to that country,' Heap said. 'I suppose if the government wants to destroy it, it can.'

'There is an argument that it belongs to the world and they just happen to be living on the land where it was found,' Rutherford interjected. 'If you're suggesting these people are descendants of the people who built these things that is a bit of a stretch. Seems to me there is no such thing as owner-occupiers. Just occupiers.'

'What happens if there is a civil war going on as in Syria?' Gilchrist said.

'There is a Hague convention to protect property during armed conflict but it's pretty ineffectual,' Byng said. 'Both sides in any civil war loot treasures to buy weapons. And there are opportunistic thefts from criminal gangs. Remember when all of Iraq's museums got sacked during that war?'

Rutherford leaned forward. 'In the antiquities world cultural preservation and national ownership often collide,' she said. 'If the French and other western collectors had not preserved this art, what would be the understanding of Khmer culture today?'

'Is Windsor a collector as well as a dealer?' Gilchrist said, trying to get the conversation back on track.

'Most dealers are both,' Byng said. 'Windsor is getting on, so he's probably spent half a century putting together his own collection. He has donated works to Phnom Penh's National Museum and prestige museums in America. The irony about the National Museum donations is that for all we know it had all been looted from there in the first place during the Khmer Rouge period.'

'Nobody gives something for nothing,' Heap said. Then flushed.

'In the case of Windsor you might be right,' Byng said. 'He has been investigated before for involvement in dodgy dealings. And when I checked with UNESCO's Phnom Penh field office they were very sceptical. They reckon his definitive book is a kind of guide to all the art looted from the country. The book has beautiful photographs of beautiful works that are all privately owned in secret places. In the book the owners are anonymous and Windsor refuses to tell Cambodia who they are or where the objects are.'

'He doesn't want his pals to risk losing their art to the country it was stolen from,' Heap said.

Byng nodded. 'He says the items are being better looked after than they would be back in Cambodia. And maybe he has a point. Who will pay for the conservation, the repatriation? Where will they be displayed? He's said he's going to donate much of his own collection to Cambodia – but not until he's dead.'

Gilchrist had heard enough. Plus she was fed up with feeling totally out of her depth. She got up from the sofa. 'We need to see this man,' she said. 'Do you know where he is in Brighton?'

'He backs a shop here and I think he has a house here but I'm not sure – he also lives in New York and Bangkok. He's a very wealthy man. In addition he spends a lot of time on a beautiful old steam-powered yacht – it was a rum-runner during Prohibition.'

'Sounds like ascertaining his current whereabouts might prove difficult,' Gilchrist said.

'I know the shop is in the Lanes,' Byng said. 'Although it's not under his name.'

Gilchrist turned to Heap.

'We also need a word with Rafferty.'

'Ma'am.'

Byng got up from her cross-legged position on the sofa with such elegance Gilchrist wanted to spit in her face.

'If I can be of any further help,' she said, holding out her hand.

'You've already been more than helpful,' Gilchrist said, resisting the urge to crush her hand in her own fierce grip. She hoped she sounded genuine. She glanced at Heap. Obviously not.

You catch up with the black Mercedes and follow it to the Terror Museum, the dreaded former home of the Hungarian secret police. Harry Nesbo gets out and enters the museum.

You abandon the taxi a street away. You take out a handful of notes to leave for the driver but someone else is going to steal this car and go through it before he ever gets it back. You stuff the notes back in your pocket.

The Terror Museum. You're too young to remember its original purpose but you're aware of its vile history as headquarters of both fascist and communist secret police.

It's a massive building on a corner at Andrassy Ut. On the outside walls are passport photographs of all those who died at the hands of occupiers of these buildings over many decades.

You do not allow yourself to get emotionally engaged, although you know how helpless each one would have been at the hands of the blunted and the sadistic. You have lived in times where you have seen such men and women all over the world. The scum of the earth. The despicable ones. The ones who feel nothing. Your aim has always been to redress that balance. You laugh harshly. How can one man do that or imagine that he can?

You go in and buy a ticket. You know your quarry is in here somewhere. Your instructions from Paradise are vague. Monitor him.

Nesbo is buying a bottle of water in the café to the left of the ticket office. You want to leave your new hat on as disguise but it is warm in here.

As you start to take it off your quarry suddenly appears in front of you. He has doubled back to collect an audio-visual guide from the bookshop and is now wearing headphones. He is fiddling with the headphones, you are fiddling with the hat. You get away with it, you think.

There is an inner courtyard beneath an internal well that rises four floors to a glass roof. People used to be hung in this court-yard. Now there is a pool and, on a large plinth in the centre of it, the hulking form of a rusty tank. In 1956 this tank rolled down the street outside to crush the uprising against the Soviet scum. You hear people say how surprisingly big it is. You have seen tanks before.

You look up. There are balconied walkways on three sides of the well on each floor. On the fourth a single wall ascends from ground floor to top floor. This wall is covered from top to bottom with blow-ups of secret police file photographs of those unfortunate enough to have been imprisoned, tortured and killed here.

There are thousands of them. It is overwhelming but you cannot allow yourself to be overwhelmed. You have a job to do.

Each blown-up photo, face front, eyes staring, has a number stamped across it. You see your quarry on the ground floor looking across at the photographs, checking them against the book in his package.

The history of this building is laid out in an exhibition that begins on the second floor and moves down the building, ending in the basement.

After your quarry has examined the photos on the wall for a little time you see him enter the lift. You stand before the closed doors and watch the indicator. The lift stops at two. You go up the stairs, two steps at a time. The heating in this museum is powerful. Now you are hot. It gives you the excuse to take your coat off.

One of your strengths is that you are forgettable. Your features are nondescript, your physique average, your demeanour modest. Except to the practised eye, taking your coat off is as good as adopting a disguise.

You find Nesbo cutting through a gallery in darkness into a long, high room with filing cabinets on every wall from floor to ceiling. The drawers of the cabinets are shallow, as if there is one per person. There are moveable ladders to access the higher drawers. You stand near the entrance, showing undue interest in a desk with absolutely nothing interesting about it.

Nesbo has opened a file drawer. You expect alarms to go off. Silence, although maybe lights are flashing somewhere. He closes the drawer, turns and leaves the room. Not quickly, not slowly. The book is no longer in his hand.

You glance around quickly but, you hope, casually. A group of young people are ushered in and cluster around the cabinet. A guide begins to talk to them.

Your brief is vague enough to give you a dilemma. Do you follow the man or the book? You are calculating how far Nesbo will have got, either by the stairs or the lift if this group are there one minute, two minutes, three minutes. You figure you have about thirty seconds before you lose him.

The man or the book?

There is movement to your left. A woman has entered the room from the wrong direction. Your height, swathed in a long coat, her head and shoulders wrapped in a shawl. Appropriate for the cold outside; suffocating, you would have thought, for the heat in here but it means her face is concealed.

She is looking towards the tour group.

Your decision is made. You loiter around other desks in the centre of the room. After what seems an age but is really only a couple of minutes the tour group moves on.

You see that they are going to block the woman's way so you make towards the drawer in the filing cabinet before she can enter the aisle. A bald-headed man with a goatee beard bumps into you.

'Sorry,' he mutters in Russian but without getting out of the way.

You glance to your left. The woman has started moving, her boots tap-tapping on the parquet floor. The man with the goatee beard is still in your way – he seems to have a problem with his shoulder bag. You try to move past him and somehow he is in your way again.

She passes behind the man and does not look your way.

You retreat down the aisle between the desks and cut into the next one. The man with the goatee is still fumbling with his bag. He may be mumbling another apology.

The woman opens the drawer, retrieves the book, closes the drawer and heads for the door by which you entered. You follow her and suddenly the bald-headed man with the goatee is in front of you again. This time his back is to you but he's still blocking your way. Intentionally?

In your line of work, there's no such thing as coincidence. Of course he is blocking your way intentionally.

You glance at the nearest surveillance camera. You turn into the next aisle and head for the other door. You zip through a couple of rooms, trying to keep the geography of this floor in your head. You push through an emergency exit door and take the stairs, three at a long stretch of the legs a time.

You're thinking: if I lose her I'll go after the goatee.

On the ground floor you come out near the entrance. You're astounded to see that snow has begun falling and sticking. You dash into the street, run to the corner. No sign of either of them. You decide – hope – they are still in the building. You walk back in more cautiously, wafting your ticket and nodding at the security man.

You can't think why the woman would still be in the museum. But if she is – where is she? You head for the basement.

You've been here before and you don't relish seeing it again. It's a bit too close to home. In the basement are the cells and the torture rooms, although the two are indistinguishable. Old stagers have told you about lying in a cell full of sewer water; of half standing, half sitting in a cell so narrow and short you couldn't easily do either.

Women have spoken quietly of implements used to hurt and dehumanise them. Basic instruments, crude instruments, laid out here in rooms where water drips from the walls and thin gunnels, crudely carved in the concrete floors some sixty years ago, aided the slow draining of innocent blood.

The corridors between the cells are narrow. They are cramped both with that narrowness and the cram of people. You zig rather than zag, hoping to come face to face with the woman. But you go from room to room, past these terrible cells, without seeing her.

Your plan for the man with the goatee beard is vague. 'Decommission' is the word that floats around in your head. It has a nice tang of guiltlessness.

Guiltlessness. What a horribly unwieldy word, you think. Like one of those German portmanteau words that go on for far too many syllables.

Kill him, then.

Not so vague after all.

You don't see her. You don't see him.

Now you're seriously pissed. And a bit scared. You're fucking up your job.

In the street the snow is falling even more heavily. There is already two inches on the pavement and the road. It's hard to see anything, never mind your two new quarries.

You lean back against the wall, against photos of the tortured and the dead. You put the hat back on. You feel the gun in your jacket pocket, the spare clip in the other. You feel the soles of your cheap shoes turning to cardboard in the snow.

You can't see anybody you're supposed to be following. You're fucked.

\*    \*    \*

Gilchrist and Heap were sitting in the office of the harbourmaster of Shoreham port. Gilchrist's head was buzzing with all that was happening.

When they were driving over Heap had said to Gilchrist: 'Do you think the dead man is Youk, ma'am?'

'Don't you?'

'And are we hypothesising that Youk's disappearance is linked to these artefacts in the Pavilion?'

'That's a reasonable assumption, Bellamy. One minute we don't know where Cambodia is, the next, two cases linked to there come up.' She glanced at him. 'Although I can't believe for a moment you didn't already know all about Cambodia.'

'I knew a little, ma'am.'

'Bodysnatching, though – that does seem to be your area of weakness.'

'I'm trying to redress that,' he said.

Now Gilchrist said to the harbourmaster: 'I've never really understood what happens here.'

'A lot,' the harbourmaster replied. She was not what Gilchrist had expected. The title had led her to expect a man, not this young, lean, clear-eyed woman. There didn't seem to be an ounce of fat on her, which made Gilchrist feel like an elephant. But she wasn't anorexic or anything. She looked supremely fit. It turned out later she ran forty miles a week. Ran, that was, not jogged. Her name was Kathleen Harrison.

'We're investigating the disappearance of a young Cambodian boy,' Heap said. 'We think he worked here.'

'Youk Chang.'

'You know him,' Gilchrist said.

'I know of him,' Harrison said.

Gilchrist glanced out of the window at a huge chute coming from a tall, grey warehouse. 'Do you export concrete?'

Harrison laughed. 'Aggregate. But not us. We have a number of private terminals here for companies that deal in aggregate. We have scrap exporters too. Our own operations division handles a range of imports and exports. Scandinavian timber and nitrates from France, for instance.'

'Goods from Cambodia?'

Harrison frowned. 'Not that I'm aware of. Not directly from

Cambodia, at any rate. You think Youk's disappearance had something to do with his work here? I thought he'd got into some
trouble in Brighton.'

'What kind of trouble?' Heap said.

Harrison scraped her bobbed hair back behind her ears. 'Well,
I've no idea – or if he did. I meant that was my assumption.'

'We're exploring all possibilities,' Gilchrist said, resisting the
urge to mirror Harrison's hair fiddling. 'It happens we have an
inquiry running parallel that involves Cambodia.'

'And you assumed a connection,' Harrison said, though not
negatively. 'Well, our ships all come from Europe – Tallin and
Riga is about as far east as we go. And that's north-east, in the
Baltic. But it's possible that a mixed cargo could contain Cambodian
goods, loaded in a European port.' Harrison looked wary. 'What
kind of goods are we talking about?'

'Antiques,' Heap said.

Harrison sat back and messed with her hair again. 'Illegally
imported?'

'Probably. Mainly we're trying to figure out how they got here.'

'And you think Youk's disappearance had something to do with
these illegal imports?'

Gilchrist spread her hands. 'To be honest, we have no idea but
a connection might help us with both cases.'

'Excuse me.' Harrison picked up her phone. 'Jack? Email me
the human resources files on Youk Chang, will you?' She listened
for a moment. 'OK – well, whatever we have.'

She hung up and looked from Gilchrist to Heap. 'Goods leaving
Cambodia would almost certainly go via China. Cambodia is in
hock to its neighbour. China is lending Cambodia a couple of hundred
million pounds to pay for various projects, including a huge new
port just completed about thirty kilometres east of Phnom Penh.'

'The capital,' Heap murmured to Gilchrist. She gave him a look.

'Phnom Penh has been jammed up for years,' Harrison went
on. 'It handled ninety-five thousand containers in 2012 – double
the number it was handling five years earlier. The new port can
handle a third more – and eventually three hundred thousand.'

'You're remarkably well informed,' Gilchrist said.

Harrison put her palms together. 'How else am I going to end
up running the company?'

Gilchrist smiled. 'How easy is it to smuggle something in a container?'

Harrison glanced at her computer screen. She tapped at her keyboard with bright blue-nailed fingers. 'How big is this something?' she said as a printer whirred in the corner of her office.

'Not huge,' Gilchrist said.

Harrison laughed. 'Could you be more specific?'

'The boxes we found the goods in are about sixty cubic metres in total,' Heap said.

Harrison slid from behind her desk and went over to collect the printout from her computer. As she brought the thin sheaf of papers back to her desk she said:

'The China trade is now using the new Triple E cargo boat. It carries 18,000 containers, each twenty feet long. The boat is almost a quarter of a mile long and taller than a twenty-storey office block. It usually leaves China full and goes back empty – you know China prides itself on being an exporter, not an importer?'

'That's a big boat,' Gilchrist said, watching as Harrison made three piles from the pages she'd printed off.

'Someone has done the maths. To carry the containers on a railway it would need a train sixty-eight miles long. These ships are so big there are hardly any ports capable of taking them. Shoreham can't get anywhere near, though Southampton and Felixstowe can manage them. There are no ports the right size in the whole of North or South America. They won't fit through the locks of the Panama Canal though they can just about squeeze through the Suez. Antwerp is digging a bloody great hole for them. London Gateway is being built as a dock especially for them.'

'So we're way beyond the needle in the haystack,' Gilchrist said.

Harrison handed each of them a couple of sheets of paper. 'Youk's personal file. A bit skimpy, I'm afraid, but he wasn't with us that long and at his level we don't require much information.'

Gilchrist glanced at it. 'Just staying with the smuggling for a moment.'

Harrison gave her a sharp look. 'Now you're saying for certain this stuff was smuggled?'

'I understand these are objects that are not supposed to leave their country of origin,' Gilchrist said. 'So my assumption is that they were smuggled in.'

Harrison smiled. 'China does kind of quasi-legal smuggling in that it breaks tariff limits and export quotas all the time. It simply ships goods to a third country or one of its independent territories – most notably Hong Kong or Macao – before re-exporting. What kind of antiques are we talking about?'

'Big ones.'

'How big?'

'Bits of temples.'

Harrison laughed again. 'That's very big. You're kidding, right?'

'Exaggerating, maybe,' Gilchrist said. 'As I understand it, they're stripping statues and wall art from Cambodian temples and palaces.'

'If such goods came through here they would be on a standard container ship – five thousand containers. If they were exported billed as something else – in among containers of tourist goods, for instance – we wouldn't have a hope of spotting them, regardless of the size.'

Harrison looked at the sheaf of papers on her desk. 'The last ship Youk helped unload was bringing a mixed cargo from Lisbon.' She tapped at her keyboard, watching her computer screen, for a moment. 'Interesting. It had come to Lisbon from Sharjah.'

Heap and Gilchrist both looked blank.

'United Arab Emirates – south of Dubai. Nice place.' She tapped again. 'And that's where the ship is now.'

She pressed a key and her printer whirred once more.

As she started to get up from her desk, Heap stood. 'May I?'

He brought the sheet from the printer and handed it across the desk. Harrison demurred.

'It's for you,' she said.

Heap looked at it. 'The SS *Yangste*. Registered in Hong Kong.'

Gilchrist was looking at the other papers Harrison had passed her. 'Youk didn't live at home,' she said. Thinking: why had Youk's mother lied?

There's a fall-back. Some weird set of catacombs up on the hill near the castle. Your contact is there. You're thinking these people have been watching too many *Mission Impossible* films.

You slip and slide through the snow down to the river. The wide

Danube looks beautiful, the snow falling on the row of lights either side of it. Even you notice that much.

The Danube. You've been reading more about the Danube. It held back the Romans, for a little while. Then again it didn't stop Genghis Khan and the Huns or the Mongols or the Turks.

You cross the river and take the antique lift up the precipitous hill from Pest to the castle atop Buda. It moves slowly. You sit on the bench and watch the lower town reduce behind you. Lights glimmering for miles through the curtain of snow.

The catacombs, carved from the soft tufa centuries before, have been turned into an art installation. You pay a few euros and you make your way to a chamber where a fountain on the wall is spilling out red wine. There is a row of glasses on a table by one curved wall. You catch a glassful of wine and sit on a bench and wait. You refill the glass. You wait.

To get into this chamber you had to bend at the doorway. A man comes in now, almost bent double. When he stands you see the goatee beard and come up off the bench, glass in hand.

The man with the goatee touches his finger to his lips and smiles, his other hand up in a pacifying gesture.

You were taught in training you don't fall for that. You throw the glass at him. No warning. He shifts his head to the side and it sails past his ear. As you hear it break against the wall of the cavern goatee is pointing a gun at you. A bloody big gun, but that's irrelevant, since from this distance a small one would do the job just as well.

'What the hell do you think you're playing at?' the man with the goatee says in unaccented English. 'Are you deliberately trying to fuck up a highly sophisticated operation?'

You say nothing. To be honest, you're not sure what to say. 'What's your part in it?' you finally say.

'To make sure nothing goes wrong until we're ready to move.'

You're starting to feel out of your depth. 'Move on who or what?'

'The trafficking syndicate, of course.'

'Which one?' you say.

You hear footsteps and a woman bobs into the cavern. The woman you saw in the Terror Museum. You start to put your hand in your pocket. Goatee man shakes his head.

'Are you stupid or crazy?' she says to you. English again. 'Your actions could incline me either way.'

'What was going on in the street market and the Terror Museum?' you say.

'What did you think was going on?'

'Who are you people?'

'What instructions did Sal Paradise give you?' she says.

'Who's he?' you say.

'The guy you're working for. The guy who told us to expect you.'

'You work for this man Paradise too?'

The woman glances at goatee and gives a taut smile. 'He works for us, Mr Tingley.'

The fact they know your name plunges you into even more confusion.

'What the hell is going on?' you say.

# TWELVE

On the way back to the station, Gilchrist called Donaldson. He was churlish, of course.

'Any news?' she said.

'Well, the antiques have gone, I understand. And we're trying to see if that blocked up tunnel leads anywhere.'

'Antiques gone?' Gilchrist said. 'I don't get you.'

'Agent Merivale and his team took them away in a big truck just after you'd gone. He'd mentioned it in our meeting, remember.'

She told Heap what had happened.

'That was never really our investigation, was it, ma'am?'

'I suppose not,' she said quietly.

He glanced at her. 'Do you mind my asking you something?'

'Of course not,' Gilchrist said.

'Why didn't Agent Merivale chip in when Windsor was mentioned? Do you think he wasn't aware of him?'

They had stopped at the lights on the seafront near the Palace Pier. Gilchrist kept her face expressionless, especially as she knew Heap was watching her like a hawk. She wasn't sure about this brotherly interest he seemed to be taking in her welfare.

'Maybe he didn't know or didn't think it important,' she said with a shrug, hoping her confusion didn't show.

Heap had a sympathetic look on his face as the lights changed and he moved on. Gilchrist obviously hadn't done quite as well as she'd hoped on the concealment front.

Back in the office, she called Merivale's mobile. The line was dead. After some detective work she found a number for Homeland Security in the US.

'I'm trying to get hold of a George Merivale, on secondment to UNESCO from the FBI.'

'This is the State Department, ma'am. You mentioned two organizations there that might suit you better.'

'He said he was seconded from Homeland Security – doesn't that have overall responsibility for all the other agencies now?'

'That is correct. What is this gentleman's particular area of expertise, Detective Inspector?'

'Cambodian antiquities.'

'A moment if you please.' It was just a moment. 'We have no one here by that name working in or contracted to this agency.'

'If he were doing undercover work you would say that, wouldn't you?'

'Probably. So, Detective Inspector, if you choose to disbelieve me, that's your privilege. But I can tell you that our interest in Cambodia lies elsewhere.'

'Where exactly?'

He paused again. She wondered if he was conferring with a colleague.

'I don't know, ma'am. You mentioned this agent. I'm embarrassed to say that whilst we've been talking I've fed him into our computer – I apologize for my rudeness in not paying total attention to you but we live in the age of multi-tasking. I am that rare man who can do that.'

Gilchrist chuckled. She liked this man.

'I'm afraid this man might not be all that he seemed,' the American said. 'His name is not coming up at all. Anywhere.'

'Meaning?' Gilchrist said, not feeling quite so much like chuckling now.

'Meaning,' he said slowly, 'that if we're the good guys . . . he probably isn't.'

Gilchrist was silent for a long moment. 'Don't shoot the messenger, ma'am.'

'It's not you I'm thinking of shooting,' she said. 'It's me. How could I be so stupid?'

'Might I ask if you gave him these Cambodian artefacts?'

Gilchrist laughed again, more harshly than before. 'I did assign the artefacts to his care, yes.' Thinking: but I assigned more than that.

Maybe the man on the other end of the line heard her thoughts. He softened. 'How long have you been in law enforcement, ma'am, if I may ask?'

'Coming up to eight years.'

'A good time, but I'm approaching my thirtieth year.'

'So you have words of wisdom for me?' Gilchrist said.

His laugh was guttural. 'I had wisdom about twenty years ago – I thought. Maybe when I was your age. But I quickly realized as I got older that I knew less and less. Maybe *you* could give me more definite words of wisdom.'

Gilchrist's laugh was quieter. 'The mantra that is going round here at the moment is: the world belongs to those who feel nothing.'

Another pause. Maybe it was the international phone line – but weren't delays a thing of the past in this digital age?

'If I may say so, that is not an entirely cheerful piece of wisdom,' he finally said. 'I have to believe that people are generally like you and me, ma'am, with morals and integrity and basic human decency.' He paused. 'All the evidence notwithstanding.'

'You're not looking on the bright side,' Gilchrist said.

His deep laugh again. 'Which in this instance is?'

Gilchrist laughed. 'I have absolutely no idea,' she said. But to herself: but this conversation has helped me get perspective on the bastard.

The situation in the subterranean caverns below Buda castle with the goatee beard and the woman reminds you of a time in a basement wine bar on London's Embankment and a conversation with people in the same line of work.

You had been there in the days of acceptable cigarette use, when the smoke billowing round the room had made the dark so Stygian the candlelight – the only light – could scarcely penetrate. Decades of smokers in the groined alcoves had left a black cake on walls and ceilings you could almost peel off with your fingernails, if you were so inclined.

That dim light and atmosphere was appropriate enough when you were being recruited into the smoke and mirrors world of the intelligence services. Well, recruited was maybe too strong a term. They wanted to use you now and then on specific projects.

The couple in the catacombs beneath Buda castle are called Sebastian and Phyllida. You think these are probably their real names.

'We know you, Jimmy,' Sebastian says. 'Probably better than you know yourself.'

That's for sure, you think but don't say.

'We've had you checked out back in London,' Phyllida says. 'We're guessing Sal didn't realize he had a tiger by the tail.' She leans forward. 'He still doesn't.'

'Sal Paradise works for you?' you say.

'We use him, yes.'

'I wouldn't have thought he'd be the sort to collude with spooks.'

'Well, Sal is always about the bottom line,' Phyllida says. 'When his business is under threat then he's happy to collaborate.'

'And this man he's sent me after is a threat?'

'It's complicated,' Sebastian says, wrinkling his nose as he tastes the wine from the fountain. He puts his glass down on the tufa floor.

'My brain still functions pretty well,' you say.

Phyllida snorts. 'You're going to have to convince me of that,' she says.

'This guy is ripping him off selling on Asian artefacts,' you say. 'I have no idea how that links with the person and paper trail that I was following.' You look at Phyllida. 'But you picked up that book in the museum. You know what it is all about.'

'You followed a man called Slavitsky from the flea market,' she said. 'Your taxi driver is doing fine, by the way. And we secured his taxi-cab so he doesn't lose his pathetic livelihood.'

You shrug. 'I couldn't afford to lose this guy Slavitsky, who I know as Harry Nesbo. Plus the driver pissed me off.'

'We noticed,' Phyllida says drily.

'Slavitsky had a list in the book he was carrying,' Sebastian says.

'The book you took,' you say to Phyllida.

'The book it was my mission to take,' she says. She gestured at Sebastian. 'We are part of the set-up.'

'So are there antiques at that flea market more valuable than they look, or is there some stuff hidden away in a basement there?'

'No basement,' Sebastian says. 'No antiques.'

You look from one to the other.

'People,' Phyllida says quietly.

Sebastian gives his goatee a little tug and leans forward. 'This isn't about antiquities or looting ancient sites.'

You sit back. 'It isn't?'

Sebastian shakes his head.

'This is about smuggling people on a massive scale.'

'Human trafficking is a huge problem,' Phyllida says. 'It took off in the early years of this century when the Soviet Union opened up and the Balkan conflict ended. But now it has broadened.'

'Cambodia has been on various watch lists since 2007 because it doesn't do enough to combat trafficking of adults,' Sebastian says. 'It has a National Anti-Human Trafficking Day but it's mostly for show. About ten years ago the deputy director of the police department charged with stopping trafficking and protecting juveniles was jailed with some of his colleagues for complicity in the trafficking.'

'And Paradise is implicated,' you say.

'Indubitably. We're pretty certain those indicted were on Paradise's payroll but we couldn't prove anything against him – he uses too many cut-outs.'

'There are big fines and long jail sentences for people caught trafficking anyone, but it still goes on,' Phyllida says. 'First, like every other Asian country, it traffics children from rural areas to cities. But what makes Cambodia special – in a horrible way – is that as well as being a key destination for sex tourists it is also a key transit point. If you know your history you'll know about the old Silk Routes. Sadly, we now live in an age of Slave Routes.'

'Sal told me he's involved in trafficking, but only within Cambodia,' you say. 'He claims to have some moral compunction about trafficking people across Cambodia's borders.'

You'd thought it was because he liked to be kingpin in Cambodia and knew he'd be mixing it with some big boys anywhere else. You've mixed it with some pretty nasty Balkan gangsters in your time and know what they are capable of.

Phyllida gives you a sour look. 'You believe him?'

'He said he focuses on slave labour. He traffics men for work in agriculture, fishing and construction. His women aren't usually sexually exploited – he puts them to work as domestic slaves or in factories.'

'And children?' Sebastian says.

'Some kids he uses in organized begging rings and for street-selling,' you say. 'Drug mules too.' You spread your hands. 'Look, I know he's involved in prostitution but most of that in Cambodia is operated by Vietnamese pimps. They bring in their own, more or less willing, Vietnamese girls.'

'You're forgetting the people forced into it from other ethnic groups,' Phyllida says. 'The sex slaves don't get paid. They scarcely get fed. They're prisoners with armed criminals as warders.'

'You're saying that's Paradise?' you say.

'You know what the third most profitable criminal activity in the world is?' Sebastian says.

You smile. You think. It could be a snarl for all you know.

'No disrespect, guys, but I don't have time for a quiz.'

'Child prostitution,' Sebastian continues. 'Worth twelve billion dollars a year. And Cambodia is at the heart of it. In Cambodia itself there are about five thousand child prostitutes for the sex tourists – you know, those men who take in a bit of culture between exploiting underage girls and boys.'

'The depressing thing is that everybody is in on it,' Phyllida says. 'Not just crime syndicates but parents, relatives and neighbours.'

'Parents?' you murmur.

'When you're starving, your children become a commodity,' she explains. 'It's always been like that. It's the same situation in parts of India, say, or even Mexico. Most Cambodians earn less than fifty cents a day. When you are just about surviving on subsistence rates, selling your five-year-old makes economic sense.'

Sebastian leans forward. 'I know of one Cambodian couple who delivered their ten-year-old and twelve-year-old to some German creep's hotel room to do with them whatever he wanted. He paid them a pittance but they took it.'

You sit back and swirl your drink around in your glass.

'That's unusual though,' Phyllida says. 'Normally, virgin children are auctioned. High-ranking military, police, government officials and businessmen take part in the auctions. The highest bidder gets to deflower them and afterwards the kids are put to regular sex work.'

'And Sal Paradise is implicated in this,' you say tonelessly.

'Paradise owns a village a few miles outside Phnom Penh that is pretty much all brothels,' Sebastian says. 'There are about fifty of them. You can buy five-year-olds for sex there. And every night dozens of westerners go out there and do just that.'

'The children are starved and beaten,' Phyllida says. 'They live in cages and are brought out just for sex. Drugs keep them pliant.'

'What's that got to do with you here in Budapest?' you say.

'He's moving into the export business,' Sebastian says. 'We think he's using us to dispose of his rivals so he has a clear run.'

'This man I was asked to deal with . . .?'

Phyllida and Sebastian exchange looks.

'We've been wondering about that,' Sebastian says. 'Slavitsky is well protected. Taking him out would have disrupted things for a Russian outfit but you wouldn't have survived.'

You look from one to the other. 'I do survive.'

'Go back to England,' Phyllida says. 'Forget here. Finish the job you started in Cambodia if you must. But steer clear of Sal Paradise. Trust us. We're taking care of him.'

You look from one to the other again. The cavern reeks of this red wine splashing out of the fountain. Reeks of more than that.

'It's not Sal Paradise I'm after,' you say quietly.

'You took the words out of my mouth,' Phyllida says.

Blake Hornby was sitting just behind the new police commissioner in the Bath Arms. He wondered why Watts seemed to be keeping an eye on the antiques shop across the road. Hornby himself was definitely interested in it.

Life had been hard for Hornby since he'd lost his job on security at the museum and art gallery. That nasty piece of work, Bernard Rafferty, was behind his firing, he knew. And he knew it was because of the theft of that painting, *The Devil's Altar*, on Hornby's shift. Hornby had laughed like a drain when he'd read what a perv Rafferty was with his grave-robbing antics. He hoped he'd end up in jail. But that hadn't helped him find work.

So Hornby was making a bit of a departure, branching out into a new line of business. Blackmail. He hadn't quite figured out how to do it but he thought the thing Youk Chang had told him must be worth something to keep quiet about.

He sipped his beer and smiled when he saw a familiar figure walk up the alley and step into the antiques shop.

\*   \*   \*

You call your friend's mobile. There's a little background noise when he answers.

'You out and about, Bob?'

'In the Bath Arms, Jimmy,' Bob Watts says. 'Shall I set them up?'

'Soon,' you say.

'You're coming back from Cambodia?'

You look out of the window at the planes on the Gatwick runway. You're waiting for the queue to die down at the hire-car counter.

'Oh, I've been to Budapest since then.'

'You're moving right along, aren't you?'

'Have you had a chance to find out about the antiques shop?'

'Sort of. I'm sitting looking at it now. But your man isn't there.'

'The owner?'

'Not sure,' Watts said. 'Listen, I want to know how you're doing. You know, when you told me about your wife I was stunned and sorry for you, but I was also cross with myself that in all this time I've never asked you about personal stuff.'

'That's not the currency we trade in. Our friendship goes deeper.'

Watts is silent for a moment.

'I hope so. Nevertheless, tell me about your wife. You've never known what happened to her? Is the not knowing the worst?'

You toy with your beer. 'That's not the way my mind works. I don't quantify bad things. Bad is bad.'

The truth is you have not allowed yourself to think about what might have happened. That way madness lies. But you have allowed yourself to hope that one day you will find out what did actually happen.

'There was this Cambodian girl,' you say. 'Michelle. I married her. My friends died trying to save her life. I thought.'

'When was this?'

'Towards the end of the Khmer Rouge.'

'You were there?'

'Unofficially.'

'This girl? What happened?'

'Hell.'

'They were rough times,' Watts says. 'You say she died in an ambush?'

'With my friends. I thought.'

'You mean she didn't die?'

'She definitely died. I thought the others died too.'

'And these best friends are the men you asked me to find out about?'

'One of them,' you say. 'Fucker is still alive. Which changes pretty much everything.'

You sip on your Hungarian beer. You were surprised to find it here. It is called Freaky Wheaty but tastes better than the name might suggest.

'What are you doing in Budapest, Jimmy? Hunting him down?'

You don't say you're not there any more.

'Sort of. A side trip. It just got more complicated.'

'You have a plan?'

You are quiet for a moment. 'Not any more.'

Watts laughs. 'Jimmy – you always have a plan. And a back-up.'

'That was back in the day. The day when the plan involved mostly killing people.'

'Does that mean you're not planning to kill anybody now? I'm relieved to hear it.'

You are silent. Then: 'You've read about doppelgängers?'

'I know what they are,' Watts says.

'Wilkie Collins believed for years he had one called Bad Wilkie.'

'The guy from Dr Feelgood?'

'The writer.'

'I know,' Watts says. 'Well, first of all he was a dope fiend so his judgement should not necessarily be relied on. Second, I'm not sure I like where this is going. If you're about to say it's not you who is going to be killing but your doppelgänger then I won't be impressed.'

'That would be a bit of an opt-out,' you agree. 'I'm happy to take all the blame for whatever I do. What I mean is that ever since Italy I have not been connected to myself, if that makes any kind of sense.'

Watts is silent for a moment. Then: 'How has it got more complicated in Budapest?'

'I made a deal with a man who only deals in misery.'

'What kind of misery?'

'The worst kind.'

'Well, we've both dealt in our share of that, Jimmy.'

'No, not killing in war. Not like that. We had some kind of right on our side.'

'You believe that?' Watts says.

'Of course. You don't?'

'I guess,' Watts says after a moment. 'Who is this guy you've made an arrangement with?'

'His name is Sal Paradise.'

'Catchy.'

'The deal was he'd let me go after my man if I dealt with a problem he had with another man here in Budapest.'

'Dealt with?'

'We left that kind of vague.'

'The Jimmy I know wouldn't agree to that kind of deal.'

'That's what I've been telling you. I don't think I am the Jimmy either of us know any more.'

Watts doesn't respond to that. He says instead: 'How has it got more complicated?'

'There's a different game being played. A long game.'

'And you're in the middle of it?'

'Dead centre.'

'And that's also what is bringing you to Brighton?'

You clear your throat but say nothing.

'Jimmy, I hope you're not going to cause trouble here.'

You give a little cough. 'I hope so too. That wouldn't be a good idea.'

'For any of us,' Watts says.

Another pause.

'If you want to think of it like that,' you say and hang up your phone.


Blake Hornby listened in shamelessly on the lengthy conversation Watts was having with someone called Jimmy. If you're going to have a private conversation with somebody don't do it in a bloody pub on a mobile phone. It was the same on buses, especially with girls. He didn't want a blow-by-blow account of their problems with their boyfriends, but what choice did he have when he could hear them loud and clear, however far away he was sitting from them?

He was intrigued by the conversation he was earwigging because it was definitely something to do with the antiques shop across the alley.

Hornby snuffled and blew his nose loudly. Watts left his tablet on the table and went to the bar for another glass of wine. He glanced back and saw Hornby staring at him. Hornby quickly dropped his eyes. He stood and put his coat on then walked out of the pub without looking at Watts again.

He had recognized Bob Watts because the disgraced ex-chief constable had once been his next-door neighbour. Hornby lived in a tiny cottage in Frederick Gardens. He'd been born in it. His mother had been born in it before him. She used to go on about growing up in this narrow alley with the row of cottages on one side and the Regent Iron and Brass Foundry on the other belching out heat and noise and sooty smoke.

'And we had an orchard at the end of the alley,' she'd cackle. Daft bint. All he knew was that his tiny bedroom when he'd been growing up had looked out on the back wall of the Royal Mail's sorting office about five yards away. The orchard and the foundry were long gone.

As he'd grown up he'd outgrown his tiny room and the tiny house. There certainly wasn't room for the two of them, his mother with all her clutter. Once he'd solved that problem though he'd been able to spread out a bit.

He'd been surprised when Watts had turned up one day with a pile of boxes and moved in next door. Hornby had hoped for sight of him with that policewoman he'd been shagging. She was a bit of a heifer, but then so was Kelly Brooks according to some, and no man in his right mind would turn her down.

Hornby's lascivious thoughts were disturbed when he turned into his gate and saw a short, red-faced man in a dark suit standing on his doorstep. By the time he'd switched his mind to carrying on down the alley the man had turned.

He looked no more than a boy, actually – and he looked familiar. He seemed to recognize Hornby too.

'Mr Hornby, isn't it? From the museum and art gallery?' The man stepped forward. 'Detective Sergeant Heap. We met when the Gluck painting was stolen.'

Hornby nodded.

'I don't work there any more.'

'Oh. Right.' Heap frowned. 'I'm actually here because I understood a Youk Chang lodged at this address.'

Bob Watts was still thinking about his old friend, Jimmy Tingley, but he was also wondering about the tall man with the crew cut who had dipped his head to enter the antiques shop across from the pub whilst they were talking on the phone. He looked familiar but it took a moment for Watts to realize it was the skipper of the steam yacht he'd seen a few days earlier. Interesting.

Watts took his drink back to his table and speed-dialled Sarah Gilchrist. When she answered she sounded like she was on the move.

'Bob – I mean, Police Commissioner.'

'Bob is fine.' He lowered his voice. 'Listen, there's an antiques shop in the Lanes you might want to take a look at.'

'Because?'

'Jimmy Tingley asked me to check it out.'

'Did he say why?'

'Nope.' Watts spread his big hands. 'I was wondering about illegal import of antiques.'

'From Italy?'

Watts frowned, then remembered the last Gilchrist had heard about Tingley he was still recuperating in Italy. 'Asia.'

'Big continent,' Gilchrist said. 'Is it a continent?'

Watts shrugged, although there was no point doing so. 'I would know that how?'

'University education.'

He snorted. The phone was muffled for a moment then: 'Bellamy says it is,' Gilchrist said.

'I take his word,' Watts said. 'The guy has offices in Budapest and Cambodia. Jimmy is in Hungary. On some kind of pursuit over there.'

'An office in Cambodia?' Gilchrist said. 'And Jimmy is in Budapest?'

Her voice was flat. Watts picked up on it.

'Is there something I'm not getting?' he said.

'Not at all. There's probably something I'm not getting. This shop in the Lanes . . .'

'Full of statues of the Buddha and other Asian stuff. What aren't you getting?'

'I can't say. Ongoing investigation and all that. Sorry, Bob.'

'You're doing your job,' Watts said. 'You're not supposed to discuss ongoing investigations with anyone outside the force.'

Gilchrist laughed. 'And when has that ever stopped me? Remember when Rafferty found the Trunk Murder stuff in a basement storeroom of the Pavilion?'

'How could I forget?' Watts said.

'Well, he put something in the storeroom in its place.'

Watts made a face, again pointlessly. 'Bones?'

'We did find bones, yes. But we also found some crates full of antiques. Well, not antiques exactly. Statues and carvings – you know, of the Buddha, but Hindu stuff as well.'

'Angkor Wat,' Watts said slowly.

'Possibly,' Gilchrist said. 'And we've just found a murder victim down there. Recent.'

'I should make inquiries at this shop if I were you. It's called Charles Windsor Antiques.'

'Yes, I know,' Gilchrist said. 'Mr Windsor is a person of interest to us. We're trying to locate him now but we understand he could be anywhere in the world.'

'He's in Brighton,' Watts said. 'Or at least he was a couple of days ago. I think he's still here since I've just seen the skipper of his yacht go into the shop.'

'I'm on my way,' Gilchrist said. 'Are you there?'

'I'm in the Bath Arms. I can't come in with you, though. That would be overstepping the mark as police commissioner. And you'd better hurry – the shop closes in ten.'

'I'll be there in five.'

Gilchrist reached the shop in about eight minutes. It smelled heavily of incense. A woman was just locking a glass case halfway down the room. She was alone in the shop and obviously closing up. The woman's hair was pulled back tightly off her oval face. She couldn't hide a frown at the sight of Gilchrist. Shopkeepers hate people who come in just before closing.

Gilchrist took out her warrant card and showed it to her. Now she would hate her even more as there would be no sale.

'And you are . . .?' Gilchrist said.

'Monique. I run this shop.'

Sexy French accent *and* petite. Jesus Christ – couldn't Gilchrist get a break?

'I'm looking for a Charles Windsor.'

'I don't know where he is,' Monique said.

'This is his shop, though?' Gilchrist said.

'It is but he's not involved day-to-day. To be honest, I can't remember the last time he was in here.'

'But he's in the city.'

Monique shrugged. 'I wouldn't know.'

'I understand his boat is moored in the Marina,' Gilchrist said.

'You know more than I do,' Monique said.

'I understood its skipper was in here not long ago.'

The woman frowned. 'Now how would you know that unless someone was spying on us? Is this linked to the visit by the police commissioner?'

'This has nothing to do with him. Was the skipper in?'

'No. Mr Windsor's assistant was.'

'So Mr Windsor is around.'

Monique smiled. 'The presence of his assistant does not necessarily indicate the presence of Mr Windsor.'

Gilchrist nodded slowly, looking around. 'We have found a number of objects like this in the cellars of the Royal Pavilion.'

'Really? How exciting.' Monique sounded sincere. 'And you want Mr Windsor to authenticate?' She smiled. 'Why didn't you just say that?'

Gilchrist gave a little smile. 'Do you have an address for Mr Windsor?'

'From what you say he may well be on his boat.'

'If he isn't – and a phone number?'

'No phone number. He has a house here in the Lanes though.'

'I didn't know there were houses in the Lanes.'

The woman gestured around her. 'This used to be one. His house is in that very narrow alley, Fitzwarren Wynd.'

Monique walked over to the desk. She held herself and moved like a dancer. Gracefully. Gilchrist wondered again whether the women she was meeting at the moment had clubbed together to make her feel lumpen and inelegant.

Monique handed her a business card. She had written Windsor's full address on the back.

'Thanks,' Gilchrist said. 'This assistant – is he around?'

'I think he's on the boat,' Monique said. 'That's your best bet.'

'Do you have a number for him? And a name to go with it?'

Monique nodded. 'Coming right up.'


'The Chink?' Hornby said to Heap. 'Used to rent a room here.'

'Cambodian, actually. I wondered if I could look at his room?'

'Nothing in there. When he buggered off I boxed everything up.'

'Where's the box?'

Hornby looked at Heap.

'Well, it's in the back yard.'

'And how long ago did he vacate the room?'

'A few months.'

'Did he say why?'

Hornby scratched his chin. How much did the midget know? Did he know the Chink had just disappeared at a sensitive time in their negotiations?

'Didn't say. Didn't say much though. His English wasn't that good, you know.'

Heap nodded and stepped to one side. 'If I could take a look at the room?'

Hornby fiddled with his keys at the door, wondering if there was anything incriminating he'd left lying around. Well, not *incriminating*, more embarrassing. It wasn't right police could just turn up on your doorstep and demand entry.

He half-turned. 'Shouldn't you have a warrant or something?' he said.

'We're getting asked that a lot lately,' Heap said. 'This is a missing persons inquiry, possibly a murder investigation, and it's the victim's room I want to see, not the whole house.'

Heap smiled up at Hornby. 'Should we need to search the entire house, rest assured, we'll have the appropriate paperwork.'

Hornby huffed as he opened the door, recognizing the steel behind the polite words. He stepped straight into the living room, his eyes giving it a quick once-over. He'd left his computer on. He turned. 'It's up the stairs at the front,' he said. 'Help yourself.'

Heap didn't so much as glance at the living room, just kept his eyes on Hornby's face. He started up the stairs.

'Watch your head – the ceilings are really low in these old cottages,' Hornby called. Adding: 'Oh, but you're probably all right being the size you are.'

That'll teach the little sod, he thought, as he went over to his computer to turn it off. Not that he had any kiddy porn or anything like that on it – couldn't get his head round that paedophile stuff – but, well, he was a normal, healthy male . . . Plus, there was this other stuff he was working on.

With hindsight he should have just turned it off at the mains. But when he pressed down on the power button of the computer to kill it dead the screen lit up and a message in a rectangular box came up: 'Are you sure you want to close down this computer?'

'Yes, are you sure?' Heap said from behind Hornby, his voice low.

Hornby jumped and stepped to the side.

'Sorry,' Heap said, giving an apologetic shrug. 'Youk's room is locked. I came down for the key.' He pointed at Hornby's computer screen. 'But why have you got what looks like a surveillance photograph of an FBI agent on your computer?'

# THIRTEEN

B ob Watts watched Sarah Gilchrist go into the antiques shop. He'd been checking his emails and had just received one from Christian Aid asking for donations for Syrian refugees fleeing the violence. All Christian Aid wanted was for you to text Syria2 to 70060 and donate £5.

Watts looked at the email address this had come from and sighed. Sure Christian Aid was using an email address whose sender was: duqqncpezcddkehffs.

This scum. There was no limit to how low those who felt nothing would stoop. He wasn't sure who was worse – those who inflicted horrible suffering on people or those who used this suffering to profit from people's good, naïve hearts. He figured they belonged in about the same circle of hell.

When Watts saw Gilchrist leave the shop he went to the door of the pub and waved her over. She had her phone glued to her ear but she ended the call as she reached him. She offered her hand to shake but he pulled her close and kissed her on her cheeks.

'Don't start getting stupid,' he said in her ear. 'We're friends, remember?'

'Start getting stupid?' she said.

'Continue, then,' he said. He stood to one side. 'Come in and let me know what's going on.' He saw her look. 'As your friend, not as the police commissioner.'

She ordered a sparkling water. He glanced at her but said nothing.

'Bellamy is tied up somewhere and I really want to doorstep this Charles Windsor guy,' she said. She showed Watts the card.

'I have his address.'

'Use DS Donaldson?' Watts suggested.

She gave him a look.

'I need a scalpel, not a sledgehammer.'

'Well, I can come with you if you want.'

Gilchrist gulped down most of her drink. 'I'm not sure I should go there with an Irregular.'

'What's holding Bellamy up?'

'He's being a bit vague but it's linked to a murder inquiry. A Cambodian boy.'

'Well, that does sound linked to this,' Watts said. He drained his glass. 'So do you want to do this?'

As they were leaving the pub, Watts said: 'How was the skipper?'

'He wasn't there.'

Watts stopped on the pavement.

'Well, he never came out. I was watching.'

Gilchrist stopped beside him and thought for a moment.

'Maybe he went down the rabbit hole,' she said. 'Anyway, Monique said he wasn't the skipper, he was Windsor's assistant.'

She fished out the card.

'Name of Klingman.'

Blake Hornby was seriously pissed off. He had a plan to get rich and this pint-sized policeman was getting in the way.

'Where was the photograph taken?' Heap repeated.

'I've told you – I can't remember. I take lots of photographs. It's one of my hobbies. With digital cameras you can go berserk.'

Heap shrugged. 'Fair enough. So you don't know who it is either.'

'Haven't a clue.'

Hornby kept his expression deliberately blank, aware that Heap's eyes never left his face.

'So don't you want to look at that bloke's things?'

'We'll see what forensics come up with,' Heap said. 'I'll arrange for somebody to come round to collect his things later today – can you ensure that you're in?'

'I have quite a few things to do today, actually.'

Heap leaned in. 'Mr Hornby, I'm not entirely sure what you're up to but I'm pretty certain you're up to something. If I were you I'd regard cooperation with the police as my top priority.'

Little prick, Hornby thought. He wanted to smash his fist into the plod's smug face. For a moment he seriously contemplated doing it. Perhaps Heap saw it in his eyes because he stepped away.

'We're investigating what might prove to be a murder here, Mr Hornby,' he said. 'Best be careful how you act.'

The policeman's phone buzzed. He glanced at the screen. 'I'll be going now, Mr Hornby. Think about what I said now.'

'Of course, Officer. Will do, Officer.'

The cop tried to give Hornby a hard look but it didn't have any effect. The thing that was having an effect was the possibility he wouldn't be able to take his plan forward.

Heap let himself out but stopped in the garden and made a call. Hornby got as near to the window as he could without being seen but he couldn't hear anything. Heap mostly listened. When he ended the call he looked at his phone for a moment, clenching his jaw, then hurried out of the garden.

You drive down from Gatwick over the Downs, the rapeseed impossibly yellow either side of you. The light is steamy and it sends you right back to Cambodia and the way the green, green jungle trembled in the morning heat haze.

You come off the Downs on to the Ditchling Road. The road winds past the golf course and rises to the crest of a hill. You stop at the traffic lights there. You look down at Brighton spread out below you, the sea glittering beyond it, a ferry from Newhaven on the horizon heading for France. You feel that something is soon to be resolved. One way or the other.

The front door was inset into a long, blank, dark brick wall. There was a stale smell of urine as Watts and Gilchrist entered the alley but the door wasn't set far enough in for people to relieve themselves against it.

The door was unexceptional, with only one big lock. It was painted black but the paint was scuffed and graffiti had been badly removed.

Watts rang the bell and the lock was released with a click. Gilchrist looked up and saw the glitter of a tiny lens pointing down from the corner of the stone lintel.

Watts led the way into a small, low ceilinged, dimly lit foyer, bare of furniture. Another black door two steps up and ahead of them. Another camera in the angle between wall and ceiling.

They heard another click and this time Gilchrist pushed open the door and led the way into a tiled second foyer with a low rack on the left wall.

'Please take your shoes off and put them on the rack,' a disem-
bodied male voice said.

Watts complied. Gilchrist hesitated. She was wearing pop-socks
underneath her boots and didn't think that look without boots did
anything for her. Plus her nail varnish on her toes was chipped if
she took the pop-socks off. Plus she was self-conscious about her
feet after teenage years cramming her toes into too small, too tight
shoes. She disliked Charles Windsor already.

She was expecting a white carpet to justify the shoeless state
but when she stepped through the archway into the house proper
it was on to bare wood: long wide planks of seasoned pine. She
disliked him even more.

'Impressive,' Watts muttered.

They stepped into a large atrium with balconies on two levels
running round all four walls and rooms leading off it on every side.
In the centre of the room lilies floated on a rectangle of water in
a shaft of light from the glazed roof far above.

A haze of incense drifted across the light shaft, its smell strong
in the room.

Gilchrist was thinking this secret house must occupy the entire
block behind the shops on the other three sides of the alley.

High up on the walls were semi-shuttered windows. Some
soothing drone-like music wafted from an unseen source. It
reminded Gilchrist of a posh spa she'd splashed out on once.
Except that in place of massage beds and recliners lining the walls
there were full-sized stone statues with seraphic smiles, hung with
jewellery.

'It's a museum,' Watts whispered, looking from side to side in
the dim light. There were artefacts on stands and pedestals, glass
cases filled with smaller objects. They were all spot-lit from above,
casting long shadows down the faces.

A tall, broad-shouldered man emerged from the gloom at the
far end of the room. He stepped into the shaft of light. It made
his shock of white hair look like a halo around his head. His face
was ruddy. He wore a black, oriental-looking silk jacket with
toggles for buttons and loose black trousers. There were gold
bangles on both his wrists.

He walked a little stiffly over to a stone statue, standing guard
over the pool. He made a small gesture.

'All Khmer sculpture was lit from above when in situ.' His voice was gravelly, smoke-damaged. It wasn't the voice on the intercom. 'It emphasized the shadows under the nose and mouth and over the pectorals, giving them definition.'

He gestured for them to come closer.

'Beautiful objects,' Watts said.

The man seemed to appraise the room.

'The pieces are the best of their kind. That Chinese horse, the Indian Chola bronze of Rama. Those bronze bells are older than the Khmer. Second century, actually. The lingam and yoni are pre-Angkor too.' He pointed. 'That finial for a palanquin is twelfth century.'

'Chola?' Gilchrist said, picking out just one of the words she hadn't understood.

'Another name for the Tamil empire. It was one of the longest ruling dynasties in southern India. Third century BC to thirteenth century AD.'

He indicated a long sofa covered in brightly coloured throws and cushions.

'But you're not here for an art history lesson. Please be seated.'

Gilchrist and Watts sat side by side.

'Actually we are sort of here for an art history lesson,' Gilchrist said.

'In what sense?' Windsor said. His face was sculpted to the bone.

'Some Cambodian treasures have been discovered beneath the Royal Pavilion and we're trying to ascertain who the owner is,' Watts said. 'We thought you might know.'

'We're also investigating a murder,' Gilchrist said. 'A young Cambodian boy.'

'And you think I can help with both these things? That puzzles me.'

'I think I saw you on a beautiful yacht a few days ago,' Watts said. 'A steam yacht.'

Windsor looked at Watts but didn't respond.

'I had no idea this palace was hidden in the middle of the Lanes,' Gilchrist said.

Windsor turned his hard face to her. 'Scarcely anyone does. I prefer it that way.'

'Of course. Was it a warehouse or something originally?'

He was taking a disconcerting length of time to respond to questions or comments. She couldn't decide whether it was age, disdain or calculation.

'Or something,' he eventually said. 'Mostly it is created from the old brewery and its yards that were surrounded by tenements. I bought parcels of it one by one and created this out of what I had purchased.'

'Planning permission must have been a bitch,' Gilchrist said.

Windsor looked at her but said nothing. Then: 'I like the fact it is hidden. A secret behind a blank façade.' He turned his cold gaze upon her. 'I suppose we're oddly similar in that respect, Detective Inspector.'

'What respect would that be, Mr Windsor?'

'You look for secrets behind blank façades – by which I mean the faces of criminals – whilst I attempt to keep my secrets hidden by such a façade.'

'What secrets are you keeping, Mr Windsor?'

He took his time again. Finally: 'Nothing murderous, I assure you.'

A beautiful Cambodian boy in a maroon tunic and trousers padded quietly across the floor carrying a tray with an iron teapot and three bowls. Averting his eyes he placed it on the table between them, poured tea into the bowls and padded away.

'Leaping Tiger white tea,' Windsor said, leaning forward to pick up a bowl. He inhaled the scent and took a sip. Gilchrist and Watts followed suit. The bowls were hot.

Gilchrist put her bowl down. 'Your secrets, Mr Windsor?'

'I meant only the secret of the very existence of my house. Do you know Edinburgh, Detective Inspector – or you, Commissioner?'

'A little,' Watts said, as Gilchrist shook her head.

'I've always liked the fact that in the Middle Ages the aristocrat might live cheek by jowl with the poor. The tenements in the Old Town are side by side with mansions. Sometimes they enfold them. There is one particular house, now a museum, in Lady Stair's Close, by the Royal Mile. Early seventeenth century. Splendid looking. Across a shallow yard, tenements tower around it. Extraordinary.'

'You regard yourself as an aristocrat?' Watts said, a bland expression on his face.

Windsor turned his pitiless look on him. 'I was making an analogy about buildings, not people. But if you equate wealth with rank . . . well, I am certainly wealthy.' He put his palms together in front of his chest. 'Do you have any specific questions to put to me?'

Gilchrist was admiring the pond. The base was black slate. It made the goldfish in the water seem luminescent in the shaft of sunlight.

'You mentioned part of your house was the old brewery,' Watts said. 'Presumably that means there are tunnels beneath us.'

'Probably. I wouldn't know.'

'You haven't investigated?' Gilchrist said.

'I think tunnels would qualify as Below Stairs. I do not concern myself with there.'

'Would you mind if we had people explore your tunnels?'

'If they exist,' Windsor said. 'And if you have all the appropriate documentation – warrants and such?'

'We can get all that if necessary,' Gilchrist said. 'But your permission is enough.'

Watts gestured round the room. 'We'd also like your permission to examine your collection.'

Gilchrist looked at him sharply. She didn't want him screwing things up by overstepping the mark.

'Why is that?' Windsor said, his voice like slate.

'Experts tell us that many South-East Asian antiquities are looted and illegally imported,' Watts said.

Windsor gave him a cold look. 'You are suggesting that is the case with my collection?'

'We'd like to be sure.'

Windsor sat back. 'I was born here in Brighton, you know. Before the Second War. It was a rough place in the thirties.'

'I've heard,' Watts said, his mind flashing briefly to his father's time as a police constable then.

Windsor may or may not have acknowledged the remark with a slight flicker of the eye. It was hard to tell.

He continued. 'I first went to Asia in 1951, as a shipping clerk. I was based in Bangkok but moved all around the South China

Seas as I rose quickly in the company.' He cleared his throat. 'I
fell in love with Khmer art visiting a new friend's house in the
late fifties. My host was showing off a piece he had just purchased.
I loved the purity and simplicity of it. I went to the shop where
my host had made the purchase. There was another piece, equally
beautiful. I paid far more than I could afford for it. I borrowed
the money from the bank, in fact.

'I moved from shipping to shipping insurance and soon added
building insurance. I had realized that leeching on the back of
industries that actually did things was the way to make risk-free
money. I quickly prospered. And with my prospering my collection
grew.'

'Do you have a favourite piece?' Watts asked.

'My best piece I keep in my bedroom,' Windsor said – but there
was no softening of his voice or tone. 'It is a ninth-century bronze
from north-west Cambodia. I bought it from a dealer in Hong
Kong. It was delivered wrapped in jute and when I had the jute
carbon-dated it was eighth century. That too is now an object for
me.'

'Do all your pieces have provenance, Mr Windsor?' Gilchrist
said.

Windsor pushed himself off the sofa and looked up at the
balcony.

'I used to drive out from Bangkok or Phnom Penh of a weekend
and take rutted dirt roads into the jungles of Cambodia to explore
vine-entangled, shattered temples and palaces of a forgotten, one-
thousand-year-old empire. The free-standing statues were long
gone, stolen by the French and local dealers. But at Phnom Rung
or Muang Tam I would walk around these open-air museums and
soak up eleventh- and twelfth-century Khmer.'

'You didn't help yourself to things?' Gilchrist persisted.

He looked down at her. 'I had photos or engravings of sculptures
and I would visit the local governor and ask him if he had seen
anything similar. Often, such objects were lying discarded in fields.
I would buy them and take them to Bangkok. I was in touch with
the wealthy American collectors. John D. Rockefeller bought one
such piece from me and donated it to the Asia Society in San
Francisco.'

'So you were both dealer and collector,' Watts said.

'Correct, sir.' Windsor looked from one to the other of them. 'Forgive me if this sounds rude, but I somehow doubt either of you have known the passion of collecting.'

'True,' Gilchrist said. Watts assented with an incline of his head.

'I bought from dealers in France, London and Hong Kong.' Windsor was walking toward a sandstone statue on a plinth. 'I would buy what I could afford but the best then was nowhere near as good as things you could buy later.'

He stood before a statue and talked to it rather than them.

'In the sixties and early seventies farmers started digging up pieces buried for centuries – like this Vishnu. Bakheng, ninth century. Suddenly in the thieves' markets of Bangkok Khmer stone and bronze antiquities and ornaments began to appear. We didn't worry about provenance, either out in the jungles or in the dealers' shops. We were rescuers, not plunderers.'

He looked up again at the balcony behind Gilchrist and Watts and seemed to see something there. Gilchrist resisted the urge to turn around. Watts was staring into the pond.

'With the Khmer Rouge the supply stopped,' he continued. 'Now, the authorities discourage the farmers from digging. I would be surprised if any more really good pieces are unearthed. That's partly why the buyers of Khmer art have dwindled. Where today are the Annenbergs or the Rockefellers?'

Watts coughed. 'I read that an anonymous buyer spent over seven million dollars on four pieces in a Montague Pyke sale a few months ago,' he said. 'You don't know about that?'

Again Windsor looked at him with a basilisk stare but said nothing. Gilchrist stood and walked over to a statue draped with gold jewellery.

'And the jewellery?'

'That is the goddess Uma. Eleventh century. There are only five sculptures like that in the world. In the temple she would have been dressed in gold jewellery – most of the jewellery manufactured before she was. An elaborate crown, necklace, pendant and belt.'

'Is jewellery the kind of thing you could also dig up?'

'Rarely, but yes, there have been discoveries of jewellery stashes. They would be buried in earthenware pots in difficult times. A lot of broken empty pots have been found where the jewellery has already been stolen.'

The music had stopped. Windsor made a gesture and a few moments later it started again.

'I donated some royal regalia to Cambodia's National Museum last year. I'm trying to persuade other collectors to do the same so the art is preserved in its country of origin. I also gave money to install a modern security system – now the gold is in a special room with locks, alarm systems, track lighting and camera.'

Windsor was looking back up at the balcony.

'I raised hundreds of thousands of dollars to light the museum – and to fix the ceiling. You know, since the Khmer Rouge allowed the museum to fall into disrepair it has been an uphill struggle. The ceiling was infested with bats for decades. The basements where most of the collection was stored – badly – flooded every monsoon season. I've been awarded the country's highest honour for all that I've done. Do you really think I would at the same time be looting the country I love?' He shook his head vigorously. 'I hope to retire to Cambodia to live what few years I have left there.'

'How many pieces do you have?' Gilchrist said, as she walked over to him. She glanced up. Whoever he had looked up at on the balcony was no longer there.

'Here? Probably one hundred in bronze, gold and stone. I only buy what I feel I can live with and what improves my collection.'

'And the things in your shop?' Watts said.

'One or two have been in my collection. But you know these days I do swaps. A friend of mine has a companion piece to that Vishnu. I've coveted it for ten years. I think I've finally persuaded him to part with it in return for several south Indian pieces I've tired of.'

'You're a patient man,' Gilchrist said.

He nodded and walked over to a sculpture that was a kind of tableau: someone cross-legged with someone else bowing to him. 'This is Shiva being worshipped by his son, Skanda. It was probably made for the new capital at Lingapura – Koh Ker, it is called today – around AD 940. It is a single piece of sandstone. I've wanted it since 1967. When I saw it then Shiva's head was separate, and his arms and Skanda's feet were broken. An American dealer bought it. He sold it on to a California museum who put it seamlessly

back together. They sold it to buy some French Impressionist paintings – as if there weren't enough of those on display in the world's
art galleries. I traced the private collector who had bought it and
cultivated him.'

Windsor had a small coughing fit then he continued: 'He is fond
of baccarat. I persuaded him that we should wager on the piece.'

'You won it in a game of cards?' Gilchrist said. 'I thought that
only happened in fiction.'

'I think it does. No, not that. But he agreed that if I beat him
over an evening's baccarat he would sell it or swap it. It was a
long, long night but by dawn's early light I had the Shiva and he
had four particularly nice pieces of mine from Sri Lanka. I had
picked them up for a song but he didn't know that – and they are
indeed worth much, much more than I paid.'

He beckoned to Gilchrist. 'Come closer then you can see the
sheer bliss on Skanda's adoring face.'

Gilchrist did as she was asked, then nodded. 'Lovely,' she said.
She really was out of her depth.

'Do you mind my asking how many staff you have here?' Watts
said, moving over to join them.

'Oh, I'd need to check that with my major-domo. He handles
all that kind of thing.'

'Did a young man called Youk Chang work for you?' Watts
continued as he drew close.

Windsor frowned. 'The name does not sound familiar but again
you should perhaps talk to my major-domo.'

'Would that be Mr Klingman? Is he here now?'

'Alas not. He is down at my boat overseeing its provisioning.'

'You're going somewhere?'

'Evidently. But then I am always going somewhere. My root-
lessness is, alas, my curse. Perhaps my collecting is an attempt to
anchor myself in one place.'

He looked up at the balconies.

'You know, I love all good art. And I deal in atrocious art. I'm
so grateful for BritArt as it makes money to allow me to buy good
art. Pickled this, unmade that, childish scrawls, adolescent
ramblings, the whiff of formaldehyde. All rubbish, but it allows
me to collect Fabergé. He was in Siam in 1904 and made pieces
for the royal family there and in Cambodia.'

'Fabergé pieces?' Gilchrist said, remembering some had been looted.

'I only buy what I feel I can live with and what improves my collection,' he said.

'How soon are you leaving?' Watts said, out of the blue but getting to the point.

'Soon,' Windsor said.

'Then perhaps you could allow us to see the tunnels beneath your property now?' Gilchrist said. 'As we're here.'

Windsor smiled. 'I'd love to oblige but perhaps it would be better if we did that strictly by the book. Those warrants we spoke of?'

'Of course,' Gilchrist said. 'Absolutely. When we have them perhaps you'd be good enough to ensure that your major-domo is here to answer our questions. What is his name?'

'His name is Rogers. William Rogers.' Windsor gave a little bow. 'If that is all?'

Gilchrist smiled. 'More than enough for now, Mr Windsor. More than enough.'

# FOURTEEN

'Right,' said Gilchrist into her phone as she and Watts hurried through the Lanes. 'I want Windsor's boat located – I assume it's in the Marina – and a watch put on it. I want a watch on this house. I don't want this bird to fly.'

'Yes, ma'am.' Donaldson sounded bored. 'But we can't stop him, ma'am, as we have nothing to charge him with.'

'At least I want to keep track of his movements. I also want work on clearing that tunnel to go on full steam ahead. I want to see where it leads.'

'Ma'am. There's other news, however.'

Gilchrist thought she'd lost the signal when nothing followed. 'You still there, Detective Sergeant Donaldson?'

'Ma'am.'

'Well, spit it out. What kind of news?'

'The nancy boy nutter is dead.'

'The nancy boy nutter?' Gilchrist said, glancing at Watts and raising her eyes. 'Is that a technical expression?'

'Yeah. I don't think we're going to get any answers from him.'

'Detective Sergeant, I have no idea who you're talking about.'

'Not that we ever would have got answers from him. Excuse me, ma'am, but some people you just have to give up on, recognising that they are inexplicable.'

'And how do you choose who they are?'

'Well, you start with Bernard Rafferty and work your way down. Digging up skeletons – seems an open and shut case of a nut.'

'I'm sure you're right.' She jerked to a halt. 'Is he the nancy boy nutter you are referring to?'

'He's dead,' Donaldson said. 'Your trick cyclist went round to interview him and found the front door wide open and Rafferty hanging in the hallway in a pair of bloomers.'

Watts had walked a few yards ahead, his own phone glued to his ear.

'Bloomers?' Gilchrist said.

'Apparently so.'

Fuck the fuck. Gilchrist slapped her hand against the nearest wall and then wished she hadn't. It hurt. Watts looked over.

'OK,' she said into her phone. 'Well, I need you to do something urgently. Forget just watching the boat – I need it securing at Brighton Marina. We need a search warrant and for Windsor's house.'

'The grounds?'

'Smuggling.'


You enter the Lanes from the back-end so you can go into the Bath Arms without passing the antiques shop. However, you walk straight into Bob Watts and Sarah Gilchrist, loitering in the narrow lane between the two. Gilchrist seems stiff with Bob, which is a shame as you think they'd make a good couple. They see you and both look surprised.

Watts embraces you, drowning you in his long-armed hug. Gilchrist knows you less well and contents herself with a kiss on each cheek.

'What are you doing here?' you say.

'Deciding what to do next,' Gilchrist says shortly.

'We may as well wait in the Bath Arms until we hear back from people,' Watts says. He indicates the antiques shop across the road. 'Keep an eye on that.'

'That's the shop?' you say.

Watts nods. He looks you up and down. 'You look well,' he says, a nervous grin on his face.

'I look like shit,' you say. Which is true. Haggard and ravaged.

'Rum and pep?' Watts says.

'When in Brighton . . .' you say. You want to sound cheerful but you think you sound dead.

'Sarah?' Watts says.

She shakes her head. 'We should be doing something.'

'Such as?' Watts says. 'We're stymied without warrants. Where's your boy Heap?'

'He's gone to see Youk's mother, Prak Chang.'

'Come on then,' Watts says. 'Have a coffee at least.'

You all go in. Watts goes to the bar and Gilchrist watches you almost warily.

'Bob has been telling me about your wife and the Cambodian mission,' she says. 'I'm sorry.'

You smile at her. You think you smile. She doesn't recoil so you assume your smile is an approximation of the right thing.

Watts comes back with the drinks. He looks at you both. 'What is under discussion?'

'Cambodia,' you say, raising your glass and taking a sip of your rum and pep. You put the glass down and line your cigarettes and lighter up alongside them.

Gilchrist frowns.

'Are you chasing these ancient artefacts?' she says to you.

You shake your head. 'No, but I know what was stolen.'

'From Angkor Wat?' Watts says.

You shake your head again. 'From the National Museum in Phnom Penh. I was there when they were stolen.'

'These things we found in the tunnels.'

'Possibly – I don't know what you found. I'm referring to three particular things.'

'The Ganesh?' Gilchrist says.

You frown. 'Not that I recall.'

'What then?' Gilchrist says impatiently. Then her phone rings.

Worried about the trajectory Watts had spelled out for Tingley's return to Brighton, Gilchrist had asked Bellamy Heap to check on the story Watts had passed on to her about the 1979 mission.

'Can you talk, ma'am?' Heap said now.

'I can listen,' Gilchrist said, consciously not looking at Tingley. Perhaps Tingley sensed something, however, for he gestured to the bathroom and slipped from his seat. She watched him go and gestured to Watts to approach and listen in to the conversation.

'This story Mr Tingley told,' Heap said. 'There is no record of the three English sailors nor of anyone called Michelle imprisoned at the time. The records list only one British person, a John D. Dewhirst, aged twenty-six. He'd been invited to go sailing with new friends he'd met in Bangkok – a New Zealander and a Canadian.

'They drifted into Kampuchean waters. Glass was shot dead during the capture of the boat. Hamill and Dewhirst were taken to SP-21. They signed a number of false confessions during months

of torture. Eventually both were executed and their bodies burned.
Dewhirst may have been burned alive.'

'Tingley wouldn't make this stuff up,' Watts said to Gilchrist.
They heard Heap click his tongue.

'It does say the records for foreign prisoners in SP-21 are incomplete. Seventy-nine foreigners are recorded as being imprisoned but
it's assumed that is an underestimate. One of the photographers who
recorded the inmates on arrival has said that many photographs and
files were destroyed before the Khmer Rouge fled.'

'There you are then,' Watts said.

'The more important point is that Jimmy might be attempting
something unlawful,' Gilchrist said. 'We can't allow that.' She
looked at Watts. 'I think we should detain him.'

They both looked to the toilet at the rear of the bar in time to
see Tingley exit and head straight for the back door to the pub.

'Good luck with that,' Watts said.

You have an address in your pocket. Phyllida gave it to you. You
take a taxi. The driver is chatty but you don't want to talk to her.
You are remembering when you came round, trussed to a tree, in
the temple in Angkor Wat. There was something unreal standing
before you, pulsating in the moonlight.

'It's beautiful, isn't it?' a voice said close by. Westbrook,
Michelle's father. 'We can't let it be lost to posterity or destroyed
by these barbaric Khmer Rouge.'

'What is it?' you said.

'The Buddhist goddess Tara, the bodhisattva of compassion.
Gilded bronze, eighth century AD. From Sri Lanka originally.'

'What's it doing in Cambodia?'

'War booty, tribute – who knows? Nobody probably did know
it was here until Francis Garnier came along.'

'Who's he?' you said, as you tested your bindings.

'A nineteenth-century explorer, in love with the Mekong. He
was convinced the Mekong went all the way to China, and in 1866
he took two paddle-driven gunboats from Saigon upriver through
the Mekong Delta to Cambodia. When his expedition reached
Phnom Penh he docked the boats and took a small party across
country to Angkor Wat. This party returned with a large crate.

'The crate was loaded on the boat but the monsoons came so

they were obliged to proceed up the Mekong in pirogues. Nobody is certain if the crate went with them or what its fate was because Garnier was killed in an ambush by the Black Flag.'

'The Black Flag?' you said.

'The Vietnamese resistance to French rule,' Westbrook said. 'And the crate was never seen again.'

You raised your chin at the statue. 'This was in the crate?'

Westbrook looked at the statue wreathed in moonlight. 'Rumours of the crate's survival have passed down through the centuries. You know the story of the Maltese Falcon?'

You nod. 'The jewel-encrusted bird.'

'And modern treasure seekers have been tracking it down the centuries by sightings and rumours and written accounts.'

'And that's what has happened with this?'

'This and what she is wearing on her head.'

You shook your own head. 'I can't see. What is it?'

'A helmet. Well, really a ceremonial crown. Emeralds, rubies, lapis and diamonds on hammered silver. Priceless.'

'And you took both these from the National Museum?'

'Nobody knew their value except me. So, yes, we took them – and a few Fabergé eggs.'

'Where's Michelle?' you said.

'She's safe. She's helping us in return for them not hurting you. The Boy Scout.'

'So what's going to happen to me?' you said.

'Nothing bad. We're just going to leave you here. A resourceful fellow like you should be fine.' He raised his voice. 'You know, I'm lucky to be alive. Tall men always die first in prison camps.'

'Really?' you said.

'Sure. We get treated worse by the guards. They are usually shorter and like humiliating us. Plus we have less fat on us so we starve quicker.'

'Can I speak to Michelle?'

He touched you. Barely.

'I don't think so. And, Jimmy, probably wisest to think of this as *adieu*. Not *au revoir*.'

Gilchrist was in Watts' car heading for the Marina. Watts had told her Tingley was looking for revenge.

She was on the phone to Bellamy Heap, who was also in transit.

'Who is this Jimmy Tingley?' Heap said.

'A lovely man,' Gilchrist said, glancing at Watts. 'But a lethal one.'

'We've both dealt with those before, ma'am.'

Gilchrist shook her head. 'Not someone like Tingley. If you come across him, don't even try.'

'It's our job, ma'am.'

'We're not up to it.'

Heap was silent for a moment.

'He's much, much, much better than us,' she added.

'Speak for yourself, ma'am.'

Gilchrist sighed.

'Know your limits, Bellamy.'

'Ma'am,' he said and she could tell he was grinning.

'Tell me about Youk's rented flat.'

'Just a room, ma'am. I'm heading over to his mother's now.'

'Does she know?'

'I sent Constable Wade round to tell her.'

'Sylvia? Good choice. She's good with people.'

And technology. PC Sylvia Wade had been invaluable as part of Gilchrist's recent team investigating black magic goings-on in and around Brighton.

'OK, Bellamy. Keep in touch.'

'Ma'am – there is just one curious thing.'

'We seem to be surrounded by curious things. Go on.'

'His landlord had a photo of Agent Merivale on his computer. A snatched shot – I would guess taken from inside the Bath Arms.'

'You recognized it?'

'I recognized the antique shop he was going into.'

Gilchrist closed her phone and looked at Watts.

'What?' he said.

'Windsor's skipper or major-domo or whatever he called him – the one who went into the antique shop today and didn't come out – what does he look like?'

'Klingman? Big, tanned, my sort of age.'

'Looks like Jon Hamm?'

'I don't know who that is.'

'Crew cut?'

'Yes.'

He glanced at her when she groaned. 'Is that the sound of a penny dropping?' he said.


You get out of the taxi at the end of a street in Hove and scope it out. All quiet. You approach the house casually. It is in darkness. It looks shuttered up.

There's a man walking down the street towards you from the other direction. A few inches shorter, which puts him in the category of short-arse. He's observant, you can see. A policeman?

You slow. He's counting house numbers. You're pretty sure you're both heading for the same place. This isn't what you want. Legality isn't going to work for you here.

The man stops in front of the house you're aiming for. You keep walking. He glances at you as you walk by. You're conscious of his eyes on your back.

'Excuse me, sir.' You walk on. 'Excuse me, sir.' Louder. Fuck the fucking fuck.

You turn.

'I was taught very early on in life not to talk to strangers,' you say. The young man is shorter than you but you can see he's in good shape. He has a shyness about him but there's confidence in his eyes.

'Mr Tingley, is it?' he says. Oh dear.

The man moves closer. 'I'm Detective Sergeant Bellamy Heap. We have friends in common. Detective Inspector Gilchrist and Police Commissioner Watts?'

'That we do.'

Heap flushes. 'I'm sorry, sir, but I need to detain you.'

'You are detaining me and I need to get on.'

'I need you to come with me,' Heap says.

You're wondering how much of a fighter Heap is. You don't want to hurt him more than necessary to get away and that will inhibit you. You know how to kill more than you know how to damage.

'For what reason do you need me to come with you?'

He's now only three yards away from you. 'Mine is not to reason why,' Heap says.

'Well, young man, I want you neither to do nor die. And I'm sorry. I can't let you detain me.'

Heap shrugged. 'That's my job.'

You stand very still.

'I know who you are, Bellamy. May I call you Bellamy?' Heap gave the slightest of nods. 'Thank you. Well, Bellamy. Don't be a dick. Neither of us wants what is about to go down.'

Heap shrugs again. 'It is what it is.'

You look down at your hands. 'No. It's not. It's something else. Please walk away.'

Heap shakes his head. 'Can't do that.'

You look at your hands again. Close your eyes. You are aware of your phone ringing in your trouser pocket. Heap hears it too.

'You want to answer that?'

You shake your head. 'It will wait.'

Heap takes a torch from his belt. Except it's not a torch. You recognize it as an incapacitating flashlight. You look at him warily.

'We've been asked to trial this by Police Commissioner Watts.'

You nod. 'I'm not sure he intended you to trial it on me.'

Nevertheless, you don't want to be vomiting up your guts any time soon.

'Why are you at this address?' Heap says.

'Why are you?' you say.

'I have to take a DNA sample and inform the woman who lives here that we may have found her son,' Heap says. 'Dead. What about you? Why are you here?'

You look at Heap. He's so fresh-faced.

'Because the woman who lives here handles the Cambodian slave trade in the UK for a certain Sal Paradise and a certain Charles Windsor.'

# FIFTEEN

B righton Marina always reminded Watts of John Hathaway, the Last King of Brighton, with whom he'd had a curious relationship. Hathaway had had a bar here that had been burned to the ground by a barbaric Balkan gangster. There was no sign now it had ever existed.

Watts saw the beautiful wooden boat at the near dock of the marina. The steam was up. It was bigger than he had realized, taking up three berths. Hathaway used to berth a boat here that he used for smuggling runs. Watts wondered whether Windsor's participation in the Great Escape had been entirely altruistic. What cargo might he have smuggled in or out of England?

Gilchrist was clearly having the same thought. 'I wouldn't be surprised if the ballast wasn't made of bronze and sandstone – or those three things Jimmy mentioned but didn't specify.'

'Given that he went on the lam when your phone rang, you mean,' Watts said.

'Given that,' she said.

'How long before that warrant arrives?' he said.

She chewed the inside of her cheek. 'Could be hours.'

'Of course, if there is believed to be a terrorist danger no warrant is needed.'

Gilchrist gave him a slow look. 'That still needs permission.'

'Who from?'

She smiled. 'The police commissioner. Sir.'

'Consider it given,' he called back as he strode towards the boat.

'But hang on,' she said in a loud whisper as she headed after him. 'You can't be involved in anything operational.'

'I'm not – I'm just there to ensure that the letter of the law is observed with regard to the Protection Against Terrorism Act.' He turned and grinned. 'You're on your own, kiddo.'

Heap follows as you walk round the back of the house.

'What are you doing?' he says quietly.

You try the back door then break a pane of glass in it with your elbow. There is a curtain draped on the other side of the glass so the noise is not as bad as you feared. You put your hand through carefully and feel for a key in the lock. You're in luck.

DS Heap shuffles his feet as the door swings inward.

'You coming in?' you say back over your shoulder to him.

You catch him shaking his head. 'Can't. I'm an officer of the law.'

'I heard there was a burglary in progress. Shouldn't you be investigating that?'

Heap breaks the smallest smile. 'I suppose I should.'

He follows you in. 'What you said—'

You put your finger to your lips, cock an ear. The house is dark and silent. You are in the kitchen. There is a door ahead of you. A cellar door. It has four bolts on it.

'Does that torch work just as a torch?'

'Unfortunately not,' Heap says. He reaches into one of his capacious pockets. 'This should do, though.'

It's a pencil torch but it will, indeed, do.

You draw the bolts quietly. They are well oiled because, you can see, well used. You turn the key in the lock painfully slowly.

'You wait here,' you whisper as you pull the door open. 'Watch my back.'

Heap nods and you start slowly down the stairs.

Gilchrist led the way up the gangplank. There was no sign of life on the deck although the fore-hold doors were open and the empty hook of a crane swayed over it in the wind.

'Ahoy on deck,' Watts muttered. 'Coming on board.'

'Ready or not,' Gilchrist said more loudly.

There was a tall, glossily varnished double door leading below, its brass handles gleaming. Watts stepped forward but Gilchrist held him back and reached for the handles.

'You're just observing, remember?' she said.

A short flight of polished steps led down into a cabin the size of a hotel suite. It was high ceilinged and should have been plush but Windsor had decorated austerely, as with his house. The room had dim wall-lights but a spotlight's beam was directed from the ceiling down on a life-size, gleaming golden statue of a full-breasted woman. She was naked to the waist but a long lower garment covered her to her ankles. Her right hand was held out as if she was giving something; her left hand looked like it should be holding something. She shimmered in the light. She was beautiful.

Another spotlight was directed to a glass case in which there was some kind of helmet. A third light illuminated a smaller case, the contents of which were obscured.

Charles Windsor was standing in front of the statue, gazing at it. He turned when their steps clattered on the stairs and frowned. 'I'm sure this is trespass,' he said icily.

'We have reason to believe terrorism is being aided by what is happening on this boat,' Gilchrist said.

Watts looked at her and raised an eyebrow. She almost shrugged – it was the best she could come up with.

'Are you insane?' Windsor said. He raised his voice. 'Rogers, get in here.'

Nothing happened.

'What is that?' Watts said, indicating the statue.

'The goddess Tara in gilded bronze,' Windsor said. He was clearly unable to keep his knowledge to himself as he continued: 'It is solid cast, unlike the majority of bronze images that were cast on a clay core. It was gilded after it was cast.'

Gilchrist stepped closer. The statue had a headdress with a surround like a flame encrusted with precious stones. She looked down into one of the glass cases. A gem-studded helmet was propped up inside. Windsor followed her look.

'See those images on each side? That's Tara again, in precious stone. In the centre is Amitayus, the Buddha of infinite life.' He gestured to the statue. 'This is her helmet.'

He waved at the other glass case. 'Fabergé eggs from Cambodia and Thailand. Frivolities, merely.'

'And these are stolen goods, Mr Windsor?' Gilchrist said.

'Haven't we gone through all that once?' he almost snarled. He raised his voice again. 'Rogers, where the hell are you?' Then he gestured at the helmet. 'That beautiful object? It was in the local history section of the National Museum for decades. Those morons didn't know what they had. I'm not talking about the Cambodians, I'm talking about the French. You know, a Frenchman designed

the museum during the Great War. The French ran it until
Cambodian independence in 1953 but they hadn't a clue.

'It was left to fall down during the Khmer Rouge period. Most
of the people running it were killed. Bats colonised it. I've been
trying to help since, as I told you, in collaboration with UNESCO,
but ninety per cent of the collection is in store in the basement.
And every rainy season it floods. They have two thousand works
on display and twelve thousand suffering water damage in the
basement. They only got rid of the bats five years ago. So, please,
spare me your "this stuff is better there than here" crap.'

'I wasn't making that point,' Gilchrist said.

'Do you know Sal Paradise?' Watts intruded, also moving closer
to Windsor.

'I'm not good with names as I get older,' Windsor said.

'Cambodian fixer, smuggler, antiques dealer. Your Mr Rogers
worked for him back in the day.'

'Is that so? Rogers, where the hell are you?'

'May still do so,' Watts said. 'As may you.'

'Me work for somebody else?' Windsor scowled and walked
over to a wing-backed chair in the far corner of the cabin. He
lowered himself into it. 'Not for sixty years.'

'Then maybe Paradise works for you,' Watts said, joining
Gilchrist in front of the statue.

Windsor looked at his clasped hands, liver-spotted and gnarled.
'You know, Cambodia has never come to terms with those Pol Pot
years. How could it?' He reached for a drink on the table beside
the chair. 'The Khmer Rouge left behind a devastated country. A
quarter of the population killed. But there has been no closure.
Successive governments have tried to ignore what happened. The
Khmer Rouge period was only made part of the school curriculum
in 2009.'

'What about charging people with war crimes?' Watts said, even
as he knew this was a diversion.

'The government was pressured by the west into setting up a
war crimes tribunal back in 1996, to operate in partnership with
the UN.' Windsor scowled. 'One hundred and fifty million dollars
and nearly twenty years later it has prosecuted one case, with two
more pending. A number of the European judges, representing the
UN, have resigned in disgust at the way a couple of cases were

handled that never came to trial. The cases involved a couple of men who switched sides in 1978 and now have positions of great power in the country.'

Gilchrist was getting impatient. She also wondered where this man Rogers was.

'Only last year the war crimes tribunal freed a former leader of the Khmer Rouge,' Windsor continued. 'Ieng Thirith. She was Pol Pot's sister. They were a middle-class pair, both educated at the Sorbonne. She was a Shakespeare scholar. She was also the Khmer Rouge's highest-ranking woman, the social affairs minister – there is an ironic title if ever there was. She faced charges of crimes against humanity, genocide, homicide and torture. But she was eighty and suffering from Alzheimer's so she was declared mentally unfit for trial.' Windsor waved his hand. 'And I was supposed to leave the world's treasures in the hands of people like that?'

Watts was trying to remember.

'What happened to Pol Pot?' he said.

'He ran his own, mad illegal state on the Thai border until 1998. On the evening before the twenty-third anniversary of his takeover of Phnom Penh he either killed himself or was murdered. He was under house arrest in the hands of a faction of the Khmer Rouge. One version has it that he heard on the Voice of America that the Khmer Rouge faction holding him had agreed to hand him over to be tried for war crimes, so he killed himself. The other story goes that the faction poisoned him so he couldn't be handed over.'

'Time's a ticking, Mr Windsor,' Gilchrist said. 'We're going to have to impound this boat.'

'Oh for God's sake. Rogers – get in here!'

Finally they heard footsteps from the back of the room. A man ducked into it. When he stood and looked round the room he saw Gilchrist and grinned.

'Hi, Sarah,' Agent Merivale said.

Watts looked from him to Gilchrist.

'I'm not sure what to call you,' she said. 'Merivale or Klingman or Rogers.'

'Not Rogers, but try "Killer",' a voice behind her said. Merivale looked beyond her. They all turned. Jimmy Tingley was standing there, with Bellamy Heap on the steps behind him.

'Do I know you?' Merivale said.

Tingley stepped down into the room and walked up to Merivale. The American dwarfed him.

'I know you,' Tingley said. He nodded at Windsor. 'The mechanic for this gentleman.' He looked at Gilchrist. 'Klingman here killed an art expert who had been working with Mr Windsor – while she was in prison. Very ingenious and very nasty.'

Merivale shrugged. 'Anybody can be bought,' he said. 'Especially prison guards.'

'Hilary Black?' Gilchrist said, remembering Merivale's description of the poor woman's death. 'Did you have to make it so horrible for her?'

Merivale glanced at Windsor. 'Following instructions.'

Windsor was saying nothing. He sat in the corner, looking from person to person. His tongue darted out to lick his lips and he took another sip of his drink.

'You killed Rafferty too, didn't you?' Heap said. 'Tried to pass it off as suicide.'

'He couldn't be trusted,' Merivale said shortly. He smiled down at Tingley. 'So – what is to be done?'

'Give up your cargo,' Tingley said.

Merivale grinned. 'Which cargo?'

'These relics,' Gilchrist said. 'And the others from the Pavilion tunnels. We know what you have.'

'Fuck the antiques,' Tingley said. 'We want the rest of the children.'

Gilchrist spun to face him. He kept his eyes on Merivale.

'What?' Gilchrist said.

'This was only partly about antiques,' Tingley said. 'Mostly it was about trafficking children for sexual exploitation. Am I right, Klingman?'

'Whatever,' Merivale said. 'The point is, we're leaving here in about five minutes and your raggle-taggle army isn't going to stop us. What you have to decide is whether you all want to come along for the ride – well, half the ride, until we're mid-Channel where we can dump you – or you want to get off now and let us get on with our work.'

'No way any of that's happening,' Tingley said, fronting up to Merivale.

Watts stepped forward. 'I think he's mine, Jimmy.'

Merivale ignored him and looked at Gilchrist.

'Look – just let us go on our way. We made a mistake here. Let us go and we won't bother you any more.'

'There's the death of a young boy to be paid for,' Gilchrist said. 'Youk Chang. I'm guessing that was you too, Merivale.'

Merivale flashed his American choppers. 'How's that make you feel about your night with me, Sarah?'

Watts hit him. Gilchrist knew Watts was fast – she'd seen him in action before – but there seemed no gap between thought and execution. But the punch was precise. A short uppercut to the point of Merivale's chin. Merivale's head snapped back and he crumpled to the floor like a puppet whose strings had been cut.

Windsor looked sour. 'All right,' he said gruffly. 'What will it take for me to be allowed to leave here?'

'If you're people trafficking you're not going anywhere,' Gilchrist said. She was puzzled that neither he nor Merivale had seemed unduly concerned at their arrival.

Tingley walked past the prone Merivale and stopped in front of Windsor. 'Where is Will Rogers?'

'Right here,' a deep, tired voice said from the stairs.

They looked round. A man about Tingley's age: big, broad-shouldered, bit of a belly on him, holding a semi-automatic in meaty hands.

'Where the hell have you been?' Windsor said.

'On shore, sir,' Rogers said. He looked at Tingley. 'Hello, Jimmy.'

Tingley nodded at him.

Rogers sighed. 'Well, this is a mess,' he said. 'Mr Windsor, sir, I think we have to cast these people loose and make a run for it.'

'Do you, Rogers. Do you really?'

'We can hardly shoot them all or drop them over the side.' He glanced down at Merivale. 'Frankly there has been too much killing.'

'What happened to Michelle?' Tingley said to Rogers.

'Sal must have told you,' Rogers said.

'How did she die?' Tingley said. 'Did you kill her because she was slowing you down?'

'Of course not,' Rogers said, almost indignant. 'It was in an ambush. I believe you were told that a long time ago.'

'What I was told and what is true are very different things,' Tingley said.

'A fib more than a lie,' Rogers said. 'Howe and I got away. Everyone else died.'

'How did you get away?' Tingley said.

Rogers gave a little shrug. 'Ran like hell,' he said.

'You abandoned Michelle and her father,' Tingley stated.

'It was every man for himself. And every woman.'

'She was helpless!' Tingley said, raising his voice for the first time.

Rogers looked round the room and sighed. 'Jimmy, this is something we should be talking about over a pint. The timing isn't exactly great just now.'

'I killed Howe,' Tingley said.

'Is that some kind of veiled threat?' Rogers said.

'Not so veiled,' Tingley said.

'I know you killed him. Sal was very pissed off about that. Said if I was to see you I should do my worst.'

Tingley spread his arms. 'Go ahead.'

Rogers nodded at Windsor. 'I work for Windsor, not Paradise.'

'How does that work, exactly?' Gilchrist said.

Windsor scowled. 'Paradise works for me and does exactly what I say if he wants to keep living his sordid life.'

'You're one to speak,' Gilchrist said, surprised at the heat in her voice. 'You think your love of art justifies your abhorrent exploitation of children.'

Windsor looked at her coolly. 'Not just children, my dear. But who cares? What world are you living in? Mine is a world where there are exploiters and exploited. Anyone with half a brain wants to side with the former rather than the latter.'

'I live in a world where people look out for each other,' Gilchrist said. 'Where fairness is the norm.'

Windsor bared his teeth. 'Your name is Pollyanna? No such world exists.'

'How can you have become so warped?' Watts said. 'Is there no decency in you at all?'

'Decency.' Windsor savoured the word. 'Do you want the long or the short answer?'

Watts didn't respond. Windsor cracked his knuckles. It sounded like a gunshot in the cabin.

'OK – long answer,' he said. 'No, there isn't. Short answer: no.'

Merivale started to stir, rolling on to his side. Gilchrist walked over and looked down at him. She took out her Taser.

'Ma'am,' Heap said. There was a warning in his voice.

She looked at him. Merivale sat up. She stepped back as he stood.

'Careful, sir,' Heap said.

Merivale looked at the torch in Heap's hand. He frowned. He looked at Rogers and took a step forward.

'Look away, ma'am,' Heap said as he turned the torch on.

Watts too turned away from the witheringly bright light. Merivale was caught in its beam. He tried to shield his eyes with his hand then reeled against the side of the cabin.

As he began vomiting, Rogers said: 'Very clever – but if you turn it on me I'll shoot you.'

# EPILOGUE

'Here's to Jimmy Tingley,' Watts said, raising his glass, the blue light on his balcony turning its contents an aqueous green.

'Jimmy Tingley,' Sarah Gilchrist, Kate Simpson and Bellamy Heap said in unison.

Tingley bowed his head but said nothing.

Watts walked over and put his arm round him. 'Welcome back, Jimmy.'

Frankly, he was relieved that Tingley was still alive. Watts had seen him move on Rogers whilst Rogers was focusing on Heap's torch. Rogers was big but slow and Tingley had him down on the floor in moments. However, Rogers still had hold of the gun and started firing wildly.

Watts moved to help Tingley but stopped when he saw Tingley raise his foot and bring his heel down. The crack as Rogers' neck broke silenced the room. Silent except for an odd wheezing coming from Windsor. The wheezing explained by the blood spreading across his black jacket as he lay sprawled on his back.

Watts looked round to see if anyone else had taken a stray bullet. Everyone looked OK, though seemingly frozen in time. Tingley's movement broke the tableau. He swept the semi-automatic away from Rogers and walked over to Windsor and looked down on him.

Watts walked over to join him.

Windsor's eyes were open, watching them both.

'Does it hurt?' Tingley said.

'I feel nothing,' Windsor said. And died.

Watts kept his attention on Tingley now for a moment until Kate turned to the telescope in the corner of the balcony.

She peered through it then called out to Watts: 'You know, you wasted your money if you were expecting to see the nudist beach from here, Bob. As you've probably discovered, the beach-front curves.'

Watts smiled. 'It's for the night sky.'

'Yeah, right,' Kate said, fiddling with the focus.

Bob Watts was fond of Kate. He had discovered too late in his – and her – life that he was her half-uncle. He had decided it was not worth doing anything about that. Not that he was sure what to do about it anyway.

Heap went and stood beside Simpson.

Watts turned to Tingley and Gilchrist. 'I was certain there would be children on the boat,' he said.

'I don't think Windsor wanted to sully himself with that side of the business,' Gilchrist said. 'He left that to Prak Chang and Rogers.'

'I'm still not clear what happened with her and her son,' Watts said.

'Prak Chang had a rough time of it in Cambodia,' Tingley said. 'Gang-raped – that's why she didn't know who Youk's father was. To get out she had to go into business with Paradise. She'd been forced to work for him as a prostitute anyway but he agreed to let her come here if she ran the human trafficking for him from this end.'

'And Youk knew about this?' Watts said.

Tingley looked to Gilchrist to answer that.

'At some point, but I don't know for how long.'

'The children were in his mother's basement,' Watts pointed out.

'Only after he left home, I think,' Gilchrist said. 'And those children hadn't been put to work yet. Thank God. Among Prak's things we found the name of the nursing home she mentioned. That was where the brothel was. We found another dozen there.'

'But Youk was in on the antiques smuggling?' Watts said.

Gilchrist nodded. 'He was down in the tunnel, presumably because he was helping to store all the stuff we found. When he found out about the more disgusting side of the business I'm not sure. Hornby is not talking yet but our hypothesis is that Youk told him about the trafficking when he moved in and they concocted a half-arsed plan to blackmail the traffickers. Youk approached them and they – or rather Merivale – killed him.'

'Why wasn't Hornby killed?'

'I presume they didn't know about him. Yet. But he was clearly planning a move that would have been fatal for him.'

'About that tunnel?' Watts said.

'You mean how did the stuff get in there?' Gilchrist said. 'Well, Windsor was being investigated and needed somewhere to hide his stuff. He came to some sort of agreement with Rafferty. You can actually reach the Royal Pavilion from Windsor's house – it's circuitous but do-able. You go right under the Theatre Royal, actually.'

'But it was blocked at the Pavilion end.'

'Only very recently and just enough to make it seem there was no way through.'

'Why would Rafferty collaborate?' Watts said.

Gilchrist's expression turned sour. 'They both liked young boys.'

'And Prak Chang wandering around the town lamenting the loss of her son?'

'She thought her son had either run off or was dead but didn't know her employers had killed him. She hoped he was coming back and felt she was somehow responsible. When she found out he had been murdered she knew her employers must have done it and felt she really was responsible. She blamed herself for his exposure to them. Hence her attempt to slash her wrists.'

Kate and Heap came in from the balcony.

'This place is great,' Kate said. 'But the balcony is noisier than I thought it would be. The traffic.'

'Do you remember Philippa's flat out beyond Hove?' Gilchrist said to Watts. 'The racket on her balcony?'

Watts nodded. Philippa had been another officer in the debacle of the armed intervention gone wrong in Milldean. He couldn't remember her last name but had heard she'd gone into social work after leaving the force.

'This isn't quite as noisy,' he said. 'And, to be honest, you get used to it.'

Kate turned to Gilchrist. 'What's going to happen to the bones now that Rafferty is dead?'

'They'll be reinterred somewhere appropriate,' Heap said.

'He dug up the trunk murder victim's remains,' Kate told Watts and Tingley.

Gilchrist raised her eyes.

'You've found the trunk murder victim's remains in his house?' Watts said.

'Maybe,' Gilchrist said. 'But we've no way of knowing. All the bones are jumbled up together.'

'I think it's worth doing DNA on all the bones to find her,' Kate said.

Watts saw Gilchrist's mouth tighten as she said: 'Kate – I've told you, that's only of any use if the DNA is taken from every bone to figure out who is who. And that's a non-starter.'

'What do you think, Bob?' Kate said.

Watts set his glass down. 'I think it would be good to know but I take Sarah's point. I certainly couldn't approve of such spending.'

'Oh yeah, I forgot, you're the police commissioner now,' Kate said with a little *salaam* gesture.

'That I am.'

'Are you going to appoint a commissioner for youth like that young girl over in Hastings?'

'Given how well that turned out, you mean?' Watts smiled.

'OK then – a deputy for you at least?'

'Probably.'

'You don't think deputies should be elected, as you were?' Gilchrist said, glancing at Heap.

Watts nodded. 'Of course – but I don't make the rules.'

'But you'll do all that equal opportunities stuff, won't you?' Kate said. 'Advert in the paper and all that.'

Watts shook his head. 'It's entirely down to me.'

'Democracy is a wonderful thing,' Gilchrist said flatly. 'In that case, in the best traditions of cronyism you should give the deputy job to Kate.'

'Me?' Simpson said.

'Sure – you said you wanted to get out of Southern Shores.'

'I think you'd be very good,' Heap said.

Gilchrist looked at him in surprise, then at Simpson.

'Bellamy – what a sweet things to say,' Simpson said. Heap flushed and ducked his head. Gilchrist smiled to herself.

Watts looked at Kate. She was bright, young and energetic. Certainly she was too intelligent to be on the dopey local radio station. The problem was that he needed somebody less naïve, someone good at nuance. He had such a person in mind.

Simpson and Gilchrist caught something in his expression.

'Hey, I didn't mean to put you on the spot,' Gilchrist said.

'I'd probably be hopeless,' Kate added quickly.

'You'd probably be bored,' Watts said. He reached over and

squeezed her hand. 'The truth is I already have someone in mind. But, you know, I'm not sure if mine isn't just a Mickey Mouse job, which means my deputy's job would be even more – what's the term I'm looking for . . .?'

'Minnie Mouse?' Gilchrist said.

'Exactly! And I can see by Sarah's expression that she doesn't have much respect for the job – or probably the man who is doing it.'

'Hey,' Gilchrist protested. 'I've got nothing but respect for you, you know that.'

He turned to Tingley. 'Actually, I wondered if you might like the job.'

Tingley looked startled. 'What – I look like Minnie Mouse and it's OK for me to be bored?'

'A bit of boredom might do you good right now,' Watts said. 'And it would get you out of the firing line.'

All eyes were on Tingley. 'I'll think about it. Thanks.' He put his drink down. 'Where's the bathroom?'

As Tingley walked away Gilchrist said to Watts: 'Let me ask you a question. What did you think of the Police Committee – and particularly its chairman – when you were the chief constable?'

Watts grinned back. 'Point taken.' He scratched his head. 'Funny you should mention the chairman. I bumped into Hart the other day.'

'What – the father of the Evil One?' Gilchrist said, only half-joking. She was the one who had arrested his repulsive son and been obliged to have dealings with him. She felt she needed a shower just thinking about him. 'What's he up to?'

'Drinking himself to death, I think,' Watts said. 'He was coming out of the Bath Arms four sheets to the wind before one in the afternoon.'

'I think the correct expression is "three sheets", Bob,' Simpson said.

He looked blank for a moment. 'You know where the expression "three dog night" comes from?' he finally said.

'I don't know the expression "three dog night",' Sarah said.

'It was the name of a band a few years ago,' Watts said.

'Victorian times?' Simpson said.

'The Inuit judge how cold it is by how many dogs they need

to snuggle next to for warmth. One dog night, not so cold; two dogs, getting cold; three dog night – seriously low temperatures out there.'

'Aside from the number three, what has that got to do with the expression "three sheets to the wind"?' Kate said.

'Four sheets,' Watts said. 'It was a four sheets day.'

You approach the mirror in the bathroom. The man reflected looks familiar, not foreign to you for the first time in an age. You try a smile. Not great, but something. You don't look quite so much like a man running from himself. You nod to your reflection.

'Jimmy,' you whisper to yourself.

You hope that Sebastian and Phyllida will keep their promise and take care of Sal Paradise and his wretched enterprises. If you can help them, you will, they know that.

You are not sure how you feel about taking revenge on Rogers and Howe. It has changed nothing. You are not sure how you feel about Michelle. You had lost her long before she died. But you failed her. You feel that and will have to live with that. You are not sure about your friend's job offer.

You remember the words written as graffiti in the toilet of a café in Lisbon. Outside was a bronze statue of their original author, sitting at his favourite table in his favourite café in the city his writing made eternal.

*The world belongs to those who feel nothing*, the indelible graffiti read in solid black. You had a felt pen in your pocket. The nib was thin and on the wall the ink was faint but still you wrote two words in front of the inscription and put a line through the 's' of 'belongs'.

Whether any of the words are still there you don't know, but it doesn't matter. They remain the words you live by. *Don't let the world belong to those who feel nothing.*

# AUTHOR'S NOTE

All characters in this book are entirely and utterly fictional and bear no resemblance to any real person, even if I have some characters working for real institutions. The illegal art and artefacts trade does exist pretty much as I have described it but none of the characters I have invented relate to anyone involved in any way in the art, artefacts and museums world. Tragically, Pol Pot and the Khmer Rouge regime were all too horribly real.

**Peter Guttridge**